# Speak To Me

by **BEN RATERMAN**

design by **THEO HALL**

APRIL GLOAMING

©2024 by Ben Raterman
Design ©2024 by Theo Hall

-First Edition

Publisher's Cataloguing-in-Publication Data

Raterman, Ben
Speak to Me / written by Ben Raterman / designed by Theo Hall
ISBN: 978-1-953932-25-9


1. Fiction - General 2. Fiction - Literary 3. Fiction - Southern

Library of Congress Control Number: 2024930304

*To Leslie, for whom what is lost can always be found amongst the puzzle of words before her.*

Speak to me, quiet earth,
Tell me stories I will never hear
And show me colors,
Those I cannot see.
Now gather your leaves and soil,
And spread them on my knees.

Pray with me, pray by the river
Where the Kingfisher flies
And the acorns fall.
Pray that I may see
Far beyond the windows
Far beyond the trees.

Bury me if you will
In a field with no stones
Or next others I do not know—
It matters not. See—
I will listen for their stories,
I will give them to thee.

—Jannie Thomas

# ONE

It was early summer after the rains when the woods were thick with leaves, and hiding was easy. This was the best time, Justine determined, standing on the back stoop of her trailer. Time to find Nonna Jannie's jewels. She opened the rear door, listening, then closed it softly. Her mother would sleep for another two hours. She skipped down the wooden steps into the small yard.

"Joseph, it's time."

The boy pushed a truck across the mangy grass then stood. He was ready. The plan involved walking into town, a place that promised adventure, somewhere different from his familiar neighborhood. He smiled and followed his sister into the shadows not thirty feet from the rear of their trailer. They would disappear between the oak and the gnarly bushes that grew close where a path formed that forked one way to the river, the opposite to the gravel road that led to the big road and town.

At the oak tree, Joseph turned and looked at their home. It sat upon cinder blocks. Dirty pink insulation hung from beneath its belly like so many lampreys. He followed his sister, disappearing from the trailer that was his home and all its scary noises that came from within the weary structure.

They walked on the shoulder of the gravel road where weeds grew beneath the reaching limbs. Justine began to jog. The post office was her destination. It was close to the church where her grandmother sometimes took them. Two landmarks she was familiar with.

"The post office people will probably know where Nonna Jannie's house is," Justine had told Joseph.

"But how will we get inside?"

Justine had considered this. Her home with its broken rear door and the key to the front door lying under the step. Would Nonna Jannie's house be like hers? she wondered.

"There'll be a way."

At the highway, heat rose from the pavement. Justine and Joseph watched the hurrying vehicles, timing their crossing, then ran. Overhead, a crow flew, unseen but for its faint shadow upon the asphalt. They ran toward what Justine hoped would free them from the monotony of the trailer park, but most of all, from the confusion and fear she and her brother lived with daily. They ran, determined.

Passing an industrial park and a perch of old homes set back from the sidewalk was the new swimming pool they longed to visit. Quickening their pace, they passed beneath a bridge where the vehicles above amplified the noise. Just beyond, the road narrowed, curving into the small town on two lanes. It approached a gray rectangular grain tower encircled near the top, with red and white checkerboard squares in faded paint. Joseph saw the tower as a soldier, with its two small windows near the top, a sentinel guarding the railroad bridge ahead. Shaded beneath the railroad bridge, he craned his neck, examining its concrete underside. Crumbling, pitted. Rust-colored stains, a natural graffiti borne of years of wear and neglect, bled from the exposed rebar. He lowered his eyes. They emerged back into the harsh sunlight.

To their right, the church, Justine's landmark. And the post office farther to the left, its flag hanging, motionless. A blunder of white clouds spoiled the light blue sky.

Standing in line, Justine watched Joseph, two years younger than her. He pulled mailing envelopes from a stand near the door, examining each envelope, then replacing it.

"Joseph," she hissed. He looked at her, an envelope in his hand. He shoved the envelope back and stood beside her.

"Who's next?" the clerk said. Justine walked up, her eyes level with the top of the counter. "Can you tell me what the address for Jannie Thomas is? She lived on Main Street."

"Jannie Thomas, you said? Main Street?" The clerk leaned forward, her eyes moving from Justine to Joseph and back. "Who is this Jannie Thomas you need an address for?"

"She's our great-great-great-grandmother."

"Oh, my." The woman motioned for the next person to come forward. "Whatchu need, sir?"

Justine and Joseph stood beside the man needing stamps, looking up at the counter lady. She glanced at the two kids as she counted out change. "Where are your parents? You two are mighty small to be traipsing about town without a grownup." Joseph glanced at his sister.

Justine said, "Our mom's waiting for us. You don't know the address?"

"Honey, we don't keep addresses for people who are dead. Why don't you check over at the courthouse?" She pointed. "On the corner. Charlotte Street. They might be able to help. Or maybe the library."

Half a block and across the street sat an imposing building.

Justine pointed. "That looks like it could be the courthouse."

The building towered before them, its four white columns almost touching the facade gave it the look of importance without creating a portico. Up close, it appeared almost two-dimensional. Justine pulled on the double door. The door inched open, then pulled itself shut. It was as if the building didn't want their company, Joseph thought.

"OK," Justine said as the two of them grabbed the handle. The door opened of its own accord. A police officer stared down at them.

"Do you two have business in here?" The officer's uniform was tan, pressed. Joseph stared at the man's wide black belt with a black gun sitting high on his hip. Justine looked at his face, his eyes.

"We were looking for the library," she said, turning away.

"It's on Caroline Street," the officer said.

They continued on at a quick pace.

"I guess the courthouse is where the police live."

"Yeah." Justine took her brother's hand.

For weeks, she had thought of nothing but her desire to find the house where her Nonna Jannie once worked. To find the jewelry so she and Joseph and their mother could move from the trailer park. To a house where the locks worked, and the screens kept out the insects in the summer. And, in winter, the wind didn't crawl through the cracks, making you cold. Where she could have her own room. A house in a neighborhood with kids.

3

Joseph pulled his hand away from his sister, jogging along the wide brick sidewalk beneath the shade trees. Justine walked without looking, her mind on her purpose. They would sell the jewelry—like on the television show with the pawn dealer. He would use a small magnifying glass, one that fit close to his eye, and examine each piece and give its worth.

Her mind shifted. "Rachelle," she heard Terrell say to her mother. "It ain't gonna hurt nothing. It'll make you feel better." Brother and sister sat with their eyes on the television. Joseph leaned against the sofa arm, stained a dark brown from where his mother had fed him when he was a baby. The sofa's fourth leg, at the front, was missing, its corner supported unevenly by a thickness of crushed cereal boxes.

The bedroom was quiet for a time. Then there was laughter and yelling. Happy yelling, Justine thought. The trailer shook. The television images created flickering shadows, and the yelling from the bedroom turned to screams, shouts. Justine tried the door. She ran outside beneath the bedroom window, shouting at her mother to come out. Joseph stood next to his sister, crying. Their grandmother, Nonna Etta, arrived just as a police car pulled up. Beyond, they saw neighbors looking on as they ran to their grandmother and watched as the police entered the trailer. Watching from a distance, along with the neighbors, as if the trailer were on fire.

Justine wanted a house far from Terrell. She watched, smiling, as her brother hopped down the sidewalk. She was happy now, walking the streets of town, away from the trailer park. Soon their lives would change, she told herself. First, they needed to find the library.

"Let's walk across the street and sit on those steps and wait." She pointed to the white brick church. "Until someone comes. We can ask where the library is."

Up against the red arched double door, they found shade.

"How long?" Joseph said, looking at his sister's face. Without speaking, Justine's face often told him things before his mind could respond to events around him.

"Look for someone who looks nice," she said. "They'll know where the library is." To Justine, looking nice meant she could trust them to act nicely, unlike the police. She did not trust the police. They had visited her trailer several times. They had guns. And their talk was often curt. Like Terrell. Terrell, the on-again-off-again man who slips in the back door unannounced.

They sat on the cool sandstone steps. Justine watched as two people walked along the sidewalk across the street. Should she cross and question them? She heard one say, Steen. No, Stephen. She thought of her name and Joseph's and her mother's name, Rachelle.

It was because of Terrell. Terrell was the reason her mother changed her name, the name Nonna Etta gave her—Rachel. Rachel had heard the story of her namesake in the Bible. As a child, she didn't give her name a thought. As a teen, though, she longed for a different name, a real name, not some religious oddity. When Rachel's children were born, it was her mother, Etta, who named them. Rachel reacted with contempt when her mother chided her to come up with a name. She refused, saying she would decide when the time was right. Time passed. Etta filled out the birth certificates—at each birth—ensuring the children would have proper names. When Rachel met Terrell, though, she knew she had to change her name. Rather than have it officially changed, she simply changed the spelling. Now it rhymed with Terrell and was a modern name. She considered herself a modern woman. Now she was truly modern. And she had two modern kids named Steen and Jobo.

The church's red door opened. A woman said hello.

Justine saw the silver bracelet hanging from her pale wrist. "Do you know how to get to the library?"

"If you're walking, go down to the next street." The woman pointed in the direction the kids had been traveling. "Then turn right one block..." She shifted her gaze. "Are you two alone? No babysitter?" The woman's face changed. Justine saw the look of alarm. She took Joseph's hand and pulled him toward her.

"She's waiting for us," Justine said, jumping to the sidewalk. They ran to the next block and turned.

Joseph followed his sister's lead and asked a woman where the library was. They walked on until Justine saw the sign, red with white letters.

"That's it, Joseph."

"It's big."

# TWO

Inside, light from the windows and doors flooded the entrance. Joseph turned on his toes. He had never seen so many books.

To their left was a counter. A woman stood behind it, peering at a computer screen. Justine was already walking toward her. Joseph ran ahead, excited.

"Do you know where Jannie Thomas lived on Main Street?" Joseph put his hands on the counter.

"Jannie Thomas on Main Street," the woman said with a smile. "Who is—"

"She's our great-great-great-grandmother," Justine said. "And we need to know what house she lived in."

"Well, if she lived on Main Street, then she lived on this street here. The one we're on now, Caroline Street. Main Street was an older name for Caroline. Why don't you go downstairs and talk to Katy Aldridge? In the Virginiana Room. She may be able to help."

"Thank you." It was then that Justine took in the full scope of the library. So much larger than the one at school. Her mind had been on the jewels. Now there was hope—Katy Aldridge...able to help. She slowed, looking around, seeing the books—on desks, in displays, on shelves, on laps being read. People standing, reading, talking. Maybe she could return—after she and Joseph found the jewels—and find a book on snakes.

They took the stairs to the basement and walked around a small glass partition. Joseph looked up at the glass, wavy, distorting his view of the room beyond. Was something wrong with the glass, or maybe, the room? It was small with a low drop ceiling lit by fluorescents. Filing cabinets and two microfilm readers. At the far end of the room, an L-shaped modular desk.

The young woman at the desk looked up as the kids entered. She watched without speaking as they walked toward her. Justine looked at the woman's face. A slight smile with a tiny tilt of curiosity. Joseph walked even with his sister, watching the woman. Would she have the answer? he wondered. He looked to his left. A smaller room with rolling stack shelving against one wall. Three heavy tables with chairs. Joseph sensed a level of importance removed from the floor above and far removed from the trailer park where he lived. Justine knew that this woman could help. She saw it in her eyes, her smile.

Katy Aldridge said, "You're looking for something."

Justine moved closer. "We need to know where our great-great-great-grandmother lived." She paused, searching Katy's eyes once more, knowing. "She lived on Main Street—"

"And her name is Jannie Thomas," Joseph said.

Katy sat back. "My name is Katy. What are your names?"

"I'm Justine and he's Joseph. He's my brother."

"Two Js. And Jannie was your 3rd-great-grandmother. Another J." Katy mulled over the name Justine, tripping through its literary history, then turned to her computer. "Let's see what we can find." She brought up census information. "Your third-great grandmother would have probably lived somewhere between 1900 and 1920, I'd guess." Katy turned to the kids. "How old are you two?"

"He's six and I'm eight," Justine said.

Katy searched the 1910 census and found no Jannie Thomas. Two Jannies came up: Jannie Pratt and Jannie Wilson. The 1920 census included a Jannie Thomas, but no Jannie Wilson. Pratt in 1910 was listed as twenty years old and working as a maid. Thomas in 1920 was thirty years old, married with three children, no occupation listed. Could they be the same person? Katy thought so—for now.

Joseph and Justine watched the woman at the computer. Justine wished she had such a thing. She had used the computers at school but to have one of her own…

"OK, here's what I see," Katy said. "Jannie Thomas is listed in the 1920 census. She was thirty years old and married to Joshua Thomas. They had three kids and lived on Sophia Street. Do you think that might be your grandmother, 3rd-great?"

"She lived on Sophia Street?" Justine said. "But…that's not Main Street, is it?"

"No."

Justine's face turned worried. "But she lived on.... No, she worked on Main Street. She worked for a lady on Main Street."

"Ah, that's a different question. And somewhat more difficult to answer."

Joseph's eyes reached for Katy's face. Justine too watched her face, choosing not to hear her words.

Katy saw their looks. "But not impossible. Tell me what you know about your grandmother."

"Great-great-great-grandmother," Justine said.

"Let's call her grandmother Jannie, then. It's simpler."

"Nonna Jannie," Joseph said.

"Perfect. Tell me about Nonna Jannie. Do you know whom she worked for? What kind of work she did?"

Justine shook her head no.

"Could she have been a maid?" Katy said.

Joseph said, "What's a maid?"

"A person who cleans the house," Justine told him. "Maybe," she said to Katy.

"There're jewels in the house," Joseph said. Justine turned to her brother. Katy saw the look on her face. Jewels, she said to herself. Could it be the Fitzhugh place? Justine turned back to Katy. The two kids stood side by side like mannequins waiting for her to speak.

"There was a story about a woman who went missing," Katy said. "She was a wealthy woman, and she had lots of jewelry. No one knows what happened to her or her jewels. It was in the papers many years ago—over a hundred. Could your Nonna Jannie have worked for this lady? Her name was Anna Fitzhugh."

Stares from across the desk. Katy paused. Anna and Jannie, she said to herself, recalling research she had done a couple years ago. Blayden Fitzhugh owned the largest lumber operation at the turn of the century. His wife, Anna, had taken a train to New York and never arrived. Later, the jewelry she owned was determined missing as well. The police assumed she was killed and her jewelry taken, but there was no evidence to support the theory. Blayden told the police it would have been unusual for Anna to have taken all her jewelry with her.

Justine said, "Did Anna Fitzhugh live on Main Street?"

"Let me see." Katy went to a file cabinet. "Here's a story about the event...where Anna Fitzhugh went missing." She opened the folder and laid a photocopy of the article on her desk. The kids stood looking down at the old newsprint as Katy read. When she finished scanning the article, she looked up.

"311 Caroline Street. That's where the Fitzhughs lived. It was 311 Main Street back then. What do you think? Did Nonna Jannie pass down any stories about when she worked there? Does the name Fitzhugh sound familiar?"

Joseph looked at his sister. She was pumping her toes so that her whole body rose and fell as if she were riding a horse. He watched her, looking down at her feet, then back at her head as she faced Katy.

"I think that's the place," Justine said. Joseph stood close to his sister, nodding. "It's on this street, right?" Justine said.

"It's at the far end of Caroline, beyond the railroad tracks. Let me see if I can show you a picture." Katy brought up a street view of that part of Caroline Street. She pulled the screen toward the kids. A Dutch Colonial with gray shingles and a large oak tree in front, close to the sidewalk. Justine bobbed up and down and clapped. Joseph jumped. Katy smiled.

"That's it," Justine said. "Thank you. Thank you."

Katy sat back in her chair. "So, Justine and Joseph. Did your Nonna Jannie say that there were jewels in the house?"

Justine stopped moving and looked into Katy's eyes. Katy had performed a miracle. She had solved a mystery that no one in her family had ever solved. Or maybe they hadn't tried. Maybe they didn't believe what Nonna Jannie said was true. Maybe it was all made up.

Justine said, "Nonna Etta told us Nonna Jannie was sure the jewels were in the house when the lady didn't come home."

"And who is Nonna Etta?"

"She's our grandmother," Joseph said. "She knows a lotta stuff."

"So, what next? Will you ask the owners if you can come in and look for the jewelry?"

Justine considered. Her Nonna Etta said the jewels were buried in the cellar. She and Joseph would dig them up. She hadn't worked out all the details.

"What should we do?" Justine said.

Katy wasn't expecting this question. "Justine, you know if there are jewels in the house, they won't be yours. They didn't belong to your Nonna Jannie. They belonged to Anna Fitzhugh—"

"But some of them belonged to Nonna."

"How do you know that?" Katy sat up, her eyes on Justine.

"Nonna Etta said so," Joseph said.

Justine held Katy's eyes. "Nonna said that the lady promised Nonna Jannie some of her jewelry. But when she was killed, she couldn't give them to Nonna Jannie."

"When she was killed? How do you know Anna was killed, Justine?"

"That's what Nonna Etta said."

"Your grandmother."

"Uh-huh. She said Nonna Jannie said so."

"Did your Nonna Jannie see Anna being killed?"

Justine shrugged. "I don't know."

"Hmm." Katy thought about the old newspaper story. She was sure it hadn't mentioned a maid, and there was no proof that Anna Fitzhugh was killed. But here is a maid who may have witnessed a murder.

"Tell you what. Let me do some research on the Fitzhughs, then we can decide how to proceed. Have you told your parents and your grandmother about your investigations?" Katy saw blank looks. "I mean, do they know you are here at the library to find your Nonna Jannie's work address?"

"We just decided to find it ourselves," Justine said.

Joseph looked at the computer screen. "It's Nonna Jannie's jewels."

"Don't you think you should tell your parents that you're searching for the jewels?"

"My mom would take them." Justine said, looking down at Katy's desk.

"What about your dad?"

"We don't have a dad," Joseph said.

Katy put her elbows on the desk and propped her chin on the back of her palms. She sensed this was the case. "And what about your grandmother Etta? She sounds like a sensible person. Don't you think you should tell her what you found out?"

Justine and Joseph watched as Katy's chin moved over her knuckle. They liked Katy. But...

Justine put her hand on the desk. "Could you write the address on a piece of paper?"

"Sure."

Justine read 'Blayden & Anna Fitzhugh, 311 Caroline Street.' "Thanks." She pushed the paper into her pocket, looked at Joseph, and turned to the door. "Bye," she said.

"Bye. Oh, where do you guys live?"

They stopped at the glass partition. "Tidewater Trailer Park," Justine said.

Katy watched them pass behind the glass, like reflections in a trembling pond, and disappear up the stairs. What would they do with the jewelry if they found it? she wondered. She turned to the computer. Fitzhugh. It was five minutes into her search when she stopped and typed Tidewater Trailer Park. "That's a long walk," she said aloud and went back to Fitzhugh and the lost jewelry.

# THREE

The police cruiser turned off Tidewater Trail onto a pot-holed street that led into the trees. A sign on the corner some distance ahead announced: 'Tidewater Trailer Park.' The sign lunged to the left, looking for support.

"Here we go again," the driver said. "3212 Greenshadow Lane."

"Our favorite address." The partner looked at the clipboard in his lap. "And Rachelle Parker, our favorite perp."

"With a gun, this time. That's new. Hit the lights and siren. Let's have some fun."

The white cruiser with its black and gold stripe along the side pulled up to the trailer.

Rachelle stood outside, next to the door, having heard the siren, knowing her situation was dire. Two neighbors stood in their doorways watching.

"It was an accident," Rachelle cried, rushing to the first officer as he approached. He held up his hand.

"Slow down, Rachelle. Is there anyone in the trailer?"

Rachelle looked behind her. "No. It's just me."

"Where are your two kids?"

"Oh. They're with their grandmother."

"And the gun?"

"It was an accident." Rachelle's hands shook. Her head swiveled back and forth, scanning the officers, the neighbors, searching within for answers she'd forgotten the questions to. "It's inside."

The officer looked at his partner and nodded. "Rachelle, we're going to enter your trailer. Is that OK?"

"Yes, sure. The gun is on the counter." The partner had walked behind the trailer.

"Alright, I want you to sit in the car while I go inside." He ushered Rachelle to the patrol car and walked to the front door.

"There's nobody inside," Rachelle said, sliding into the seat. She pressed her palms against her forehead, leaning her head against the seat. "Going to jail," she whispered, sobbing.

The officer opened the front door and entered the trailer. He walked out with the pistol. His partner approached from the opposite side of the trailer. Rachelle looked up. He motioned to her.

"You can get out. Where is Terrell?"

"Terrell?"

"Your boyfriend."

"How do you know I have a boyfriend?"

"Rachelle," the first officer, holding the pistol, said, "how many times have we come to visit you in the past six months?"

"Um...you're the same guys?"

"That's us. This your gun?" He had removed the magazine and the bullet in the chamber.

"Well, I guess it's Terrell's."

The partner walked to the cruiser and pulled out his clipboard. "Terrell Jackson?"

"Yeah." Rachelle looked at the ground. She wondered where Terrell was now. He had run into the woods behind the trailer.

A car drove up and stopped next to the police car. Etta got out. Rachelle looked at her mother. She saw the anger on her face. Tears crawled down Rachelle's cheeks. The officer with the gun waved at Etta. From the rear doors emerged Justine and Joseph. Etta walked up to Rachelle. They stood eye to eye. Etta put her hands on her hips and glared at her daughter.

"I got a call from Francine," Etta said, trying to control herself. Rachelle looked over at Francine, who stood leaning on her porch railing watching the proceedings. The nosy white neighbor who loved to call the police.

"You look at me when I'm speaking, girl," Etta said as if her daughter were six instead of twenty-six. Rachelle stiffened and faced her mother. Justine looked up at Rachelle. What has Mama done? she wondered. Joseph looked at the policeman holding the pistol.

Inside the trailer, Etta faced her daughter and told her she had found Joseph and Justine walking along the road. "Cars and trucks everywhere—you know how that road is. They were at the library. In town. All the way in town. That's got to be at least three or four miles, Rachel. And you didn't know where they were, did you?"

Rachelle scrutinized her mother. She was still shaking, thankful she would not go to jail. She told the police that it was Terrell who shot the gun. He was teaching her how to defend herself, she explained. "You're going to jail the next time this happens." The police officer pointed at her chest. "You didn't pull the trigger, you're saying." The officer stared. Rachelle's eyes focused on his finger, six inches from her chest. "Did you?"

"Did you?" Etta repeated, waiting for her daughter to respond.

"What?"

"I said," Etta raised her voice, "you did not know where your children were, did you?"

"They said they would play around here. You always say they should get out. Well, they were out."

"And a good thing. Otherwise, they might be dead. With you and that gun." Etta walked to the sink. Dishes lay in it, unwashed. The cabinet door below, broken off. A thin piece of wood hanging from the two hinges remained, revealing the plumbing along with an array of cleaning products that rarely left their lair.

"Where's your fool boyfriend?" Etta stared out the rear window. Justine and Joseph sat on the listing sofa. Joseph bounced on the corner, making it tilt up, down. Justine looked at him. He stopped. They listened to their mother and grandmother talk. They heard their mother explain that Terrell brought the gun by because he was worried about Rachelle and the kids. It was for their protection.

Etta listened to her daughter tell her story, the same story she had been telling since she was sixteen, the same lies, the same feigned innocence, the same excuses. And the same boyfriends. Etta no longer heard the words pouring from Rachelle's mouth. She stood at the sink and saw herself standing before her. The same boyfriends, she heard a voice say. It is your story, the story of poverty. Poverty as penury, absence, inferiority. Poverty of imagination, of determination, of intelligence, of belief, of principle. Was she born this way? Born with shackles strapped to her ankles and told to swim.

Swim to the other side. To the side where dreams are true. She looked at her contemporaries along the shore, the ones without shackles with whom she was born. They dove in and swam. Some struggled, but they moved along, their heads above the water. When she dove into the water, she sank to the bottom. The weights about her ankles prevented any movement. She looked up through a veil of dark water and saw failure and disappointment. And there she stayed, born to be a bottom feeder. It must be so.

"It was my fault," Etta whispered.

"What, Mama?" Rachelle frowned. Joseph and Justine looked at their grandmother. She held onto the sink as if it were a life raft, then turned.

"It's not your fault, Rachel," Etta said, hugging her daughter. "It's mine. I never learned to swim."

"But Nonna," Joseph said, hopping off the sofa. "You can swim. Remember when you taught me at that pool?"

"Yes, Joseph. I remember—"

"Mama, what are you talking about?" Rachelle broke her mother's embrace, looking into her eyes.

Etta smiled. "I'm just yammerin'. Got to get back to work. I want no more calls from Francine, you hear. Nor anyone else in this neighborhood. The police will have Terrell in for questioning soon. He's a bad influence, Rachel. Please consider dumping him, will you?" Etta walked to the door. "I'll be back by 5:30." She looked at Justine. The only one in the family with any intelligence, she thought. "You two stay out of trouble till I get here, understand?"

"We will," Justine said, thinking of the house at 311 Caroline Street. How would she and Joseph get inside?

Rachelle usually caught the bus for work at five, but she was thinking she would leave early today and meet Terrell first.

# FOUR

Katy sat beneath the first floor of the library among the books and documents related to the history of the town and its neighboring counties. She looked around her small office with the filing cabinets full of old photos and letters, news articles, bits of research. Some started, then forgotten. The stuff of past lives. She loved stories, authentic stories, and made-up stories. Upstairs were the made-up stories, the adventures, and romances, the mysteries, and the dramas of people who never existed. Stories of people writers invented so that real people could pretend they were a part of the story. Downstairs, in the basement, Katy sat amidst stories, all fragments, of real people. It was here that Katy would often read the fragments, the letters, and documents, the mentions in an old newspaper. Staring at the microfilm screen, she would drop the reins on her imagination. The fragments filled the confines of her mind, and there, between the library and home, Katy constructed stories she felt were just as good as the fictions lining the walls on the floors above her.

She pushed her hair back over her right ear and typed, querying her computer for articles on Anna Fitzhugh. Fitzhugh being a common name in the area, she narrowed her search, finding four articles mentioning Anna: marriage to Blayden Fitzhugh, return from honeymoon, visit sick mother, and disappearance of. There was nothing on Jannie Pratt.

Katy retrieved the microfilm reel for 1908, the first reference to Anna.

Beautiful Church Wedding
Miss Anna Darla Stromberg becomes the bride of Mr. Blayden Thomas Fitzhugh.

The interior of St. George's Church was ablaze with light Wednesday evening. The pulpit was converted into a bower of beauty; the decorations being composed of growing plants and cut flowers. The church was packed to its doors, with people eager to witness the scene to be enacted.

Katy read on. The effusive reporter described the bride and her gown ('white crepe de chine over white taffeta') and the gown of her maid of honor ('white silk, artistically made'). Describing the groom, the reporter called him 'a man who has won the esteem and confidence of our businesspeople and has many friends.' The article ended: 'Mr. Blayden Fitzhugh and his new wife, Mrs. Anna Fitzhugh, left on the late northbound train for a trip of several weeks. The presents were many and costly.'

Katy jotted down the other three article references and turned off her computer. She looked at her watch. Long lunch. She took the stairs two at a time, heading for daylight and the courthouse.

Handing her purse to the officer behind the desk, she walked through the metal detector, a contraption that was fitted after they built the building. Ugly, she thought, retrieving her purse on the opposite side of the fence. Walking into the archive's preservation room, she waved to the bow-tied man at the desk to her left.

"Hey, Travis." She walked quickly past to the next room.

"Katy. I haven't seen you in a while."

"Got a new house on Caroline. I need to know who the owners were."

She glanced at the heavy deed books stacked on metal shelves in the middle of the room. Short shelves with angled tops designed to support the old books and other documents researchers perused while standing over them. She moved to a computer along the side wall. The city's real estate data revealed a Beverly Langston had owned the house for the last twenty-one years. The deed listed the previous owners and deeds. Katy walked back and forth between deed books and a General Index to Deeds and Wills until she had compiled a list of owners back to Fitzhugh. There were four owners before she got to Blayden and Anna Fitzhugh, who bought it in 1908, the same year they were married.

She breezed past Travis. "Next time stay a while," he said.

Outside, the sun sat high above the buildings. Katy squinted down Princess Anne Street to the railroad bridge. She looked across the street to the house where her friend worked. Meghan Foster. A recently graduated architect working for Marlboro Associates. Peter Marlboro, a well-known architect from DC, preferred the solitude of this small town to his main offices in the capital. Meghan was his sole associate in this office.

Katy crossed the street and entered the Victorian house, ringing the bell to announce her entry on the ground floor. She climbed the stairs to the second floor, walking past Peter Marlboro's office to Meghan's office.

"Meghan. You busy?" She peeked past the door frame into what was once a bedroom.

Meghan sat before a computer and two screens. She looked up, her dark hair and eyes dominant.

"Katy. Come in. What's doin'?"

"I'm researching a new house. 311 Caroline. I'm on my way to talk to the owner. See if I can convince her to let me snoop around. You interested? I'm hoping for Saturday."

"Of course. I love old houses."

"Yeah. I didn't know how busy you would be." Katy sat on a stool next to the table behind Meghan's desk. Atop the table were two rolls of drawings. Meghan swiveled her chair.

"I'll make time. Do you know the history? How old is it?"

"I'm just starting the research, but I know it was the house where Anna Fitzhugh lived in 1908. She was famous at the time because she took the train to visit her mother in New York and never arrived. She was never seen again."

"A mystery."

"Yeah. And she had quite a collection of jewelry. The jewelry went missing as well. The suspicion was that she was murdered on her way to New York and her jewelry stolen."

Meghan's eyes widened.

Peter Marlboro stuck his head in the door. "My favorite females. How are you, Katy?"

"Just fine, Peter. You?" Katy glanced at Meghan with a wary eye.

"Oh, you know. Progress can be difficult sometimes without the appropriate stimulus."

"Peter, go back to your cave," Meghan said. "Katy has no interest in that kind of progress."

"Of course," the man said. "Another time, then. Ladies." He tipped his forehead and disappeared.

"How can you deal with that man?" Katy whispered.

"Day to day. He's proven to be harmless. So, this weekend?"

"Yeah. I'll text you." Katy got up and leaned into the display on Meghan's desk. "What are you working on?"

"I'm designing a corbel for a house Peter is designing. It's a concept at this point."

"Neat. What's a corbel?"

"A fancy support."

"That's why I need you to look at this house. You're my corbel." Katy raised her hand. Meghan smacked it with her open hand.

"Later, Kater."

She parked opposite 311 Caroline and sat sizing the house, the mature tree by the sidewalk, the bushes up close, the condition of the clapboard siding. She wondered how old Beverly Langston was. How receptive would she be to having people explore her house under the guise of research? Would she know anything of its history? Would she be home?

Katy practiced different greetings: Hello, Mrs. Langston, or should it be Ms. Langston or Beverly? She crossed the street and walked up the stone path to the front door and knocked. Waited. Knocked again, then walked around the side of the house to a gate that entered the backyard. Walking into the yard, she surveyed the bounds, turning to the rear of the house, scanning the small patio. It lay off the back door, a French door, set between four large floor-to-ceiling windows that looked out on the yard.

Standing in the room's shadow and just visible through the windows was a woman waving at Katy. Katy froze, staring at the woman, a mere outline in the window. She walked closer, stepping to the door. She saw the smile on the woman's face, saw her mouth say, "Come in." Katy opened the door.

"Kate, I wasn't expecting you today. Come in. Come in."

Katy studied the woman, confused, excited, pleased. She stepped into a sunroom that appeared to have been an addition to the small kitchen where the woman stood.

"Mrs. Langston?" Katy said, walking closer.

"It's so good to see you, Kate." She showed Katy to a small table in the kitchen's corner. Katy's eyes adjusted to the dim light as she took in the visage of Beverly Langston. She wore a faded dress that dropped well below her knees. Thin socks rolled down to her ankles, just above a pair of black lace-up shoes. The dress was not of recent vintage, Katy thought.

"Beverly…" Katy started.

"Let's have tea, shall we?" Beverly walked toward the counter on the opposite wall.

Katy smiled at her new friend. "Sure. Tea would be fine."

Katy's eyes took in the extended and enlarged area that made up the kitchen-cum-sunroom. A long farm table separated the two areas. She followed Beverly and stood watching as the woman fixed the tea.

Beverly glanced at Katy. "You're wearing men's clothes these days," she commented.

Katy looked down at her jeans, then back at Beverly.

"Beverly…" Katy watched as the old woman filled the teapot. "How do you know me? I don't think I've ever met you."

"What?" Beverly was surprised. "I think you are the funniest person I know. Always making up stories for the amusement of those around. Have you written any new poems? I so love your poetry."

Katy stood at the corner of the stove and decided that Mrs. Langston must have her confused with someone else, someone with her name.

"No. I've had little time to devote to poetry lately. I've been doing research." She watched as Beverly measured tea into a strainer. The blue flames on the gas stove slapped the bottom of the teapot like so many salamander tails.

"Research? Goodness. What sort of research?" Beverly looked at her visitor with searching dark brown eyes. Katy saw the white hair pulled back in a ponytail, hair that was once the color of her eyes.

"Research on this house. To determine its age, its history, and anything I can find on its owners over the years."

"Kate," Beverly said in a low voice, pouring hot water through a strainer. "You know this house."

"Yes." Katy went along with her host. "I do. But, you know, I've never recorded it—in my notebooks. I would like to capture all the details."

Beverly gave Katy a look of some concern. "You mean to put it down on paper?" she said, holding Katy's cup close to her chest. Katy reached out and took the cup.

"Don't you think it would be a good idea? For posterity?"

Beverly studied Katy's eyes, then turned toward the large windows overlooking the garden. "I suppose," she said. "Shall we sit?" They moved to the round table in the kitchen's corner.

Katy wasn't sure how best to proceed with Beverly. The old woman seemed uncertain, maybe fearful. Would she allow Katy to tour the house in pursuit of her research? She was certainly welcoming. But if Beverly has confused her with someone else and later discovers her mistake, then she may drop her welcoming attitude. How can she keep Beverly in the dark long enough to accomplish her in-house research?

"Why don't we just talk about the house, what you know of it?" Katy looked at her host over her cup, sipping cautiously.

"But Kate, I have told you everything. We are friends. You know all that I know."

Katy knew for certain, now, that she was masquerading as someone else. A pretense. She was taking advantage of this woman's trust, and she felt bad about it. She also felt compelled to continue probing, balancing on the word 'pretense,' hoping not to fall off.

"You are right, of course," Katy said. "My memory is not always accurate. That's why I came by. And to ask if it would be alright if a couple of my friends and I could walk through the house, take measurements, notes. It's important to see the basement if there is one—and the attic. Those areas are usually unfinished and so will show the bones of the house. Would that be alright?" Katy needed to get this basic permission. She would circle back, if she felt it safe, and ask personal questions about the inhabitants later. If Beverly was indeed knowledgeable of the past owners.

"The bones?"

Katy saw the look on Beverly's face, a look of confusion and concern.

"The wooden frame. The foundation."

"Oh. The materials. Yes. I don't see why not, dear."

"That's excellent. When is the best time for you? Would this Saturday be alright?"

Beverly studied her teacup. She looked up suddenly and said, "Kate Aldridge, you have changed so. I dare say I may not know you." She gave a quick smile.

Katy was taken aback. How did Beverly know her last name? The old woman got up and walked to the kitchen counter.

"Maybe you're getting me mixed up with someone else," Katy said. "Did someone come by earlier or call and say I would come to visit?" She searched for some explanation, knowing with some certainty that neither Justine nor Joseph would have done such a thing. But who? She watched as Beverly reached to the cupboard and retrieved a box of cookies and a plate, then unwrapped the cookies. Katy saw her rounded shoulders and the way the dress fell off them. Beverly carefully placed the cookies on the plate.

"That's alright, Beverly. I need to be going. I skipped lunch." Katy stood and walked to the woman. Beverly turned and walked right into Katy, spilling several cookies on the floor. Katy apologized and picked up the broken cookies.

"I should go," Katy said, placing the cookies on the counter, looking at Beverly.

"You just got here, Kate. Come, sit with me." Beverly walked to the table.

"Beverly, can you hear me?" Beverly's back was to Katy. She did not answer. Katy walked to the table and sat, looking at Beverly's face. "Your hearing isn't too good, is it?"

"No. I have difficulty hearing. It was not always so. Now I can hardly hear myself sing. And I love to sing. Remember when we celebrated our second anniversary at Pythian Hall? We sang a duet together."

"Second anniversary?" Katy's mind tumbled.

"Pythian Sisters. Your memory is as bad as my hearing. We were so young." Beverly focused her eyes on some invisible image just beyond the range of Katy's sight.

Katy said, "That's why I need to write these things down. It's my memory. But I must go. I can come back soon, though. Would this coming Saturday be alright?"

"Yes, dear. You are always welcome. You know that." Beverly reached out and touched Katy's hand.

"Thank you," Katy said, looking down at the frail hand. The veins raised, the skin furrowed and loose.

"Goodbye, dear."

"Bye." Katy smiled at her new friend and walked through the sunroom door. She held her hand before the glaring light. The garden needed care.

\* \* \*

The microfilm screen flashed black and white print in a blur, then slowed and stopped. Katy advanced the spool, waiting for the Free Lance banner to appear. Who is Kate Aldridge? At the banner, page 1, she advanced two pages and stopped, waiting for the image to come into focus. Column three. Kate Aldridge married to Frederick Aldridge. She threaded an earlier article from 1908. It mentioned Kate as an attendee at a Pythian Sisters concert. And that she and her friend, Anna Stromberg, had sung a duet together. "Wow," Katy said under her breath. Kate and Anna were friends before Anna married. So, who is Beverly Langston, and what is her relation to these two women?

Katy stared at the wall behind the reader. A blank white wall. Pythian Sisters? What is that? She went to her desk and consulted the internet oracle. Pythian Sisters appeared first on the list. Founded in 1888. Fraternal order. Their mission stated that the Pythian Sisters "bring together women of diverse backgrounds and provide opportunities for them to help themselves and others grow through the principles of Purity, Love, Equality and Fidelity." So, my namesake and Anna Fitzhugh knew each other, were singing buddies. And belonged to this sister's organization.

She now had three articles on Kate Aldridge, one covering her marriage, one about the Pythian sisters, and the latest from 1956 talking about Kate's self-published book of poetry. And four articles on Anna Fitzhugh. Set for the evening.

What a life, she thought as she gathered her papers and purse. Twenty-eight years old, living in a town only history knows about, no love interest, excitement measured by the presence of books and the words of the past. I am without hope, she thought.

# FIVE

As soon as Rachelle Parker left her trailer, Justine looked at the clock. Almost two hours. That's when Nonna Etta would arrive to look after Joseph and her. Would that be long enough to walk into town and back with time to get into the house and dig up the jewels? What if the house was locked? She looked at Joseph, who sat at the edge of the sofa, bouncing, watching images on the TV screen. School had been out now for three weeks.

There were two kids in this geriatric park who were close in age to her and her brother. Justine considered them vermin, a word she had learned when Nonna Etta called for pest control to rid the area beneath their trailer of destructive animals. "They chewed through a pipe and now there is water running across the yard and down the road," Etta yelled into her phone.

"Joseph, we have to go now. We don't have much time to get to the house." She would figure out how to get in when they got there.

"OK," Joseph said, catapulting off his seat. "Let's go."

Justine told Joseph they should leave by the back door and walk down the path through the woods to the road. The same path Terrell took, Justine thought, as they pushed aside the low branches. Often Terrell would park on the feeder road rather than next to the trailer and walk to the back door through the woods. He told Rachelle he liked to mix up his routine.

Once on the feeder road, they jogged to the main road and crossed to the other side. Justine hoped no one she knew would see them. When she reviewed the number of people that might be, she felt better. She didn't have many friends, none living in this trailer park. And her mother and her grandmother had so few friends close by that the chance of one of them spotting her and Joseph was small. Maybe Reverend Sharp and his wife, and a couple of other parishioners at Shiloh Baptist. But they didn't live out here. They always wore nice clothes. They must live in nice houses too, Justine thought.

Justine was confident, happy, thanks to Katy Aldridge. Katy had found the house where her great-great-great-grandmother had once worked. Where the lost jewels were buried. She walked along the gravel shoulder with a bounce, holding onto her brother's hand. Walking on the balls of her feet helped keep the small stones from entering the hole at her toe. Joseph always bounced. He wasn't big enough yet to feel the rocks that could and would hinder his advancing steps.

When the road entered the town, Justine wasn't sure which way to go to get to Caroline Street. So, she followed the route she and Joseph had taken into town that morning. It passed their church, Nonna Etta's church. From the church, all the roads looked the same. But she knew Caroline Street was one street over. "This way," she said to Joseph.

"Is that the street?" Joseph said.

"See that sign over there? It says Caroline." They walked to the corner. To their left, a train station and a parking lot. Justine looked right, where old homes sat on either side of the street. "Look for 3-1-1. There's a number on each house."

They sauntered along the sidewalk. There were walls with ivy crawling over them, bushes that reached out as they walked by, bricks that lifted above gnarly tree roots, then flattened back down as they passed. In and out of shadow, they peered toward the front steps and porches looking for numbers.

"I think we're on the wrong side of the street," Justine said. They crossed to the opposite side. No cars or trucks moved along this street. No person walking their dog, no person in their yard. It was as if this end of Caroline Street had stopped in time.

"This way," Justine said. "It's there." She pointed. Joseph ran toward the house. They stopped in front of the house and stared at it. It looked old and small, sitting back from the road, overwhelmed by the tree in front. The small front yard of anemic grass needed trimming. Two large brick chimneys held it in place, like hands pressing, holding something valuable and vulnerable. Two windows on either side of an entry door. Above, on the gambrel roof, three windows framed in white looked out at the street. A black carriage lamp perched on the shoulder of the entry door. The cobbled driveway to the right of the house was without a car.

"Should we knock on the door?" Joseph said.

"No. Let's go around back."

"What if they don't let us in?"

"We have to sneak in."

They ran across the small front yard to the far corner of the house and the narrow gap between this house and its neighbor. Down the gap, they ran to the backyard. Justine stopped Joseph. They looked over the yard and the back of the house. The rear of the house was a modern addition to the much older front. Joseph pointed to the rear door of the sunroom. Gray flagstones led up to it from a garden path that meandered among flower beds and low growing hedges. He looked at his sister. She nodded, and they ran to the door. Locked. They peered in and saw a table, chairs, a kitchen island, cabinets behind. Justine shook the door.

"It won't open," Joseph said. "There's windows." He pointed to small casement windows at the bottom of the fixed glass of the sunroom. The two of them crouched down and examined the windows. Joseph pushed on one. It didn't give.

"They're all locked," Justine said. "Let's go to the other side." She was disappointed. She had hoped the house would be open, be easy to get in, like her own.

On the opposite side of the house was a small gate opening to the driveway and the street beyond. There were no doors or windows on this side of the house.

"Maybe there's a key by the front door," Justine said. She ran toward the gate when she heard a voice.

"Hey! What are you kids doing there?" a woman yelled.

Joseph froze and turned toward the voice. The woman stepped off her porch and began walking toward them. Justine looked back at Joseph, then ran toward him. Joseph made an about-face, running to the backyard and around to the opposite side of the house. A muffled yell. "You two stop."

The kids ran along the narrow gap between Nonna Jannie's house and the neighboring house. Joseph spied a small window at ground level close to the front of the house. He followed Justine to the street. They ran across the street, down the sidewalk and parallel to the train station, stopping at the next street.

"We made it," Joseph said, looking back, breathing hard.

"We need to come after dark," Justine said. Her mind was churning fast. "If we can't find a key, then we will have to break in. And we have to bring a shovel, something to dig with. And we need a bag for the jewels."

"I can bring my backpack," Joseph said. "But where will we find a shovel?"

They walked toward home. Justine was even more determined now that she knew where her Nonna Jannie once worked. "Francine has a small shovel she uses for her flowers. I know where she keeps it."

"I saw a small window when we were running. Maybe we could get in there."

"We'll come back tonight," Justine said. "Come on." She began to jog.

They heard noises in the trailer when they came upon it from the path in the woods. The back door was open. Joseph looked at his sister and said, "Terrell." She frowned. Terrell, the bully. He was loud and demanding and had an answer for everything. Answers that always favored him. Joseph was afraid of him. Justine didn't understand why her mother liked him. And now he was in their trailer. How did he get in? But she knew.

"Terrell, what are you doing in here?" she yelled. A yelled question like one her grandmother might produce. A learned bravado, one she found useful both at home and at school. She discovered she could use words to her advantage. She was good at taking someone's words—often barbed and hurtful—and twisting them back toward her provocateur. The surprise in their eyes was usually enough to derail their attempt at mastery over her. Justine felt a growing power every time she was challenged and countered the challenge with her words alone.

Terrell turned toward the small voice. Justine and Joseph stared at him. The sofa cushions were on the floor. The cereal boxes supporting the sofa's one gimp leg were strewn. Cabinet doors askew, drawers emptied. The trailer was a shamble, well beyond its normal state.

"Where's my gun?" he scowled.

"The police took it," Justine said. "Get out of our house."

"The police." A cold, wary stare, calculating the truth in her eyes. He looked at Joseph for confirmation. Joseph stared back, confident in his position by the door.

"Yes. Now leave." Justine stood aside at the corner of the sofa, giving him room to pass. Joseph moved toward Justine. Terrell eyed the two, considering his next move. The police would be looking for him. He bolted out the door and into the woods behind the trailer.

They watched from the back door as he disappeared beyond the low branches. Justine swung the door closed.

The two kids looked at the shaken trailer.

"Put the cushions back," Justine said. She restocked the cabinets and drawers with the fallen items from Terrell's desperate searching. "We need to look around the back door at Nonna Jannie's house. Maybe a key will be hidden somewhere there."

"But what if the people are home?"

Justine held a box of crackers. "I don't think anyone lives there." She wondered how she knew such a thing.

"When will we go?"

"Tonight, after Mama gets home and goes to sleep."

Joseph gave this some thought. He knew he would be tired, but this was important. He would dig for treasure. Nonna Jannie's treasure. "We need to get a shovel."

Justine pulled aside the curtain and looked at the trailer across the street, where Francine lived. With her dog. "She keeps her garden stuff in the shed behind the trailer. Let's see if we can sneak behind without that dog hearing us. Come on."

They exited the back door and walked into the woods, circling the park until they came out on the street above Francine's trailer, then walked down the street and behind two trailers to Francine's. The shed was locked, but a bucket and a small cart sat beside the back door. Justine pointed. "You go," she said. "Be quick."

He returned with a tiny shovel and the two of them made their way back to their trailer, back to the failing insulation and the door that would not lock.

# SIX

Katy sat at her desk at home in the dining room of this single bedroom apartment, the rear of which overlooked a creek, Alum Springs. The sound of crickets outside and the call of frogs. She could hear those creatures if she chose, but her mind blanked all else but the words on the display before her. She read and re-read the news story in the Free Lance. It was August 1910 and Anna Fitzhugh was missing. A brief article just three days prior had announced Anna's departure for New York to visit her sick mother. This article stated that Anna never arrived.

> One of this town's most upstanding citizens, Mr. Blayden Fitzhugh, is distraught at the news. He reported his wife had left on the 14th on the train for Washington, where she was to board a train for New York. Mr. Fitzhugh told the police that his wife had with her many pieces of jewelry. There is speculation that this may be a motive for foul play. Could Mrs. Anna Fitzhugh have been murdered for her jewelry? The police have informed this reporter that they will not indulge in such a theory. Mr. Fitzhugh has offered a reward for information pertaining to his wife's disappearance.

Katy finished the article and smiled. She loved the homespun style of these old news articles. She checked the time. After ten. She was not tired. She felt like telling a story, exploring possibilities. This had the makings of a story.

'The Disappearance of Anna Fitzhugh.' Katy sat back in her chair and looked out at the creek. Tree shadows and dark beyond. Where should she start? A young woman, newly married, with a black maid. And much jewelry. A small town in Virginia. Eight years past the turn of the century. She would have a friend, Kate Aldridge. The two would belong to the Pythian Sisters. They would dine together, the Aldridges and the Fitzhughs. Jannie Pratt and Anna would confide in each other. Anna would share her jewelry with Jannie. And then...Katy began typing.

It was late in the summer of 1908 when Anna and Blayden Fitzhugh drove into town in their new automobile. They had honeymooned at Lake George in New York. Blayden had purchased the car from a dealer in Boston prior to leaving for New York and had it shipped to Washington, DC, where it was waiting when he and Anna detrained. They drove south for several hours and when the vehicle finally crossed the bridge into the small town, it was met with wonder. Anna waved from her seat as the boys running alongside hooted and whistled. The next day, the Free Lance announced the couples' return from their honeymoon. 'Mr. Fitzhugh has brought with him a fine automobile. His lumber business is surely one of the most profitable in the area', the paper reported.

She sat back and re-read that last sentence. Interesting comment by the reporter, she thought. She wondered if Fitzhugh might have a reputation as a successful but pompous business owner.

She continued her fiction tied with the small twine of newspaper opinion and questionable fact.

The next day Anna arranged her house, the house that Blayden had bought, knowing he and Anna would soon wed. She had in mind to add wallpaper to the small dining room. And they needed proper furniture for entertaining. The barn-like furniture that Blayden brought from his office above the lumber warehouse had to go.

"I'll need a maid," Anna said to Blayden as he left for work the next morning. "I'm going to consult with Kate. Her maid is quite nice. She may know someone."

"You need not ask my approval, Anna," he said. "We should have the Aldridges over once you've put your stamp on the house."

Anna smiled. "I was thinking just that."

After lunch, she phoned Kate Aldridge. Henrietta, the operator, put her through, then listened to their conversation. Anna and Kate had both been stenographers. They met at a luncheon organized by a woman who wanted to start a stenographer's union. The luncheon went fine; the union died the next day.

"How has your day been, Henrietta?" Anna said.

"Oh my, Anna. You should know that Mr. Tunnley took ill Saturday. But how was your honeymoon? I heard you have a new Packard car. How wonderful."

"Yes. Thank you, Henrietta. I'm so sorry to hear about Mr. Tunnley. But I must talk with Kate. Can you excuse us?"

"Of course. Hi Kate."

"It's always nice to hear your voice, Henrietta," Kate said. "Bye now."

"Bye."

"Kate," Anna said in a low voice, "I am in need of a good maid."

Three days later, Jannie Pratt met Anna Fitzhugh. From her house on Sophia Street, Jannie walked south past the new train station being built on Prussia Street, not two blocks from Anna's house. She knocked on the door.

It wasn't long before the two young women were friends. They were two years apart in age, Anna the older. Jannie had an eye for fashion and skill with the sewing machine. Her father, who worked as a carpenter, acquired a broken Singer machine. He fixed it and Jannie taught herself to use it. When Anna saw that her new maid was an accomplished seamstress, she put her to work. She and Anna would model the new creations and soon Jannie was selling dresses to Anna's friends. They were seen walking through town together, carrying material they had picked out. In J.T. Lowery's they looked over the lady's suits. Later, Jannie said she could make such a suit.

That night, Anna told her husband about her outing with Jannie. She showed him a picture of the suit that Lowery's was selling for $5.95. "Jannie can make this suit for less than a dollar,

she told Blayden. Let me show you the material we bought today."
Blayden was impressed. Could she teach others to sew? He
wondered. He was fond of Jannie and happy that his wife had a
companion for a maid—and now a seamstress. Blayden, the
businessman, proposed that Anna should consider establishing
a dressmaking establishment. He knew how she enjoyed
working as a stenographer. This would allow her to operate a
proper business. Even if she made little profit, it would establish
her as a presence in the community and burnish his reputation
as well.

Katy read it over, always surprised by how her stories just seemed
to flow from behind her eyes onto the page. Jannie the seamstress. J.T.
Lowery. What a marvelous thing is imagination. Katy made a note to
look for newspaper citations for Blayden Fitzhugh. She had searched
for articles for Anna but didn't bother looking for articles on Blayden.
It was late. She would continue working on it tomorrow evening.

# SEVEN

Justine lay in bed waiting for her mother to get home from work. Nonna Etta was asleep on the sofa in the living room. Joseph snored softly next to her. She heard the crickets through the ajar'd window next to the bed, duct-taped to keep the mosquitoes out. And then the sound of her mother's footsteps. She reached over to Joseph and shook him awake.

"It's time," Justine whispered. Joseph rubbed his eyes and leaned up on his elbow. Justine held a small flashlight. They waited as their mother and grandmother finished talking. The front door opened, then closed. Rachelle readied for bed and minutes later, the back door opened. The two jewel seekers walked toward the wooded path, followed by short moon shadows.

"We forgot the shovel," Joseph said, stopping. Justine turned and looked back toward the trailer. "I put it under the trailer."

"Go get it." Justine interrupted her image of the Caroline Street house, the same image from earlier in the day as she stood across the street from it. Was that how the house looked to Nonna Jannie more than a hundred years ago? And what did Nonna Jannie look like? What did she do in the house? Justine had been mulling these questions over since Katy at the library identified the house. It was a real house now, just as it was real so many years ago to her great-great-great-grandmother.

Joseph returned with the shovel and Justine put her thoughts aside. At almost midnight, the busy road to town was lit sporadically. The kids let the moon guide them. They jogged and walked, ignored by the few cars that passed. Justine was now familiar with the streets and the neighborhood of this end of Caroline Street. They stopped on the opposite side of the street and watched the house and its neighboring houses. Only a few lights within the houses on the street. 311 was dark. They crossed and walked along the side of the house to the rear. Joseph pointed to the small window at ground level as they passed by, but Justine wanted to check the back door once more. Locked. She turned on the flashlight and looked at the ground for small rocks that might hide a key. Nothing. They walked back to the front door and searched. Justine turned off the flashlight and followed Joseph to the side with the window. He reached down and pushed on it. The window gave, opening in on wobbly hinges. Justine shined the light. To get in, they would have to crawl over the window since the hinge was on the bottom and it didn't open all the way.

"How do we get in?" Joseph whispered.

Justine examined the window and took the small shovel from Joseph. She jammed the shovel blade below the hinge and pushed down hard. The hinge broke and the window dropped at an angle. When she broke the opposite hinge, the window fell to the cellar floor with the sound of breaking glass. Joseph looked at his sister. Justine knelt and shined the flashlight into the cellar. She saw pipes and wires and cobwebs. The floor was less than five feet below them.

"I'll go first," Justine said. She handed the flashlight to Joseph.

"It's too far down."

"We can jump." She backed into the window opening, grabbing at the sill as she lowered herself down the inside wall. Hanging with one hand, she pushed against the wall with her other hand and dropped two feet to the floor. She used the window frame to scrape aside the broken glass. "I'll catch you," she said to Joseph, who was peering into the cellar. "Give me the flashlight and the shovel." Justine reached up. Joseph lowered the light as far as he could. "Just drop it," Justine said. It fell into her hands. Joseph dropped the shovel, then lowered himself with Justine's help.

"How do we get out?" Joseph said, looking around.

"The back door," Justine said.

"But the people will hear us."

"I don't think anyone is home. They would have heard the glass break." Justine pointed the flashlight at the floor beneath them.

"It's cement," Joseph said with alarm. "How can we dig anything?"

Justine studied the floor. Her heart stumbled. She moved the light about the room. The walls were brick and stone, stained by water and lime. Overhead, wooden beams and joists collected cobwebs and wires. White knobs projected along the inside of one beam. Justine walked to the center of the room. The floor was uneven.

There was black plastic laid on much of the floor. She picked up one end and pulled it back.

"Look," she said to Joseph. "It's dirt here. Help me pull this."

They pulled the plastic back toward one corner. It was heavy and hard to manage. The underside of the plastic was moist. Bricks held down three sheets laid side by side. They knelt and pulled the plastic as far as they could, then stood and followed the light beam as Justine scanned the dirt floor. Beneath the window was an area of concrete, a pad six-feet square. The remaining cellar floor was dirt.

"Why is that cement?" Joseph said.

"I don't know. Let's hope the jewels aren't under it. Here, hold this," Justine said, handing the flashlight to Joseph. She took the small shovel and began to dig. For half an hour, they took turns digging, then stopped and reviewed their progress. Justine held the light. Joseph took the shovel and knelt. He was tired. The light revealed a series of small mounds as if gophers had attacked the cellar.

Justine moved the beam across the floor. She wasn't following the illumination. Her mind had stalled, marveling at how easy it was to forget the darkness. The darkness that comes brings with it fear—bringing 'creaks and crawls' as Nonna Etta would say—the fear of being alone and unable to see and know what was nearby, what was familiar. Justine was not scared in this house in the near dark. There was within her a strength that was both familiar and unfamiliar. She took a deep, satisfied breath. Joseph reached up and directed the light to the hole next to his knee. She looked down and smiled. It was only later, years later, that Justine would realize that her natural fear of the dark and the unfamiliar could not overpower her determination. It was a trait she would build upon and hone her entire life to where the absence of light was a minor obstacle to be overcome or, sometimes, welcomed as a partner.

"We'll never find Nonna Jannie's jewels," Joseph said, watching as the flashlight's beam dimmed, then died altogether. The sparse moonlight from the window illuminated two small figures. Four innocent knees spackled with dirt.

"Yes, we will," Justine said. "We'll come back tomorrow. We need a bigger shovel."

# EIGHT

Nancy Bilderson stood near the side door to the library where the used-books box sat. The large plastic box was half full of books that were donated by patrons. She lifted them out in twos and threes and placed them on a wheeled cart. When she had emptied the box, she pushed the cart into the main library room behind the counter and began triaging the books, determining which the library wanted and which to be set aside for their next sale. Most were fictions, others were biographies and kids' books. One was not ordinary. She read the title: *Virginia's Attitude Toward Slavery and Secession, Beverley B. Munford* and turned to another volunteer who was checking out a book for a patron.

"Karen, this is one of our books. It was in the used book bin. A donation."

The woman shrugged. "Probably a mistake."

Nancy noted the number and checked her cheat sheet for its location. Virginiana Room.

Katy sat in front of the microfilm screen reading an article about Blayden Fitzhugh, the first of several she had found in the historic newspaper indexes. Several articles and advertisements about his lumber mill. She was familiar with this business from earlier research. The last article, dated 1918 in the index, covered the sale of the business: Fitzhugh Millwork, sold to J.W. Masters. She moved her finger up the page to an article dated four months after Anna's disappearance, noting the spool number of the microfilm.

Leaning in close at the contrasty type, she read of Fitzhugh's marriage to Sarah Tabor.

Mr. Blayden Thomas Fitzhugh and Miss Sarah Jane Tabor were married late afternoon yesterday in a small ceremony at the United Methodist Church. Miss Tabor and her bridesmaid, Miss Constance Reems, both wore white…

Katy sat back and mumbled: "They always wear white. So, four months and he has a new wife…and a new church."

She looked up at the man standing beside her. He held a sheaf of papers to his chest and leaned his head forward, his eyes magnified by his thick-rimmed glasses.

"Excuse me." His white goat-beard moved as if controlled by a ventriloquist when he spoke. "I need some help. One of my relatives was in the Confederate Army in Arkansas. I understand you have a history that might mention his regiment and the battles they fought in."

Katy took the man back into the room with the moving bookshelves. "Why don't you start with this book," she said, handing him Volume XIV from a length of red-bound books on Confederate military history.

Katy returned to the microfilm but was interrupted again. Nancy Bilderson walked around the glass partition and into the Virginiana Room.

"Nancy, what brings you to the underworld? You got your hair cut."

"It's my summer cut. I have a book that I think is yours. It was in the donation bin." She handed the book to Katy.

"I was wondering what happened to this." Katy leafed through the book, checking the pages. "Someone took it home with them rather than make notes down here. Let's hope they didn't cut a page or two from it."

"Does that happen often? Someone steals a book?"

"Not too often, but occasionally. Some of these books are one-of-a-kind. It's nice that whoever took this returned it. Looks like it's still in one piece." Katy walked the book back to its place in the adjoining room. Nancy followed.

"Don't you get lonely down here?" Nancy said, glancing at the man with the white beard. "All the people are upstairs. Reading or working in the computer room."

"I'm not lonely," white beard said. Nancy looked at him and smiled. "No. Not you." She followed Katy into the stack.

"I never get lonely here," Katy told her. "I get lonely at home sometimes, but I know I can always return to my books here in the library." Katy fit the book on Virginia slavery back into its place.

"You don't have a boyfriend?"

"I go through boyfriends like I go through books. Once the story is over, I move on." Katy walked back to her desk.

"You need to find someone with a long story." Nancy followed the younger woman like a puppy.

"Someone who is constantly revising, perfecting. Yeah, I haven't found that person. Or he hasn't found me. I'm not an active seeker." Katy sat at her desk. Nancy stood opposite, wondering how someone so intelligent, so pretty, could live among these old books and the histories they presented. While upstairs, the present world was alive, moving, talking, laughing, playing…mingling. Nancy liked to mingle. She liked the word 'mingling.' It sounded like ringing, like bells talking amongst themselves: ring-a-ling, ming-a-ling.

Nancy looked at Katy's computer screen. What was she working on? What could be so interesting that kept the girl in the basement all day? She knew Katy wrote a blog on local history and she led a book club sponsored by the library, but these were extracurricular. What was it she did during working hours?

"I'm thinking of working here full time," Nancy said.

Katy looked at her, knowing this was an opening gambit into a long conversation. She liked the woman—mid-40s, Katy figured—but she talked too much. Talking was fine, Katy believed, if it had a purpose. But talking to fill silence was just wrong. Katy leaned back in her chair.

"I think that's great. The library could use the help." She glanced at her computer screen. It had gone to sleep. She looked over at the microfilm reader. Blayden Fitzhugh. Did he kill his wife?

"Now that my girls are on their own, I need something to keep me busy. They were the ones who encouraged me to work here. I remember bringing them to the library when they were young, but I never really enjoyed it. I was never interested in books, but now that I'm surrounded by them, I have to be interested. Right?" Katy considered her reply, but before she could give it, Nancy continued. "I checked out a book last week. It's a big one with over four hundred pages, and I love it. I wasn't sure if I would, but now, I can't wait to get home to read."

"That's wonderful, Nancy." She could think of no better word to use. Full of wonder seemed to fit. She wouldn't ask the title. That would encourage more talk. She smiled and waited for her intruder to get the message that she wasn't interested in talking.

"I know. I'm so happy. It's like walking into a different world when I walk into the library now. And when I get home, I enter a new world in the book. Why has it taken a lifetime for me to discover this?"

Katy looked up at the woman standing close to her desk. Her soft blue eyes were wide and her cheeks full of smile. She waited for Katy to answer, to share in her discovery. Katy wished for solitude but knew she was trapped. She would not be rude. That was not in her character. She raised her arm, pointing to the chair next to her desk.

"Do you have time to sit for a minute, Nancy? I'm sure you're very busy upstairs—"

"Oh, thank you. That's sweet. I don't want to take up your time." Nancy sat. "I'm hoping to get involved with more important work, you know. When I come full time. And you seem to do important work down here. Maybe you could give me something to do that would help you. I could do it upstairs and when I'm done, I could bring it to you."

Katy smiled. The woman thought Katy was doing important work. "I don't do important work, Nancy. If I were to leave, no one would know I was missing—maybe two or three people would know— but the rest of the world would simply float along, oblivious to my disappearance. But the work I do requires me to be down here, mostly. So, you would have to be here as well."

"Oh. I thought maybe I could work upstairs but still help you. What things are you working on?" Nancy leaned forward with expectation. Katy looked at her and thought.

"I have an ongoing project I work on in the background. I'm creating a hyperlinked database of all the people, businesses, and houses in the city from its beginning to present day."

Nancy leaned back in her chair. "Oh."

"I'll show you how it will work. It's still very much in its infancy." Katy turned to her computer and brought up a screen showing a map of the city. "The software is in beta, but you'll get the idea. This is an early map of the city—the blocks, the streets. I'm filling in the details, showing various houses and businesses of the time. You can click on a block, and a window shows that block zoomed, like this. So, there you see the outlines of the different businesses on William Street in 1886. And if I click on one, it brings up the data for that business, what sort of business, who owns it, and so on. If I click on the owner, up comes information on him or her. Where they live, deed info on the property, family, and anything else that exists on the person or business. The problem, of course, is where does the data come from? I'm starting with a blank database and need to find the data and enter it. The data comes from deed books, insurance policies, from newspaper articles, court records, census records, genealogy records, anything I can unearth."

"Why would you want this? Who would use it?"

"Well, I would want it because it's really neat. It describes the interconnections of people and places over time. And other researchers would use it. Let me show you." Katy brought up a different map. "Here is the city in 1866. Same kind of information plus additional info I am getting from the park service. It includes which houses were destroyed in the war—Civil War—and which were hit by cannon fire. The cannon fire is cool. Look at this. I've entered data for each house that got hit, how many hits, and which walls were hit. So now, if I query for those houses, we get this map."

Nancy looked at the map. She saw the streets, the houses highlighted that received cannon fire. And she saw lines drawn from those houses going in various directions. "What are those lines?"

"That's the cool part. They show the probable directions from which the cannonballs would have come. From this, you can trace backward and determine the probable placement of the artillery." Katy looked at Nancy and said, "And where are most located?" She pointed to the screen and answered her question. "On the hills across the river from the town. Of course, we know that already from what we know historically and from general military tactics, but this ties the actual houses and structures to that cannon fire. Cool, huh?"

"Yeah." Nancy was less than impressed. Maybe there wasn't fun work here after all.

"To populate the database, I need to search all the archives available—and most aren't digitized. It's hand labor. Eye labor. Have you ever searched through a deed book that looked like it was written by a nineteenth-century doctor? I have newspapers from the 1700s there." Katy pointed to a cabinet opposite. "They're on microfilm. I need to read through each and pick out the information that corresponds with other info I know of. If I have a name from a deed book or a court record and I discover the same name in the newspaper of the same period, I may be able to correlate the two, then enter it in the database—by hand. It's tedious work. During the school year, I have help from Professor Stanton's college students, but during the summer, I'm on my own." Katy looked at Nancy, now thoroughly depressed. "That's just the work I'm doing in the background—when I have time between requests that come in from researchers trying to find out if their great-great-grandmother lived in a house that was haunted."

"Haunted?" Nancy's eyes lit. Katy realized she had said the wrong thing. She got caught up in her enthusiasms. She took a deep breath.

"Yeah. I had some kids come in and ask about a house that their 3rd-great-grandmother worked in. She was a maid for a wealthy couple. They hope to find jewelry never recovered from when the original owner went missing."

"Wow. That sounds fascinating. I could help with that, maybe. Do you think?"

Katy considered this request. "If your handlers upstairs say it's alright, I don't see why not. Of course, you would work down here much of the time."

"I guess I could deal with that for a while." Nancy waited for Katy to reply. She watched as the younger woman moved the cursor about the screen, the signal for her to move on. "Thanks," she said and got up. She waved at Katy. Katy waved back and said, "Bye."

"How was the house haunted?" Nancy said, turning at the door.

"Oh. I don't know that it's haunted. Whenever you mess with history, you're apt to encounter a ghost or two."

Nancy smiled and walked up the steps to the sunlit main floor with its many patrons mingling with each other and their books.

Katy got up and looked into the research room. "How's it going in here?" she said.

"This is just what I was looking for," said white beard. "Thank you."

Near the end of the day, Katy took her seat at the microfilm reader, continuing her search through the old newspapers. She skipped the advertisements. A short mention of Blayden having to shut down his mill because of an accident with a planing machine. One of Mr. Fitzhugh's black laborers was hurt working with the machine. Mr. Fitzhugh said the planer would need repair but would have minimal effect on production. The next article caught her interest. It stated that Blayden was arrested for selling liquor. This was two years after his second marriage. He didn't spend time in jail, though. Katy wondered if the authorities were taking advantage of Blayden's liquor. She knew Virginia was ahead of the country in prohibiting the sale of booze. But, like the rest of the country, if you were well-placed, you could buy your way out of trouble. She spooled another reel and leaned into the screen. A member of the Knights of Pythias. Blayden honored for his generous donation of timbers for the new post office on Princess Anne Street. Katy switched off the reader. Time to go home. She grabbed her purse and notes, turned off the lights, and walked to the stairs. So, he kills his wife. No. He meets Sarah, then kills his wife, then becomes a bootlegger of fine whiskey. All while maintaining his disguise as one of the town's upstanding businessmen. I like this better.

At home, Katy sloughed her shoes by the door and went into the kitchen. She pulled a bottle of beer from the refrigerator and sat at her laptop. Last night's story was history. She began anew.

"The Death of Anna Fitzhugh"

There was a knock on the door. Anna looked at her maid. "Can you see who that is, Jannie? I'm certainly not expecting anyone." Jannie was twenty-one and had been working for Anna Fitzhugh for just over a year. She and Anna became unlikely friends during that period. Jannie held the long piece of material as Anna fed it through the sewing machine. Jannie was teaching her mistress how to sew. She folded the material and hung it over a chair but was startled by a shout from outside. She looked at Anna's face.

"That's Blayden," Anna said, alarmed.

"Just open the goddam door," Blayden yelled. The women ran to the hall. The front door opened. Two men helped Blayden in. His waist was covered in blood.

"Blayden," Anna screamed. "What happened?"

"In here." Blayden motioned for the men to help him into the parlor.

"He's been shot," one man said to Anna. Jannie ran to the kitchen and brought back towels. The men laid him on the sofa, then stood back and looked at Anna.

"How?" she said, kneeling beside her husband, opening his shirt. "Is it bad? We need to take him to the doctor."

"Not too bad…" the man began.

Blayden interrupted him. "You'll have to sew it up, Anna. I don't need a doctor."

Anna knew the police had shot her husband. It was that whiskey business. He promised not to continue. Now he was injured. She opened his shirt. Jannie peered at the blood oozing from the two holes in his side, then turned for the kitchen.

"Bring hot water," Anna said, looking over her shoulder.

Jannie filled a pot and lit the stove. She was familiar with gunshot wounds, having heard from her father and uncles of the wounds suffered by men in the Civil War and having helped dress a wound that a neighbor got from a run-in with a gang of men bent on killing him.

Over the next week, Blayden lay in bed recovering, complaining, arguing with Anna about his side business. Over the next several months, Anna noted the change in his behavior. She sensed there was trouble at the mill. He had been to see his banker. Yet she did not confront him. She confided in Jannie. The two developed theories; they conspired. Anna asked Jannie to follow Blayden into town, to visit places she was sure Blayden would visit. The Exchange Hotel, the National Bank, or his lawyer.

Anna met with her friend, Kate Aldridge. Kate offered to have her husband talk with Blayden. Fred Aldridge had arranged for the delivery of some of Blayden's heavy machinery. The Fitzhugh mill was near to the railroad yard where Aldridge worked. Both men were members of the Knights of Pythias. There would be opportunities, Kate said, for Fred to "make certain inquiries." She held Anna's gloved hand outside of church and gave her friend a hug.

Two weeks later, Kate called Anna and asked to meet. She said she had important information. Anna called for a carriage and met Kate in town. Kate told Anna that she had seen Blayden with a woman standing outside the Hotel Dannehl.

"The hotel?" Anna said. "But...what were they doing?"

"They were talking, and it was intimate talk. I can tell you for certain it was."

"I am sure there is an explanation," Anna said, looking at Kate, hoping for her friend to offer it. But Kate said nothing, and Anna looked to the ground.

Anna sent Jannie on missions when the work was finished around the house. The Hotel Dannehl was her destination. Soon, Anna had evidence enough to confront Blayden.

Katy took the last swallow of beer and read over her story. It was late, and she hadn't eaten. She went to the kitchen and pulled a veggie burger from the freezer. She microwaved the burger and a bun, sloshed some tabasco sauce over it and sat at the table and thought, chewing on her less than palatable dinner. How would she incorporate Anna's jewelry? Jannie should have a more central role. Who is this Sarah Tabor? Where did she come from? Katy finished her meal and returned to her laptop, staring at the screen. Where to start? she asked herself. She got up and went to the kitchen for a glass of water, then lay on the couch and thought about how she wanted her story to proceed.

# NINE

It was morning when Katy awoke on the couch. Her mouth tasted like burnt wood. Her shoulder ached from having slept on it. She glanced at her watch and jumped up, showered, brushed her teeth, and ran out the door, shaking her wet hair like a dog.

\* \* \*

"Where you kids going?" Rachelle called from her bedroom.

Joseph held the back door open but didn't move. He waited for Justine to answer. Justine would know what to say.

"Outside," Justine replied. "We'll be in the woods."

Rachelle, not fully awake, tried to focus on the ceiling, on the words of her daughter, then said, "OK," and dozed off.

Justine closed the door and skipped down the wood steps to Joseph, who held Francine's garden trowel.

"It's bent."

"Get a rock and pound it back. We need to find a real shovel." Justine shoved the small flashlight with a new battery into her back pocket. She looked down at her knees, still marked with the dirt of the cellar from last night. She glanced at Joseph's knees. "Let's go."

They scoured the neighbors' backyards, searching for a real shovel. Two streets over, they found it—a short spade—but as they approached the woods and safety, the Corbin brothers sighted them. The Corbins had a reputation. People to be avoided. At nine and ten years, the two brothers exhibited many traits of experienced gangsters. They smoked cigarettes, and they cursed. They wore their hair long, and they had tattoos. Justine heard Nonna Etta describe Terrell as a gangster. He had these same traits.

"Do they really have tattoos?" Joseph whispered as Justine adjusted the shovel in her hands. Shahin, the oldest, and Hauk approached, grinning at Justine. Justine knew Hauk better than his brother; he was in her class, six months older than her. Joseph looked at their curly hair. He studied their arms. He saw nothing that resembled a tattoo.

"What's goin' down?" Shahin said.

"Looking for gold." Justine held the shovel across her chest, ready to strike. Joseph stared at her, waiting for further explanation. He held the trowel like his sister, its bent tip drooping, tongue-wise.

"Gold," Hauk said with derision. "Pass the shit, bro. These two wouldn't know gold from dirt."

"They've been digging the dirt, though." Shahin pointed to Justine's knee.

"Get out of our way." Joseph held his shovel toward the two gangsters as if it were an instrument of exorcism. Shahin and Hauk looked at each other. Hauk laughed. Shahin put his hand on his brother's shoulder.

"The pone's got guts, don't he," Shahin said. "Tell you what. We'll let you go, but we need to look after you. Don't want you to get in trouble." He glanced at his brother. They smiled, happy conspirators. Hauk moved, bowing his permission to allow them passage. Justine gave him a frown and motioned to Joseph.

They strode along the side street closest to the woods, then entered the path to the road. The gangsters followed. Justine considered her options. She would walk into town and hope the Corbin brothers got bored and left. If they didn't, she would walk them up one street and down another until they got tired.

"What's the flashlight for?" Hauk said. Justine swung her hand behind and touched the light in her pocket.

"For seeing in the dark."

They came to the entrance road to the trailer park and continued to the highway. The Corbins attempted conversation, but Justine ignored them. She felt safe now that she and Joseph were on the big road with all the traffic. She still held the shovel close, having Joseph lead by several yards, out of range if she had to swing it.

Justine thought back to previous encounters with the Corbins on the school bus. The bus seemed to be the prime hunting ground for these two raptors. They had an audience they could play to, and the rear of the bus afforded them cover from the driver. Making the fifth graders laugh by bullying the smaller kids was a favorite activity. They carried no books or papers. Homework was not a word in their vocabulary. Yet their report cards rarely exhibited anything less than a 'B.' Justine saw their father drive off to work in the morning sometimes. The mother appeared not to have a job. Once, Justine saw her on the river path. Alone, with a notebook in her hand. Justine followed her to the river and watched as she sat beside a sycamore and wrote in her book. It was early spring when the osprey and the eagles flew, when the shad swam from the ocean to their spawning grounds. Mrs. Corbin sat watching the birds circle above the water, seeking a meal. Justine hid in the brush along the trail and watched. Now, Justine turned and glanced at the strange woman's sons. They were shoulder to shoulder, their eyes on the ground, talking softly. Two brothers, planning. They must be up to something, Justine thought, and turned back toward Joseph, who tried to whistle, holding his trowel like a baton, tipping forward on his toes.

Justine put her shovel over her shoulder. It was heavy. The day was warming. She longed for the shade of the old trees along Caroline Street. She looked up at the bridge, and her mind presented her with the house where Nonna Jannie worked. The house with a roof that looked like a barn and its red door. Wouldn't it be nice to live in a house? A place with a backyard that tumbled in flowers and had doors that locked. Maybe, with the jewels they find, they could buy a house. Justine's mind floated over the idea like a bird searching for a safe place to land. She would have her own bedroom, one with a door that would close. It would hold the quiet close.

"Where is this gold mine, Justine?" Shahin came up behind and tapped her on the shoulder. She startled and looked into his face. The curls of his hair danced. His eyes were bright as the sun.

"It's up around the corner a ways."

"It's in somebody's yard?" Shahin moved in front of her.

"Why does your mother sit by the river?" Justine wasn't about to tell Shahin what she was up to.

"What?" His face changed. He looked back at Hauk. Hauk came up beside his brother.

"You been following our mother?" Hauk said with concern and contempt. They had reached the bridge and its shade. The rumble of the vehicles above made it sound as if they were in a kettledrum. Justine stopped, holding the shovel chest high.

"I've been doing no such thing," she told the boys. Joseph turned. "I have a right to be at the river, like anybody." The Corbins stared into Justine's eyes. Justine stared back. Joseph came to his sister holding the garden trowel, elbow cocked.

"Come on," Justine said, turning Joseph toward town. The brothers followed.

"Why do you want to know about our mom?" Shahin said. Justine said nothing.

"Everybody's a busybody," said Hauk.

Justine was weary of this harassment. She turned abruptly and faced the Corbins. They pulled up fast, almost walking into her as she held the shovel before her like a Japanese bo.

"I am not a busybody," she declared. "But you two are. We didn't ask you to come with us. Now go home."

The brothers stood shoulder to shoulder, less than two feet from Justine. The look on their faces was that of an enraged bull. Truth had cornered them. Shahin wouldn't admit it. He reached out and grabbed the shovel, yanking it from Justine's grip.

"We came along to keep you two safe," he said, throwing the shovel to the side. "You can go to hell, then." He turned and marched from the shade back into the sun. Hauk followed. The sound of the moaning bridge fell from the girders above. Justine went over and picked up the shovel.

"And stay away from our mother!" Hauk yelled.

"They really bad," Joseph said.

"Yeah," Justine agreed. "But they're gone. That's good." They strolled from under the bridge toward town.

"Why did they say keep us safe?" Joseph said, facing his sister.

"They were just trashin' us."

"They're mean. I don't like them. But they didn't have tattoos."

Justine thought back to the first time she mentioned the Corbin brothers to Joseph. She told him to stay far away from them. They were as bad as Terrell. Maybe worse.

"They never had tattoos, Joseph. That's Terrell. He has tattoos."

Joseph worked this information around in his head. "Terrell has a skull with wings on it."

Justine pictured the flying skull and the snake on Terrell's other arm. The skull was yucky, but she liked the snake. She remembered the small ringneck snake she had caught and shown Terrell last summer. He was terrified and yelled at her. Why would he have a snake on his arm if he was scared of snakes?

"Terrell has a snake," Joseph said and told Justine of the time she scared Terrell with the ringneck snake and then scared the teacher at school and scared Nonna Etta after school. "That little snake couldn't hurt a fly," Joseph informed Justine as he skipped along the sidewalk beneath the shade trees on Caroline Street. "It didn't have a mouth big enough to grab anybody's hand. It was too little and besides, it wasn't even poisonous." He stared at Justine, waiting for her to affirm his knowledge, the knowledge he received from her. Justine kept walking toward her destination, staring forward at the long truck at the end of the street. Joseph touched her arm.

"Justine. That snake was too small to bite. You told me."

"Joseph, you were as afraid as everyone else. Remember?"

Joseph looked at his shoes. He remembered. He remembered being told by Justine that he was being silly about the snake. But now he wasn't scared. He was sure the snake wouldn't hurt him.

"But I'm bigger now," he said. "And that snake wasn't even poisonous."

Justine stopped by a large maple tree on the corner. "It wasn't venomous, you mean. Look there. At the house. They're taking the furniture out."

She pointed to the moving van parked in front of 311 Caroline. Three men lifted furniture into the van. Another man inside the truck covered the furniture with blankets, stacking them.

Justine considered their options. Joseph cut his thoughts of snakes. "Why are they taking the furniture?"

"I think the people are moving. No one will be in the house," Justine said, thinking this confirmed what she already sensed. They could get into the house without worrying about the owners discovering them in the cellar. "Go over and ask the man in the truck when they'll be finished."

"Me?" Joseph watched as two men lifted a dresser onto the rear liftgate.

"Are you afraid?" Justine said.

"No."

"He's not a snake."

"I'm not afraid of snakes." Joseph was angered that his sister would consider such a thing.

"Then go ask when they'll finish moving the furniture." She pointed. "I'm going to walk around the front of the truck and see if the window on the house is still open." She leaned her shovel against the tree and walked down the sidewalk parallel to the truck, then crossed the street ahead of it. Joseph watched her. She turned to him as she got to the truck and motioned for him to go. He dropped his trowel and stepped off the curb.

"Mister," he called.

The man in the truck didn't hear him. Joseph came closer. From the front door, a man came holding two lamps. "Better stay away, kid. You'll get hurt," he said.

"When will you be done moving this stuff?" Joseph pointed to the truck.

"Probably a couple hours. Why do you want to know?"

"Just wondered." Joseph was growing confident. And curious. "Where're you taking all this?"

The man handed the lamps to the man inside the truck. He said to his co-worker, "Who's your friend?"

"He just showed up. You don't live around here, do you, kid?"

"No." Joseph's confidence was now waning.

"Yeah. Better be moving on, then. Go back to the hood where you're from."

Joseph studied the man's arms. They were bigger than Terrell's, much bigger. Justine came around the back of the truck and grabbed her brother.

"Come on." She looked at the man with big arms, then turned and walked across the street.

"Where'd she come from?"

"Beats me, but there's two more over there."

Justine held Joseph's hand and looked into his eyes. "What did they say? How long will they be?"

Joseph stared across the street at Shahin and Hauk, who stood beside the maple tree holding the two shovels. "They're back," he said as Justine looked up at her implacable guardians. She stopped in the middle of the street and scowled.

"What do you want?" she said, walking up to Shahin, taking the shovel from him. She turned to Hauk and grabbed the trowel.

"Free country," Hauk said. "Last I heard, anyway."

Justine and Joseph pranced by them.

"Better not be following us," Justine said, hurrying on.

"We were on our way home," Shahin said. "So there ain't but one way to go."

"You were on your way home a time ago, but I guess you got lost." Justine twirled around. "Why don't you two walk in front? That way, we can keep an eye on you." Hauk shrugged. Shahin gave her a smirk. "And you can protect us from the boogeyman." Justine moved to the side. The Corbin brothers' eyes conferred. They walked ahead of the Parker kids, then stopped and waited.

"Keep going," Justine said. "We'll be right behind."

"So," Shahin said, "what were you doing at that moving van? That where the gold is stashed?"

Justine ignored the question.

"None of your business," Joseph said.

"You're going to need some help with that gold," Hauk said. "You know, gold weighs almost three times as much as steel."

"Yeah," said Shahin.

Justine wasn't thinking of the weight of gold. Her thoughts were on the house that was being emptied. What if the jewels were not buried in the cellar? What if they were somewhere else in the house and the moving men found them? She leaned toward Joseph and whispered.

"What did the man say? About moving the furniture out. When will they be finished?"

"I think an hour," Joseph whispered back.

Justine thought: If it was only going to be an hour, then should they turn around and go back or wait for the men to finish?

"I believe," Shahin said, turning, walking backward, "you were going to dig in that yard back there. So, how do you know there's gold buried in that yard?"

Justine was tiring of the Corbin's curiosity. How would she lead them away?

"Gold," she began without knowing where this was going, "isn't always gold..."

The two brothers waited for her to continue, as did Joseph.

"You're talkin' trash," Hauk said.

"The sun is gold," she said. "And some snakes have a gold ring around their neck. And some flowers are gold, like sunflowers. If you go into the backyard, you will see gold flowers. That's what we were going to dig up. Flowers."

The Corbin brothers were disappointed. For a second.

"Bullshit! That's a tasty turd and you know it." Shahin stopped walking backward. Hauk stopped. Justine and Joseph stopped. They were at the corner next to a house with yellow shutters. In the small yard, a man stood up, appearing full height above the hedges that grew next to the sidewalk. He looked over the hedge at the four kids but said nothing. The kids stared, an eyed silence above the hedge.

The man spoke. "You kids lost?" He wore a tan, wide-brimmed hat which he doffed, wiping the sweat off his forehead with his arm. In his hand was a yellow-handled pruner.

"Just looking for flowers," Hauk said.

The man looked at the shovels that Joseph and Justine carried.

"Best not be lookin' 'round here. Flower thieves don't last long 'round here."

"We were going home," Justine said.

"Best be goin' with a ghost on your tail, missy. You don't visit this neighborhood without an invitation."

She frowned at the man. He put his hat back on his head and ducked below the hedge. The kids moved on. Joseph turned to Justine. "What did he mean about a ghost?"

"I don't know."

"Scary-looking n——," Hauk said to Shahin.

She followed the Corbins around the block and into the high sunlight, walking two streets over, then turned toward home, not saying another word. Joseph glanced at his sister, knowing she wasn't in the mood to be disturbed. The two brothers led the gold diggers along the road to Tidewater Trailer Park. Justine considered her next move. Her flower story wasn't convincing. She and Joseph would have to leave their trailer later today or tomorrow without the Corbin brothers knowing. They should bring a sandwich and water; she was thirsty.

Turning onto the trailer park road, the long-haired brothers began to jog, leaving Justine and Joseph well behind. They said nothing to the two jewel seekers, turning at the corner on the main park road. Justine was satisfied with this outcome but worried the bullies would continue to dog her and Joseph. She and Joseph walked past the entrance to the trailer park, circling into the woods to the rear of their trailer. As they got closer, they knew there was trouble. Loud talking and yelling penetrated the trees. It was Rachelle and Terrell. The two children stood beneath low, overhanging limbs just inside the tree canopy, watching their back door. Justine knew that if Francine, their nearest neighbor, was home, the police would soon be arriving. She dropped her shovel and whispered in Joseph's ear.

"We need to get inside quick and get a sandwich, then come back here." Joseph gave her a questioning look. "They're in the bedroom. We can sneak in, but we have to be quiet. You get the bread. I'll get the peanut butter and a knife." Joseph nodded. "And some water."

She gave Joseph a nudge, and they ran to the back steps, stopping on the landing. Justine listened, then opened the door. Joseph went to the cupboard and pulled a half loaf of bread onto the counter. Justine filled a plastic cup with water. She saw Joseph struggling with the bread, trying to release four slices. She put the water down and grabbed the bread. "Get the water," she said, shoving a knife in her back pocket and picking up the peanut butter. They heard their mother say to Terrell: "Either you get a proper job, or I'll lock your fucking ass out of this house." Finally, Justine thought, as she and Joseph jumped off the drooping back step.

"That was close," Joseph said, glancing down into the cup of water.

Justine pulled the bag of bread from her teeth. "Let's eat at the pond," she said, moving the big jar of peanut butter under her arm like it was a football. They trekked to a small pool, deep in the late winter and early spring but now shallow beneath the heavy canopy where the trees drank it near dry. They sat at the edge against an Overcup Oak and slapped peanut butter upon bread, sharing the little water that remained after Joseph's one-handed gallop down the stairs and into the woods.

This was Justine's favorite place—a place of refuge and quiet— where she could come and sit and think about better times and catch frogs and snakes and lift rotted logs searching for salamanders. It was a place of solace and safety, where anger and sadness were barred and those emotions faded and disappeared for hours, replaced with the magic of discoveries.

They sat against the tree, their knees high, chewing on dry, sticky sandwiches, watching streaks of sunlight pierce the top branches in search of shadows. Justine worked through ideas that might free jewels from their hundred-year-old burial.

"This is what we'll do," Justine said to Joseph. "Tomorrow we will walk to the house. It will be before Mama wakes—early. I saw the window. It had a piece of wood against it, but we can move the wood. It was just leaning. So, we'll be able to get in." Justine was animated.

Joseph listened to her voice and watched her face and hands as she explained the plan. He knew his sister had special powers. He watched her eyes. They burned through the shadows like Pentecostal flames. Joseph thought back to the sermon that Pastor Jacobs gave on Easter. He asked Nonna Etta what Pentecostal flames were. After Jacobs finished and turned toward the altar, she leaned over and whispered that they were flames with special powers. They could burn through anything.

"We will need to bring lunch and water," Justine continued. "We'll be there all day. It might take that long to find the jewels." She stood up and brushed the leaves from her shorts. "Let's see if Terrell is still there."

Joseph followed his sister to the backyard. They both dropped to the ground, prone, and looked under the pink-bearded trailer. Terrell's car was parked in front. "Leave the stuff here," Justine said. "We'll go to the river."

They walked through poplar and oak, beech and sycamore, over a small stream with perfectly-worn pebbles. Stopping, they scanned the wet gems. They picked favorites, pocketing them, and continued on over a fallen tree and out onto a clearing that looked east across the river at the tree-lined shore of another county. They slowed, hesitating. Not fifty feet from them sat Mrs. Corbin, leaning against a tree with a sketch pad on her knee. Justine looked upriver. The Corbin brothers stood on a sandbar, fishing.

"What do we do?" Joseph whispered.

Justine stood still and motioned with her hand to go back. Mrs. Corbin, however, heard their approach. She put her pad aside, twisting her head around. Justine saw the smile. Neither Justine nor Joseph had ever come close to the woman. Justine's only other knowledge of her—other than the time last spring—was from afar when Mrs. Corbin stood in her doorway on a snowy afternoon. The bus drove into the trailer park—a rare occurrence—and dropped off the kids. Mrs. Corbin leaned on the front door as Shahin and Hauk walked into their trailer. And then the door closed. Now the woman was smiling at them, a smile Justine knew to be genuine. In Justine's catalog of smiles, this one conveyed no falseness or possibility of harm. Yet she hesitated. Joseph's question of what to do caught her in a bind.

As a family, the Corbins were a mystery. They had moved in the previous school year and associated with few people. The boys were less of a mystery and showed themselves to be bullies and ruffians. Justine could not decide. Joseph waited, concerned, as his sister studied the woman sitting by the tree. His knowledge of her was a conflation of Justine's warnings and Pastor Jacob's sermons. Could she be a devil, like her sons, but even more dangerous? He held Justine's arm, hoping to hurry her decision, hoping he had a long enough lead to outrun the devil if she made a move to grab him.

"Come," Mrs. Corbin said. "The river welcomes all."

Justine heard the words, soft, inviting. She moved with the force of curiosity, convinced there was no danger. Joseph let go of her arm and followed close behind, uncertain but always trusting in his sister's decisions.

They walked to the sycamore tree and stood before Mrs. Corbin. It surprised Justine how young she looked and how pretty she was. But it also surprised her how frail she appeared. Her eyes glowed with a presence that stood in relief to the rest of her body. It was as if she were hidden within her body, looking out through her eyes. She was a woman of distinctive appearance, like a fragile flower, Justine determined.

"Hello," the strange woman said. "You must be Justine and Joseph. My sons were telling me about you." Justine twisted her head toward the two fishers. They were at a distance, occupied, ignorant of her presence. She turned back, spying the sketch pad in the woman's lap. "You're searching for buried treasure, I understand."

"We're looking for jewels," Joseph said, charmed by the lady at the river.

Justine was bewildered. Everything about the Corbins was now in question. "Shahin and Hauk told you about us?" Justine said.

"Yes, they did. Here. Sit with me. Tell me about yourselves. My name is Corinne." She patted the ground next to her where the strong roots of the sycamore splayed to gather a moss mat. They sat on the soft earth, mesmerized. "Justine, you're in the same grade as Hauk. Is that right?"

"Yes, ma'am." Justine knew Nonna Etta's rules applied here. There was something special about Corinne.

"Hauk says you like snakes. You brought one to school one day."

"A ring-necked snake. Joseph and I found it at the pond back there."

"You're not afraid of snakes."

"No, ma'am," Justine said. "You just have to know how to pick them up."

"And, Joseph, do you like snakes?"

Joseph was examining Corinne's nails. They had no polish, unlike his mother's. He looked up at her and thought about the question. "Sometimes," he said. "But they're scary."

Corinne smiled. "Scary. Yes. But try not to let scary rule your life. If you're scared all the time, then you'll miss much that is interesting and important and fun." Corinne watched the two siblings as they examined her. She would have to keep this conversation going. "So, tell me about this treasure you're seeking. How did you learn about it?"

"Our grandmother told us," Joseph said.

Justine heard his words but decided it was alright. "She told us about our great-great-great-grandmother who lived in town and worked for a rich person who gave Nonna Jannie some jewels, but then the lady died and Nonna Jannie never got the jewels."

Corinne listened closely while she studied the knees of the children sitting next to her. "The lady of the house promised your Nonna Jannie some jewelry, but she never received it because the lady died before she could give it to her. Is that right?"

Justine nodded. "Yes."

"And now you and Joseph are searching for the jewelry at a house in town. How do you know the jewelry is in the house?"

"Because Nonna Etta told us. That's our grandmother. She told us that Nonna Jannie said it was in the house."

Corinne mulled over this information. "I see. What do your parents think of this enterprise of yours?"

"What's 'enterprise?'" Joseph said, peering at the drawing on the sketch pad.

"It means what we're doing," Justine said. She turned to Corinne. "It's going to be a surprise."

Corinne smiled. "Yes. I'll bet it will."

"We don't have a father," Joseph said, coming from left field. "He died."

"Oh. I'm sorry."

"He didn't die," Justine said. "He just never showed up."

"Ah. An absentee father. I am aware of such a thing." Corinne looked out at the river. She saw the strandline along the mud bank. The mark of the force of a faraway object making tiny but significant adjustments to the lives of many.

The two jewel hunters looked at her, perplexed. She saw the look and added, "My father was like yours. He never showed up, either. But it was for the good. I'm sure your mother is quite busy. Where does she work?"

"She works at the IHOP," Justine said. "She doesn't get home till late."

"They make pancakes," Joseph said. "Sometimes she brings some home for us."

"Uh-huh." Corinne turned to watch her sons. They were talking, but their voices were unheard at this distance. So much hope, so many dreams, she thought. If only... "And who watches you when your mom is at work?"

"Sometimes Nonna Etta is with us," Joseph answered.

"But sometimes you're by yourselves?"

Justine studied the woman by the river. Her hair was strange, not quite real-looking. But her smile came from deep within. "Sometimes," Justine answered, looking down now at the sketch pad. "Do you draw?" she said.

Corinne looked down, then back at Justine. She was tired, but she forced a smile.

"Would you like to see?" She picked up the pad, offering it. Justine placed it in her lap. Joseph leaned in. They saw the shoreline, trees, and a bird sitting on a branch that leaned out over the water. "It's a kingfisher," Corinne said, pointing to the bird.

"A funny head," Joseph said. "With toothpick hair."

"And a white collar," Justine said. She turned the pages and saw other drawings in colored pencil. She stopped when she got to a sketch of Hauk in profile, looking off, away from the artist. His eyes were dark, contemplating. Justine looked up at Corinne and handed her the pad. These pictures were personal. It wasn't right for her and Joseph to be looking at them.

"We should go," Justine said, pushing herself up, leaning on the tree.

"I'm glad you stopped," Corinne said. "It was nice talking with you both."

"Bye," Joseph said.

"Bye."

They walked back along the path, Justine thinking about the conversation with Mrs. Corbin. Now she was certain everything she thought she knew about the woman was false. And maybe the things she believed about the Corbin brothers were false as well. But that couldn't be. She knew firsthand about them, about their behavior on the bus, and what people at school said about them. Still, something was different.

She heard a whistle and stopped. Joseph turned back toward the river.

"What was that?" Justine said. "It sounded like someone blowing a whistle."

"Yeah."

They stood on the trail and listened. There was no other sound than that of a few frogs calling.

"Maybe we should go back and see," Justine said. Joseph looked at his sister. Her eyes were on the trail back to the river. Justine stepped past him.

"OK," he said, following her.

But before they got to the fork where the two paths met, Justine saw Corinne and her sons approaching. She ducked down, pulling Joseph with her. They moved off the path into the brush and watched as Corinne walked slowly, holding onto Shahin and Hauk's shoulders. The boys held her by the waist, pushing aside the close-growing bushes along the path. The three took the fork and disappeared into the woods leading to the far end of the trailer park, the end where the Corbins lived.

Justine stood looking up the path toward her end of the trailer park. Her view of the Corbins had been forever changed.

"Come on," she whispered to Joseph. "Let's go home."

# TEN

Nancy Bilderson did not have time to visit Katy in the archives. She spent her day readying for an art exhibit. The paintings and watercolors were to be hung in the atrium between the library and the theater.

Katy spent her day, a stairway away, helping a woman research her church's early pastors while assisting a man in his search through the Westmoreland County Deeds & Wills looking for a list of belongings owned by a relative who may have arrived in the country aboard a pirate ship. And did she have a copy of *The Baylor's of Newmarket*? I think I'm a descendant. And what about *Alsop's Tables*? Which volume did you need? There's more than one? Each query led to other queries branching Katy and her searchers off into a delta of information that would have overwhelmed and confused lesser pilots. Katy had the experience to steer around the sandbars arriving at destinations satisfactory to all. By day's end, she was tired but looking forward to working on her story of Anna Fitzhugh and her maid, Jannie.

Nancy stood in the atrium admiring her work—that is, the work of several local artists—hanging on the walls with accompanying descriptive information printed and placed by Nancy. She was looking at two pieces by Corinne Corbin when Katy opened the door from the stairwell. Nancy turned and said, "Hello, Katy." Katy looked over. "Hi, Nancy. Gotta go. I'm late for work." She rushed to the side door.

"But...your work is over...isn't it?"

"Just starting. See you tomorrow."

She dropped her purse and papers on the sofa and went to the refrigerator. After a quick search, she opened a cabinet and pulled out a fig bar, ripping the wrapper. She walked over to the desk by the window and pressed the power button on the laptop. The computer was on.

"Forgot to turn it off last night," Katy said aloud, sitting, chewing on the fig. The screen lit up, asking for a password. She typed in IBFBAMS, humming the words of the Cat Stevens song. The word document appeared. Katy read the last few lines, then pushed her chair back and stared at the screen.

What she read was not what she remembered writing the night before. She scrolled up and read more. It was a diary with dates. Anna Fitzhugh's diary? She scrolled to the beginning.

1909, Feb 23rd. There is snow on the ground and in the trees. It is so lovely. I started a diary today. I have been thinking about doing so for some time and then I learned Jannie has a diary. She suggested I keep one. Jannie has such good ideas. She is so smart.

Today is a good day, sitting next to the fire and watching the snow through the window. I want this little journal to be a happy one, a compilation of my most memorable happenings. I will give it to my granddaughter when I am old and close to meeting my Lord. Maybe I will live to be 100. It would be 1986. What will it be like to live at that time in the future? And will this town look different? How different? We have so much today that our ancestors never dreamed of. I can't imagine life so different from today. With so many new devices available, there will not be a need for anything else by then. Just last week Jannie and I saw a Spangler electric suction sweeper. Jannie said she could not use such a device. It was very noisy, I will admit.

I am concerned about Blayden. The last three Sundays, he has not accompanied me to church. Reverend McBryde asked if he was ill. I told him the truth. Blayden was busy at work. But that might not be the whole truth, for I sense a divide between us. And this, less than a year from our wedding day. So, I am writing not of cheerful things but sad. It is not the way I wanted this diary to be. But it must contain the truth. I have never feared the truth.

Jannie went shopping Thursday last. When she returned home, she told me she saw Blayden with a woman outside the bank. Jannie said they acted like more than acquaintances. Of course, those were not the words Jannie used. She said, "Ma'am, there was love in them eyes. I could see plain as I see you now." I don't know if I should be alarmed. Sometimes Jannie can exaggerate. Her heart is big; it often senses more than what appears. But Jannie is my support. Indeed, she has been a close friend. Ever since she came by looking for work. It was Blayden who inquired of his workers at the molding shop. And Edgar, Jannie's father, told her to hurry to the house or someone else would get the job. Edgar runs the new planer that Blayden just had delivered. It was the planer installation that Blayden said required his time these last several weeks. But, I fear, this bank woman may have designs.

April 11th. Blayden is buying liquor from someone. He told me. It is illegal in Virginia, yet he maintains there is a demand for whiskey and if there is a demand, there will be suppliers. Just so I told him. It is still against the law. Blayden says that the law is wrong. If the demand for something is so high, then the law is wrong. Then, I told him, he should have the law changed. And so, he is having bottles of liquor delivered to establishments in town. I believe he is working with others who are looking away.

Jun 06th. Why must this diary be so much about Blayden? But I am married to him. He is my center, or so I thought. Now I am losing that center for sure. Kate came by. We had a fond luncheon. Kate makes me laugh. We are as sisters. Jannie prepared sandwiches, and we had strawberries and cream. She chilled the strawberries in ice beforehand. So close to heaven! And Kate told me about seeing Blayden with a woman called Sarah. Sarah works at the bank. When Kate described her, Jannie said it sounded like the same woman she saw several months back. Kate said that Sarah is a stenographer, like Kate. And like me, before my marriage. But that is neither here nor there. Kate is certain there is a closeness between Sarah and Blayden. Kate is so bold. She walked up to the two of them and said hello to Blayden. Kate said the look in Sarah's eyes told stories. And Blayden was as cold as the ice that cooled the strawberries. I must confront the man.

Jun 12th. Blayden has been distant this past week and now he has accused Jannie of stealing. He has a favorite pipe, and it is missing. Why does he think Jannie would take such a thing? It is an anger built from guilt. I know it. He is not the man I married. Jannie is distraught. Her distress I can measure by the stride of her walk, the angle of her face, and the tears upon it. Later this evening, when Jannie had left for the day, I went to Blayden and reproached him for his actions. He sat like a toad, glum and mum. But his eyes burned. I saw the anger. And his anger arose mine, and I lit into him. Who is Sarah? I demanded. And why is she seen with him so often? I told him I no longer believe him when he says he is too busy to go with me to church. And too busy to take me to the picture show. "You are not too busy to be with Sarah, are you?" He said nothing and got up and left the room. Where I began this diary sitting by the fire watching the snow on a cold February day, I now sit in the same chair looking at the soot, the only evidence of a fire once strong and warm. I am burdened with sadness. Blayden is upstairs. I shall sleep here and listen to the crickets.

Jul 28th. Such a happy occasion, yet sad—again. Yesterday evening was the Pythian Sisters anniversary celebration. They held it at Pythian Hall, and I invited Jannie to attend. Kate and I would sing a duet and Kate would recite a poem. The day began with mirth as we three laid out our dresses. Jannie made a wonderful costume of silk organdy over cotton. She would wear her charm bracelet—and the new charm I bought for her, a pretty bird. She loves birds, those who are free to fly, Jannie says. Excitement was on her face, it being her first concert. We arrived early. Blanche was practicing her address with others of the committee when she looked up and saw the three of us enter the hall. Her face dropped. The hall grew silent. Kate and I looked at each other, then looked at Jannie. Jannie knew. We two were confused, but our motion forward slowed as if our bodies knew before our minds. It was a serious breach of etiquette we soon realized as Blanche took my arm and steered me to the anteroom and informed us that negroes were not allowed in the hall. Blanche looked Jannie up and down with a severe eye, then turned to us. I could see Jannie's fingers tighten, then loosen. She was staring hard at Blanche as the older woman informed me and Kate. And then Blanche looked at Jannie and said, "You should know this is not acceptable. You have no shame coming here." Jannie apologized and walked out of the hall. Her dress and the way she wore it could not be surpassed by anyone in the hall that night.

This evening, when Blayden got home, he castigated me for taking Jannie to the Pythian celebration. His Pythias Knights had informed him of my mistake. I am to be banished from the Sisters, he told me. And he also told me I must let Jannie go. She was getting too close. I told him I would not. And now I sit with blackened eye for my insolence. It is more than sad. My life is splintering.

1910, Feb 3rd. Almost a full year since I began this diary. I fear writing anymore. It is becoming a documentation of mourning and despair. Today, Jannie's father, Edgar, was injured at the factory. He was running the planing machine and one knife got loose and fired back upon him like a bullet. The knife cut into his shoulder, almost severing it. There was blood upon blood. Jannie learned of the accident soon after. Her sister came by, and we three went to the factory, but Edgar had been taken away. Blayden said that a man bandaged his shoulder and then set him in a wagon for the trip to the hospital. Jannie will be with him until he is recovered, as her mother must continue to work at the woolen mill. All this happening just as Jannie and her intended, Joshua, have set a date for their wedding. This news has been the happiest I have to report. Jannie and I have been looking at wedding rings. Jannie has picked out a simple band she wants to have engraved. One for her and one for Joshua. She is so excited and I as well.

Feb 4th. Edgar was not admitted to the hospital. A doctor looked at his bandaged shoulder and declared that it would be fine. But how could it be fine? Jannie came by for a few minutes and said her father was in pain. The most horrendous pain. Could I do something? He has no savings to pay for a doctor and there are no negro doctors in this area. I walked to the pharmacy with Jannie and bought her laudanum. When Blayden came home, I implored him to take Edgar to his doctor, but he refused. He said he had more serious problems to deal with now that the planing machine was broken. He went off to drink from one of the many bottles of whiskey he has squirreled away.

May 2nd. Jannie has put off her wedding with Joshua. Her father needs her. His pain is improving, but his arm is weary and weak. It affects his whole body, she says. And his mind. He has no job and income. I can only employ Jannie three days a week, per Blayden's order, but I am paying her for the full week. Blayden does not know, but I fear he will soon find out.

Jun 30th. I saw Sarah. Sarah Tabor. Her hair is the color of mine, a bit shorter. She could be my sister. But assuredly she is not.

Katy stopped reading. Who could have typed this? she wondered. The door was locked. The computer requires a password. She got up and paced across the room. She went back to the laptop. There were more entries. She paced. And pondered. Stopped. And retrieved her phone from her purse.

"Meghan, can you talk? I need to talk to someone sane."

"Katy, are you alright?"

"No. Do you have time to talk?"

"Always."

"Would it be alright to come over? Would I be interfering with something you and Alex are doing?"

"No. It's fine. Alex is outside playing."

"I'll be right over. Thanks." Katy saved the file, unplugged her laptop, and grabbed her purse. The drive to Meghan's took twenty minutes, up Warrenton Road and down Holly, a road Katy loved because it seemed to go back in time. She filled the trip with thoughts, possibilities, and ghosts. Ghosts must be involved if there is no explanation. The road took a meandering path through trees and farmland. Old and new homes parked amongst each other, tucked back into pines and tall oaks. Meghan had told Katy that she wanted a place away from town and the busy environs surrounding it. She felt it was important for Alex, her brother's son, whom she adopted when the boy was two. Meghan's brother, also named Alex, was killed in Afghanistan. When the Army informed his wife of his death, she fell apart and took her life. Now, Meghan is mother to her brother's son and decider-in-chief of everything that is good for him. Meghan based 'good' on what she knew growing up in New York playing in the forests around Lake George. The end of Holly Road, near the river and a stream that ran to it, was 'good.'

Katy pulled off Holly into a cul-de-sac. Meghan rented the house at the far end of the small circle of three houses. Katy parked behind Meghan's Civic. On the front steps, Meghan sat with large drawings drooping across her legs. She looked up and waved.

"This must be urgent," Meghan said. She gathered her building plans and stood.

"It is." Katy held her laptop in one arm, her purse in the other, waiting for Meghan to move. "We need to go in so I can show you what's on this computer."

Katy laid her laptop on the kitchen table. Meghan pulled two beers from the refrigerator.

"OK. Start here." Katy said. "No. Wait." Meghan handed her a beer. "Let me give you the background."

Meghan grinned. "Whatever this is," she said, "It's got you riled. Take a breath, take a swig, take a seat. Let's talk." She sat at the table.

"OK. You're right." Katy poured beer into her mouth and placed the bottle on the table. "So...this is what I'm working on. I told you the other day about the kids who are looking for their grandmother's jewelry. 3rd-great, I mean. Anyway, I started doing a little research. Her name is Jannie Pratt. She was a maid for a woman named Anna Fitzhugh, who lived at 311 Caroline back in 1910. According to newspaper accounts, Anna took a trip to New York to visit her mother and was never seen after she got on the train in Washington. She apparently took her jewelry with her because that was missing as well. A motive for murder. Four months later, her husband remarries. Oh, I also found evidence that Anna's husband, Blayden, was selling illegal liquor. I don't know if that has anything to do with anything, but it's interesting. So, Anna is gone. Her jewelry's gone. These two kids told me that Jannie Pratt was promised some of Anna's jewelry.

Forgot to say that her husband had money—he ran a lumber mill in town."

"Whose husband? Anna's or Jannie's?"

"Anna's."

"OK. You're talking much too fast. Take a breath and slow this down, so I can follow."

"Right." Katy took another swig. "So, that's all I know from the newspapers and the little from the kids. However—here's where it gets interesting—I paid a visit to the house to talk to the owner and see if we could get in and look around. When I get there, she invites me in. Her name is Beverly Langston, and she seems to know me. She called me Kate, then later, after she served me tea, she called me Kate Aldridge. We were old friends. How did she know my name? So, I did more research. Turns out there was a Kate Aldridge living in town at the same time as Anna Fitzhugh. And they were friends."

"And you think Beverly Langston... Whoa!" Meghan held her beer, staring at Katy.

"I don't think anything yet. It's just a coincidence. So, I say bye to my new friend Beverly and go home and begin typing up a story involving Anna and Kate and Jannie and Blayden. You know me. I'm a sucker for stories. My mind gets stuck in that library basement, and I must invent stuff from the things I read, or my mind rebels. You following me so far?"

"Yeah. You know you don't need that beer. You're flying without wings." Katy gave Meghan a smirk. "Then what happens?"

"I go to sleep. Writing stories is tiring."

"I believe you."

"So, I wake up this morning and go to work. When I get home, I go to turn on the computer, but it's still on from last night. So, I start to read what I wrote last night." Katy leaned forward and punched her laptop. Meghan pulled her chair closer. "Here is what I last wrote," Katy said, pointing to the screen. Meghan read the last three lines.

"OK," she said, looking at Katy.

"Pure fiction. Remember, I went to sleep after I wrote that? Now, starting here...this isn't my writing. This is what I came home to just an hour ago. As you can see, it's diary entries. I read through several of the more interesting ones. I haven't finished, but this looks like an actual diary written by Anna Fitzhugh." Katy picked up her beer and watched as Meghan read. "The same Anna Fitzhugh, who has been dead since 1910, who somehow got into my apartment last night and typed this. So, tell me. What's going on?"

Meghan leaned back in her chair and studied her librarian friend. Meghan, the architect, deals in structure and analysis. She pursues beauty that flows from form and color, shadow, and shape. But if it isn't built upon structure and the mathematical formulations that define it, then it has no lasting effect. Substance, something tangible that can be measured, described, and defined. This is Meghan's world. Katy was proposing something that had no basis in the structured world. Therefore, it could not be.

"Let's start with the laptop here," Meghan said, touching the computer. "Two ways these words could be trapped in this thing: either you typed them or someone else typed them. If someone else, then they had to have had access to your computer—either physically or through the internet."

"And known my password."

"Right. So, who could have gotten in? Is Bret still around?"

"I dumped him long ago. I told you that."

"But does he have your key? You didn't change the lock, did you?"

"No. But I don't think he would do that. And how would he know about Anna Fitzhugh?"

"I'm trying to list all possibilities. Who else?"

"But what about the diary? Who could have written it? It's so real."

"You just told me. Anybody with an imagination. You're the prime suspect. You know how you invent stories from the archives you read. How your mind slips in and out of those old newspaper stories, remembering and forgetting shards of information, then bringing it back up months later in some form or other that may or may not resemble the truth. You don't care if it's the truth. You're inventing your own stories, as any author would. Placing those shards in new ways that form new shapes that only your mind sees. You could have, in a hazy stupor, typed these words."

Katy studied her friend. She knew she was right. Putting words down on a white background and much later, reading the same words, wondering how her mind ever conjured them into existence. But this is different, she thought. This just feels different.

"I have no memory of writing any of it." Katy blinked and rubbed her eyes. Meghan could see she was upset, but what other explanation was there?

"Tell me about this Beverly Langston. What did she say? It sounds like she knew about Anna and Kate."

"Beverly never mentioned Anna," Katy said. "She just wanted me to have tea with her and talk. I'm kicking myself for not staying and asking her more."

"Well, go back and talk with her. Ask her where she was last night."

Katy laughed. "She didn't look like the kind to break into an apartment and start typing on a computer."

The back door opened. Alex walked in. "Aunt Katy, why are you here?" He had shorts and a t-shirt on. No shoes. His hair dark brown, a shade lighter than the black hair his aunt had.

"Alex," Meghan said. "Try not to be so blunt."

"Blunt?"

"Try something like, Aunt Katy, it's so nice to see you."

"How will I know why she's here, though?"

"Alex," Katy said, standing up and hugging him. "It's so nice to see you."

He grinned. "So, why are you here?"

"I'm looking for a ghost." Katy sighed and sat back at the table.

Alex's eyes widened. "Can I help?" He walked to the refrigerator.

Meghan and Katy laughed. Katy said, "The problem is, I don't know where to look."

"I would start with Beverly," Meghan said.

"What's for dinner?" Alex set a glass of orange juice on the table.

Meghan looked at Katy. "Do you want to have dinner with us?" Katy thought about the state of her refrigerator and didn't hesitate.

"Good. So, go back to Beverly and get as much info from her as you can. She might have a clue to this mystery."

Katy put her head on the table and groaned. "I need more sleep."

"Of course, that might be the answer right there," Meghan said. "You slept while your mind told your fingers to go right on typing."

"No way." Katy sat up and pulled the laptop toward her. "I did not type this diary. And, if I was that tired, the words would not be coherent."

"You'd be surprised what your mind is capable of when you're not looking," Meghan said, watching as Katy scrolled up to the first diary entry.

"Excuse me," Alex said from his perch at the end of the table. "What about the ghost? I thought you were looking for a ghost, Aunt Katy."

Katy turned toward Alex, leaning back in her chair, pushing her fingers through her hair. She explained to Alex the events of the last couple of days, meeting Justine and Joseph, their quest to find their great-great-great-grandmother's lost jewelry, meeting Beverly Langston, and going home this evening to read a diary typed on her laptop that she did not write.

"The ghost wrote the story," Alex declared. "Can I read it?"

Katy smiled. "Sure, Alex. Tell me what you think." She pushed the laptop to Alex. "It's as if I'm standing on the Owl Creek Bridge hearing the thoughts of a dead woman. Knowing the thoughts."

"Her thoughts are yours," Meghan said.

"Right... No... Well..." Katy leaned toward the laptop, positioned in front of Alex, and began re-reading the diary.

"And you're typing them down as you hear them."

Katy stopped reading and looked at Meghan. "No! I can't believe that."

"Well, whether you believe it, the fact is the words are on your computer."

"Jannie had a diary too," Alex said, turning to Katy.

Katy's mind jumped. "Oh my gosh, I read right over that. Could it still exist? I need to talk to the grandmother." She told Alex he was a genius. Alex asked whose grandmother. Meghan pulled hamburgers from the refrigerator. "We have half an onion," she said.

Katy said, "You're as bad as me. At least you have burgers. What's your wi-fi password?" She wanted to see if she could find an address for Justine and Joseph. "Shit. I never got their last name. Forget that."

"Whose grandmother?" Alex said a second time.

"The kids," Katy said, slumping. "They live in a trailer park. I wonder if I could cruise the park. Maybe see them playing."

"Which one?" Meghan said, slapping patties on a cast-iron skillet.

"I forget. A water park? No. It had water in it. I don't remember. I'm useless."

"Finish your beer. It might go to your head and wash out the quarantined cobwebs you've been building up."

Katy picked up the bottle and looked at it, then drained it. "You know. This always happens to me. I dive into the past and get stuck. I get hypnotized."

"And walk around in the present, bug-eyed and confused," Meghan offered.

"I should just stay in the past."

"But then," Alex said, "you would want to go back further in the past because you wouldn't be living in the past, then. So…"

"So, I need a new career."

"Alex," Meghan said, "get the carrots out and wash them. We're having burgers and carrots for dinner."

"Let me search for trailer parks near town," Katy said. Her career still had legs.

* * *

That night, in bed, Justine raised herself on her elbow and said to Joseph, "We should invite Shahin and Hauk to go with us tomorrow to the house." Joseph was looking at the shadows on the wall, thinking of the snake tattoo on Terrell's arm. Terrell and Rachelle had made up just minutes before. Terrell said he would take Joseph fishing with him on Saturday. Joseph didn't want to fish with Terrell, but his mother thought it was a great idea. The two could get to know each other better, she told him. Joseph didn't want to get to know Terrell. He was a bully, and he made stuff up and never kept promises. And on his arm was a picture of a snake. Terrell was afraid of snakes. This was confusing to Joseph. The shadows from the streetlamp and the wavering blinds cast a mesmerizing glow. Joseph rubbed his eyes and turned to his sister.

"What?" Joseph said. Now Justine was being confusing. "Why? I thought Hauk and Shahin were bad. You said...on the bus—"

"I know. But I think I was wrong."

Joseph looked forward to riding the bus next school year. With the other kids. But he had concerns. What if the Corbins tried to hurt him?

"You think they aren't mean?" Joseph sat up and looked at his sister's silhouette.

"They could get another shovel and help us dig." Justine was beyond good and bad. She was thinking of the utility of the brothers as well. And thinking of their mother and how Hauk and Shahin helped her walk along the path in the woods. Can the demonstration of good outweigh the demonstration of bad?

Joseph had difficulty with the concept of forgiveness. He struggled with giving up his original belief, provided by Justine, that the Corbin brothers were bad. After all, it was just hours ago that Shahin had yelled at Justine, taken her shovel, and thrown it down. This was evidence of being bad. Even if he didn't have a tattoo like Terrell. But Justine was now suggesting that the Corbin brothers were not bad. Justine had always provided Joseph with the answers and direction and comfort that he counted on. No one else could do that, only Justine. To Joseph, Justine was infallible—even when she wasn't.

"OK," Joseph said. It was a weighty decision. He lay back on his pillow and was asleep. Justine fell back and stared at the window screen. Every few seconds, an insect bumped into the fiberglass weave. Tiny noises in the dark.

# ELEVEN

When the jewel seekers awoke, Rachelle was asleep. The air conditioning unit hanging in her bedroom window mumbled on like a preacher filled with sacred rocks. She could not hear the real world even if it had opened her door and screamed at her. Playing it safe, the kids snuck into the kitchen and fixed themselves breakfast—cold hot dogs, a piece of bread. They fixed themselves lunch—more hot dogs, filled a bottle of water, and exited the back door. Joseph carried their lunch in his backpack. Justine knew where the Corbins lived. The school bus would drop them off before her on snowy days. She and Joseph took the wooded paths, slipping up behind the Corbin trailer. They stopped at the edge of the trees. Justine had not seen the trailer from this side. She noted that the trailer's skirt was in place. Probably no drooling insulation, she thought. Flowers grew along the edge, wrapping toward the street side. She stepped out of the trees and into the small yard. Joseph followed. They walked around to the front door. Justine put her hand on Joseph's shoulder, then walked up the wooden steps. Joseph remained on the walkway below, watching his sister, unsure of what would happen next. His small shovel was on the path in the woods. He had nothing to defend himself with. Justine knocked. Hauk stood looking at Justine, a glance at Joseph, then back to Justine. His eyes narrowed, then showed curiosity. Justine wasn't about to let him preempt her. "You want to go with us to the house? We could use help to dig."

Hauk studied her face, considering the offer. He glanced at Joseph again, then turned and called his brother. Shahin appeared behind Hauk.

"They need help digging," Hauk said.

Shahin reviewed the troops standing before him, turning over the words his mother had shared with him and Hauk the evening before when the three walked back from the river. Shahin backed away from the door. "Let me tell Mom."

Hauk remained looking at Justine. She said, "Better bring something to eat."

Hauk took this suggestion. "Wait here." The door closed.

Justine turned to Joseph, who stood with his thumbs hooked beneath the straps of his backpack. What will the Corbin brothers do? he wondered. Justine sat on the top step and said, "I think they'll come." Joseph nodded. They waited another five minutes when the door opened. The brothers were stuffing two energy bars each into their shorts.

Shahin said, "Where's your shovels?"

"On the path by our house." Justine stood. "Can you get another?"

Hauk said, "Yeah, we have one." He ran to the back of the trailer, followed by the other three explorers. He entered an access door on the trailer's skirt. "This'll do," he said, looking at Justine for confirmation. She nodded. "We're not digging for gold, are we?"

Justine watched Hauk's face. She remembered the conversation at the river with his mother. "Jewelry," she said, turning to the trees and the nearly invisible path through them.

They walked single file through the trees. No one said a word. When they got to the road, their motion meandered like a line of ants with Joseph falling behind, then hurrying to catch up as Shahin and Hauk led the way with Justine holding her shovel over her shoulder. Hauk and Shahin whispered as they hurried along. Justine wanted to ask them about their mother. Why couldn't she walk? She heard the brothers talking—words, fragments floated back to her. What were they saying? They were talking about her... and Joseph... and their mother. Or were they? She closed her ears and let her eyes follow their feet while she thought about Nonna Jannie. Where did Nonna Jannie live? Did she walk to the house on Caroline Street every day—like she, Justine, was walking today? Did she live in a trailer park?

Hauk handed the shovel to Shahin and turned to Justine. She looked up, surprised. Joseph brought his shovel to his chest, ready for battle. Hauk held out his hand and said, "Let me carry it." Justine was dumbfounded, scrutinizing his face. He seemed genuine. She looked past him to Shahin, who was standing, waiting. His eyes weren't threatening. She pursed her lips, then opened them to a smile.

"Sure," she said, handing the shovel to Hauk. Hauk put it over his shoulder and turned toward town. Justine turned to Joseph. She still held the smile. They followed the brothers.

The house stood empty on the shaded street. A sign by the sidewalk announced it was for sale. A realtor's key box hung from the doorknob. The four kids stood by the big maple across and down the street. Hauk and Shahin looked at Justine.

"For sale. Probably empty," Shahin said.

Justine looked at the houses along the street. No one about.

"Let's go," she said, running across the street. The boys followed close behind. Justine ran for the side of the house where the cellar window was. She leaned down and moved the plywood to the side. The light from the window illuminated a patch of dirt floor, but all else was dark. The four kids knelt before the window, studying the floor, archaeologists beginning a dig into history. Justine prayed they would find her Nonna Jannie's jewels. She lowered herself onto the cellar floor, followed by the other three.

"No lights?" Shahin said, looking around.

"I have a flashlight," Joseph said, removing his backpack. He handed it to Shahin. Shahin scanned the ceiling. Cobwebs among the joists, wires, pipes, insulation. A bare bulb. Shahin walked to the stairs and found the switch. The room brightened to a dull brown. Stone and brick walls shone in contrast to the floor below and the dark wooden joists above. The small concrete pad beneath the window was stained, appearing darker than the earth beside it. A red steel column sat upon a concrete pier in the middle of the room. Shahin handed the flashlight back to Joseph and said, "Where do we start?"

Justine looked at the Corbins, now glad that they had come along. She surveyed the room. It was larger than she had remembered.

"Where would somebody hide a bunch of jewels?" Hauk said, then answered, "Maybe close to the stairs, so they wouldn't have to walk far?"

"OK," Justine said.

"We need a metal detector." Shahin walked to the stairs. He and Hauk began digging. Justine and Joseph stood watching.

Joseph lifted his small shovel. "Where do I dig?" he said.

Justine looked at him. He was almost a head shorter than her. He waited for her reply, holding his shovel like a beacon before his eyes. She turned around and pointed to the corner by the window. "Try there," she said, then turned to the Corbins. "I can help too. We can take turns."

Shahin looked up from the small mound of dirt in front of him. "When I get tired," he said. Hauk had a thin trench going along the wall next to the stair landing. Justine saw Shahin was digging down, Hauk was digging across. She twisted her head about, looking over the real estate remaining. How would they be able to dig up this whole basement? she wondered. It would take forever. She looked at Joseph. He sat on the edge of the concrete pad, digging a tiny hole. Justine went over to the steel column and sat against it, watching, thinking. Where would Nonna Jannie hide the jewels? Before she had an answer, Hauk's shovel made an odd sound. He shouted, "Something is here!" He dropped the shovel and knelt on the dirt, digging with his hand. The other three hurried to his side. Hauk uncovered a shard and lifted it. Everyone stared.

"A piece of a plate, it looks like," Shahin said. Hauk tossed it across the floor. Everyone went back to their corners.

No, thought Justine. It wasn't Nonna Jannie that hid the jewels. It was the lady. Anna. Justine stood looking at the joists above her. Upstairs? In the house? "Maybe they're not buried," Justine said. Hauk and Shahin stopped digging and looked at Justine. "Maybe they're in the house somewhere."

"Let's go see," Shahin said, leaning his shovel against the wall. He jumped on the first step. Hauk was right behind. Joseph abandoned his hole. Six inches deep with a pile of loose dirt on the edge of the concrete pad.

Upstairs, the kids stood in a corner off a central hall. Justine closed the door behind them. They stepped into the hall. To their left was the kitchen, to the right the hall went straight to the front door. Off the hall were two opposing doors opening into the two front rooms. They entered the first room to the left, square with high ceilings and plastered walls. Wood floors. A fireplace. "There," Justine pointed. A door in the corner. She ran to it and opened it. A small closet with shelves. She knelt, examining the floor beneath the bottom shelf. Nothing. They went to the other room. A similar layout with a fireplace, no closet. It led into another room. They searched them both.

"Look for a secret place on the floor," Shahin said. "Sometimes there might be a board that you can pry up. People used to hide stuff in the floor."

On their hands and knees, they searched the front room floors, looking for loose strips of pine. They searched the kitchen and walked into the sunroom, new looking with a tile floor. On the second floor, a central hall led to four rooms at the front of the house. This part of the house looked old, Justine thought. She walked into the room to the right overlooking the street and looked out the window. She put her hand on the glass pane. This is where Nonna Jannie was. The limbs from the old tree in the front reached almost to the window. Justine looked down at the shadows on the floor, shadows cast by the old tree, moving with the breeze. She felt a warmth in this room, something she hadn't felt in other parts of the house.

Standing with her back against the wall, she allowed her body to slide to the floor with her feet straight out. Bending forward, she touched her toes, then leaned back and closed her eyes. She felt the hole in her right shoe and heard the boys in the back rooms. But there were other voices. Two.

*　*　*

Jannie stood next to her and looked out the window at the top of the tree, wrapped in snow. Flakes fell fast, bumping the windowpane, then slid to the sill. Jannie placed her hand against the window, lifting it.

"Are you ready, Jannie?" Anna called from the hall.

"Miss Anna, it's snowing so hard. Are you sure we should go?"

Anna walked into the front bedroom, the one she planned to transform but was now a spare. She came to the window and stood next to her maid, watching the flakes tap against the window. Her long hair was wrapped and coiled atop her head, affixed with a silver comb. She turned to Jannie.

"Perhaps we should wait a while. Come downstairs. We forgot to make your foot outline."

Jannie followed Anna downstairs and into the kitchen. Anna took a small piece of cardboard from the table and dropped it on the floor. "Now remove your shoes. I'll trace the outline."

"You sure Brown & Crismond will allow me into their store?" Jannie said, sitting at the table.

"Of course, they'll let you in. I know the owners. They won't let you try on the shoes, though."

"I never been in that store, Miss Anna. I don't know." She reached down and unlaced her shoes.

"Step on this and I'll trace around your foot. Now, when we go in, I'll ask to see the shoes, and I'll say: 'Do you think Kate will like these?' If you like them, then say yes. If not, say no."

Jannie looked at the torn sole of her shoe and nodded, placing her foot on the cardboard.

"There's always a way to kill a cat," Anna said, holding her hand to Jannie's arch and running the pencil around her foot. "That's what my father says."

"Choke him with butter or drown him in puddin' is what I heard."

"What a waste of good butter. Now, put your other foot here." Anna, kneeling on the floor, looked up at her maid sitting on the chair. Her Christian upbringing urged her to skirt the prevailing rules of behavior. "I wish you wore the same size as me. But my foot is longer. How can you fit into my clothes but not my shoes, Jannie?"

"You were just born with big feet, I guess." They laughed. Anna stood and went to the window.

"The snow is slowing. I think it may just be the wind blowing it about. Shall we try?" She looked at Jannie with a smile. Jannie looked past her to the window. She pulled on her shoes, thinking about the snow working its way into the sole. But she thought of the new shoes that she would be getting. It would be worth the discomfort. Only six blocks up Main Street—and six back.

"It's a ways, Miss Anna, but I'm ready."

Anna wore her long fur coat and gave Jannie the long woolen one she had had since she was sixteen.

"It's not too deep," said Anna as she stepped out the front door. Jannie tested the snow. It wasn't deep, not quite at the top of her heels. She walked to the street. Every time she took a step, the sole on her right foot opened. She felt the cold wet enter.

The two women walked up the street toward town. They crossed the tracks. Anna looked west. There was the lumber mill where her husband, Blayden, worked. She wondered what he would think of her walking alone into the business district—alone with her maid. She was sure he would not be pleased. It was he who had asked his workers if they knew anyone who would make a good maid for his wife. That very evening when he came home, he had a name. "N—— Edgar has a daughter. He said he will send her over tomorrow." Now, a year later, Blayden complains. "You're too friendly," he says, looking over the newspaper.

"Too friendly? How can a person be too friendly?"

"You know what I mean, Anna." Blayden dropped the newspaper in his lap and stared at his wife. "Associating with the help, n—— help especially, isn't done. I'm hearing stories. I don't like it."

"What stories?"

"Around town. At the Knight's. Different places. It's got to stop."

Anna leaned into the wind. She knew few people would be out today. A perfect time to shop with Jannie. Of course, word would get out, but it could be explained. A present for a friend. Why bring your maid? To carry the shoes home. It would be alright. Everything would be alright. Two more blocks.

Jannie looked down at her feet and the tips of her shoes as they darted out beneath her dress like nervous mice, then disappeared beneath it as she walked along the sidewalk. Her dress swept the snow. She peered into the store windows and saw the hint of her reflection and Anna's reflection, ghostly, head down, determined. How had she come to be here? To be dressed as she was? To know this privileged person and to be close to her? Jannie felt the cold biting at her toes. Soon she would have new shoes. What would her parents say? Would they be angry? Or happy. I hope happy, Jannie thought, but knew her father had told her to repair the shoes. "We have no money for new shoes. You sew them," he told her. Her mother, home from the woolen mill, looked at her with receding eyes and tilted her head toward the closet, the closet where her father kept his tools and the sewing awl. "But if I sew it, then it won't fit. It will be too tight," Jannie explained. "Then walk around with wet feet," her father said, turning toward the front porch. They lived in a small house on Sophia Street above the river. She chose, instead, to walk barefoot to Anna's that day, carrying her shoes. Anna thought it quaint, Jannie walking barefoot, not realizing the sole had torn from the top leather. Jannie didn't mention her shoes to Anna. Later Jannie made a repair using a canvas strip. She waterproofed the canvas by dripping melted candle wax over it. But it was never truly waterproof. Now, at the first snow in December, Anna knew something more permanent and more effective was required. She examined Jannie's shoe. It could be repaired, she told Jannie, but she really needed new shoes.

"We're here," Anna said as they stood beneath the overhang and looked through the glass display window. Anna tried the door. Locked. The sign on the door showed that Brown & Crismond was open. She rattled the door, then knocked. "Why is it locked?" she said, looking at Jannie. Jannie moved closer to the display. Men's and women's shoes, children's. Jannie looked at Anna and said, "It's alright, Miss Anna. I can sew my shoe."

"I'm sure you can, Jannie. But I will not have you walking about in those shoes." Anna knocked again, peering close to the glass. A light went on. She saw someone walking toward the door. "At last." Anna moved back from the door. The door opened.

"Hello, Anna. You are out on such a dreary day. I wasn't expecting anyone today. Come in."

"Thank you, Portia." Anna and Jannie walked into the shoe store. "This is my maid, Jannie," Anna said. "We've come to pick out a present for my friend Kate."

"A present? How nice."

"Yes. I have outlines of her feet." Anna pulled the cardboard from her purse.

Portia looked at Jannie and said, "Perhaps you would like to wait outside while we look for—"

"That won't be necessary, Portia. Jannie is fine right here. Now I would like to see what styles you have that would be appropriate for my friend."

Portia hesitated, eyeing Jannie. "Let me bring out several," she said, turning and walking to the back of the store. "Please have a seat."

Jannie and Anna sat in two of the five chairs lined against a side wall. Portia returned with several pairs of shoes, placing them at Anna's feet.

"We have the side button and lace. Also, this cloth top Baby Doll style is popular. A dollar ninety-five. Do you think she would like the taller heel or the low heel military?"

Anna handed Portia the cardboard outline. "We'll need to get the right size. Can you cut these out, Portia, so we can make certain of the proper size?" Portia took the cardboard and looked at it, then looked at Jannie.

"I'll get a pair of scissors." When she returned, she handed the cardboard and the scissors to Jannie. "We have these in two colors, Anna. Brown and black. And these Mary Jane Colonials are popular."

Anna looked at Jannie and nodded. "Let me see some other styles as well. I am thinking a lace-up military."

Portia walked to the back. Anna picked up a shoe and held it up. "What do you think?"

"It's nice," Jannie said, scissoring the outline of her foot from the cardboard.

"It's very sensible."

Portia returned with three more shoes. "Two cloth tops and one full leather." She put them in front of Anna.

"That's nice," Jannie said, pointing to a shoe. Anna picked it up.

"Yes. I think this one is very nice. Do you have it in her size, Portia?" Anna reached over to Jannie and took the cutouts and handed them to Portia.

"How did you get your friend to let you make these outlines?"

"I told her I was going to knit a pair of socks for her and needed to have her foot size."

"You knit. How brave of you," Portia said.

"No, no. I don't knit, Portia."

Portia looked confused, looking at Anna, then at the foot cutouts.

"I knit," Jannie said. Portia looked at Jannie, then turned to the back of the store.

"Let me check. These are quite wide, probably 'Eddies.'"

Anna paid for the shoes, $1.58, and said, "Portia, if perchance these don't quite fit, may I bring them back?"

"Of course. Just don't have her walk outside in them."

"Thank you for being open on such a snowy day."

Portia smiled, closing the door. Anna and Jannie walked along Caroline Street, the wind at their back.

"I think they're beautiful, Miss Anna. Thank you."

"You're welcome, Jannie. Let's hurry home and try them out."

✱ ✱ ✱

The voices receded and were silent. Justine looked down at her right foot. Her little toe peeked from the shoe. She raised herself up and walked to the radiator that sat by the far wall. She put her hand on it. Cold. She looked up. Was there an attic? She walked out to the hall and ran toward the rear of the house. The boys scampered through the rooms talking, pointing, examining, opening doors, closing them. Justine searched but found no door or access that might lead to an attic. She sat down in the hall against the wall with her knees up, her chin resting on her right knee. She sighed. "Nonna Jannie," she whispered. "I need a clue." Justine sat still for several minutes thinking, not hearing the words of the boys in the near and far rooms. She sat up straight and sighed again, brushing the dirt from her chin. She stood and looked down at her knee. Particles of dirt fell to the floor.

"In the basement," she yelled. "It's got to be down there. Nonna Jannie says it's down there." Three boys appeared in the hall, all looking at Justine.

"Nonna Jannie?" Hauk said, coming up to Justine.

"She's our great-great-great-grandmother." Justine turned toward the stairs. "She owns the jewels. Come on. We need to keep digging."

83

Justine took up the spade that Shahin was using. Hauk gave Shahin his shovel and Joseph continued adding dirt to his pile by the window.

"I'm going to dig over here," Shahin said, moving to the middle of the room. Justine and Hauk remained near the stairs.

"Your Mom is sick, isn't she?" Justine said to Hauk. Shahin looked over at Hauk. Hauk stood motionless, watching Justine dig. He was starting to like her, he thought. She had hair like his mother's. Not like the wig.

"Yeah. She has cancer."

Justine stopped digging and looked up at Hauk's eyes.

"She'll be dead soon," he said.

Justine couldn't stop looking at Hauk. She tried to look away, to look down, to look in a direction where the raw truth wouldn't see her eyes. When she turned away from Hauk, the eyes of Hauk's brother were on her. She could not disappear.

"I'm sorry," Justine said.

"Yeah," Hauk said. "Me too."

"There's no medicine?"

"It doesn't work, and it costs too much." Hauk stepped up to Justine and took the shovel from her. "My turn."

Justine stepped away. Her mind was on her mother. Not much of a mother, she thought, but she could not think of living without her. She looked over at Joseph. His pile of dirt was growing. How would it be to lose Joseph?

"Sometimes it's just not fair," she said to no one. No one answered, and Justine looked at the small window above Joseph. The wall of the house next door was visible. She thought of the day before, sitting next to Mrs. Corbin, talking by the river. She knows she is going to die. How can she live knowing she will be dead soon? But what choice does she have?

✳ ✳ ✳

The library basement was quiet. No one searching. No one asking. No one reading. Katy looked up from the map on her computer. She had been adding layers of nuance to a database that only a few researchers would use. She was recreating a mundane history of a time long past. Her actions were mechanical. Her mind remained on the puzzles of the night before. It trundled on, asking questions, formulating answers. Beverly Langston. She might have answers, she told herself. Katy turned off her computer and walked to her car. How did Langston know Kate Aldridge?

* * *

Joseph's shovel struck something hard. In one hand, he held his shovel, the other held half a hot dog. He stuffed the rest of the dog into his mouth and reached down into the hole he had been working on for half an hour. It was big enough for him to sit in. He scraped away the dirt, revealing a rounded, white object, still mostly buried.

"Hey, what's this?" he said, shoveling more dirt from around the object. He knelt over the hole and scraped dirt with his hands. Shahin walked over and looked down.

"Give me the flashlight," he said. Justine, Shahin, and Hauk stood over Joseph's mound of dirt and looked down into the hole. The light settled on the white object. Joseph brushed it clean.

"Is that what I think it is?" Hauk said.

"Shit, that's a skull," Shahin said, backing away, looking at his brother.

Justine knelt, taking Joseph's shovel, and dug around the object.

* * *

Katy had determined that Kate Aldridge died in 1956. If Langston was eighty, eighty-five today—a guess on Katy's part—then she would have been in her teens, maybe early twenties, when Aldridge died. She could have known her. But why would Langston mistake Katy for Kate Aldridge?

Katy turned left onto Caroline Street. As she neared the house, she saw the 'For Sale' sign in the front yard. She pulled into the short driveway and parked. She sat looking out at the sale sign and the lockbox on the door. This is strange. She got out of the car and walked around to the back of the house. She walked up to the door to the sunroom and peeked in. There was no furniture. Beverly Langston is not here. She's moved out.

Katy turned around and looked out over the lawn and its hedges and flowers. She heard noises on the opposite side of the house. Talking. Kids talking. She followed the noise to a small window just above ground level. Joseph looked up and saw Katy staring in from the window.

"Hi, Katy," he said. Justine looked up from her archaeology work. Katy moved to the side so that the light more fully filled the small patch of cellar. She saw three kids standing over Justine who held a small garden trowel. They all stared up at her.

"Find the jewelry?" Katy said.

"No," Justine said. "But we think this is a skeleton."

Katy looked at the four kids, who were motionless, waiting for her reply. Joseph nodded his head. Shit, thought Katy. What's going on here? She pulled back from the window and gauged the opening, then looked toward the street. It was as if the entire street were as dead as this house. She turned around and eased her way through the window and dropped onto the concrete pad next to Justine. Everyone was watching Katy as she brushed her pants and shirt of dirt and dust.

"Who are your friends?" Katy said, looking at the Corbin brothers.

"I'm Shahin, and this is Hauk."

"Hi," said Hauk.

"Hi, I'm Katy. Where's the skeleton?"

Shahin pointed the flashlight into the hole. Katy leaned down and met Justine's eyes. The eyes of discovery. "That's it," Justine said, pointing. Katy saw the top of a skull. She reached into the hole and moved some dirt aside. Part of an eye socket. She dug with her hand, moving more dirt. The other socket came into view. Katy looked up, thinking Anna Fitzhugh. Who got on the train, then? Katy worked through different scenarios when Joseph interrupted her with a tap on the shoulder. He stood looking into her eyes. Katy nodded to him and stood.

"You got yourselves a real skeleton, guys. I think at this point we better call the police. This is a crime scene."

"But what if the jewels are buried here?" Justine said.

"The police will find them, then. Come on. Let's get out of here. You know you're not supposed to be here. This is private property."

"But it's Nonna Jannie's property, her jewelry," insisted Justine.

"It may well be, Justine. You'll be able to argue that point once the police put all the pieces together. Come on, I'll boost you out."

SPEAK TO ME

# TWELVE

South of town and a little east, a small house backed into the trees close to the river. On three sides were flowers, all native to Virginia. With yellow shutters and yellow fence posts across the front, it looked as if it were a canary diamond surrounded by gemstones of every color. Helen Freeman knelt by a bed of Black Cohosh that stood tall above her, waving, white furry eels standing on green tails. She heard the distinctive noise of her husband's truck pull into the bluestone driveway. She listened for him to pull the tools from the bed of the truck and walk them to the shed. But those sounds were silent. Instead, she heard his footsteps rise along the flagstone path to the house. Helen looked up at a tall man standing, watching her, his hands dangling, dirty, and still strong. She smiled. He said, "Come inside. I got a story for you."

"OK," she said, pulling off her gloves and standing. "You're home early."

"Yep. Just takin' a rest. I'll be goin' back." He walked to the porch and sat on the top step and pulled off his shoes. She sat next to him, watching his dirt-stained hands rub his feet. A ring of ankle-high dirt clung to each sock. He pulled the socks off and stood.

"Rough day?" she said, hugging him. "I hope those rich people are happy."

"Rich people are never happy...but they pay pretty good."

"Come inside and tell me about your story."

Douglas Freeman described himself as a gardener and prided himself as such. He would tell you he was not a landscaper. He considered the people who make a living landscaping as hoaxers. Some may be good at what they do, he will admit when pushed, but most are what he considered 'landscrapers.' They scrape up a little soil and plant a few bushes or flowers and leave. Douglas Freeman, gardener, pondered the land and tasted the soil and selected the best plants and put them where they would grow best, then stays with

88

them like a good parent. He tended his gardens from the season's beginning to its end and then into future seasons. His contract may define a scope of work and is interpreted by the homeowner as limited to defined extents. But those are not Douglas' limits. Those limits declare a cost and assume a payment, and upon receipt of payment, the work is considered complete. To Douglas, work is never complete, work never ends. Work is life. Life decides when to end. And when that happens, Douglas will be secure in knowing that his life was good. It was complete.

He sat at the kitchen table. A glass of lemonade sweating before him. Helen sat opposite. She examined the lines on his forehead and the crinkly fissures beneath his eyes.

"You gonna tell me what happened today?" she said.

"'Bout when I finish this lemonade, I will." He grasped the glass, feeling the wet and cold on his fingers. A good feeling against his stiff joints and now on his tongue and on the roof of his mouth. The tang and the sweet. He smiled, swallowing, and took another swig, then wiped his lips with the back of his hand.

"'Member I told you about those kids the other day?"

"Yesterday."

"That's right. Four of 'em. Three boys and the girl. They were hangin' around the Langston house watchin' some guys movin' furniture out of the house. I saw them again today. They come around the corner where I was plantin' in Faith's side yard. Didn't see me, but I watched them walk down the street toward Beverly's place. Those kids stood across the street for a bit just lookin' at it. I knew they was up to somethin', but I had my work to do. They walked to the back between the houses—between Beverly's and the Panton's house."

Helen nodded.

"I couldn't see where they went after that. But they had shovels. That's what was strange. They carried two shovels and the one kid, the smallest, he carried a garden trowel. I was going to walk down and see what they was up to, but I didn't. Figured they was kids. Kids got to explore."

"They were going to dig up your plants, weren't they?" Helen said. "In the backyard."

"I didn't know what they was doin'. But things got curiouser." Douglas took a sip of lemonade, watching his wife's eyes. She waited as he rubbed his wet hands together, kneading his knuckles. Helen had listened to his stories for over fifty years. She knew when to interrupt and when to sit and wait. "I had to go over to Roxbury and get some mulch, and when I got back, there was a car parked out front the Langston place but didn't think nothin' of it. Thought it was probably a realtor. I worked the weeds for a bit when I heard voices comin' from Beverly's. There was a woman standin' with the four kids next to her car. Then they all got in the car and drove off—shovels in the trunk." Douglas gestured with open arms.

"Now you're really wonderin'," Helen said.

"Damn right." Douglas' eyes followed a wasp as it explored the window above the sink. "So, I just get up off the ground where them weeds are, and I tell them weeds they better not go anywhere while I'm gone."

"No. Those sassy weeds. They're always disobeyin'." Helen leaned in and said, "Then what?" She looked at the man she married so many years ago and wondered what she would do if he were to go off one day and never return. She looked at his hands, worn from work with the soil, worn down from living, and wondered, What would life be worth without your second voice?

"Well, I walked across that street and direct into old Beverly's yard to the backyard. That's where I was sure those kids went. But before I get too far, there's this window to the cellar. And it's got a piece of plywood up against it. Now I know what them kids was doin'. They was in the house. But what was they doin' with the shovels? That's the real question." Douglas leaned up to the table and took the lemonade in his hand. He stared at Helen, then took a gulp and swirled it in his mouth and swallowed. "That's real lemons," he said, his eyes close up to hers.

"Course it is. I only use real lemons."

He put the glass on the table, knowing she only used real lemons, and grinned at his wife, a grin she knew.

"Well, are you gonna tell me?" Helen asked.

"Tell you what?"

"Oh, for Pete's sake. Get on with the story."

"Now, Beverly Langston moved away some time ago."

"Course."

"And her kids just let that house go. And the garden. I go over from time to time and look after it, but it needs real tendin'. More'n I can put in right now. I'll get to it sometime. It's a shame. But it looks like they're finally gettin' around to sellin' it. Sale sign and a lock on the door. And here I am lookin' down into the cellar—that little window at foot level. I can't see a thing, it's so dark. But I gotta know what those kids was up to. And that young lady that come by. What's her ante in this game? So, down I go…"

"You crawled down into that cellar?"

"Course I did. How else does a man satisfy his curiosity but to crawl around under the thing that devils him? And what do you suppose I saw, Miss Helen?"

"Lord in heaven only knows."

"Lord in heaven and me."

"And maybe me if you don't die before you finish this sorry tale."

"Oh, I won't die. But somebody did."

"What do you mean by that?" Helen leaned forward and gave Douglas a peculiar frown. "You tellin' me there's a body down there?"

"Nope. No body. But once was a body." Douglas watched his wife pull back just a tine's width, her eyes staring straight at him.

"Are you sayin'…you found a skeleton?"

"I didn't see a whole skeleton, just the head, just the skull. Those kids dug that thing up. How do you suppose they knew to do that?"

"A skeleton in Miss Beverly's house. Well, that's one for the papers. You think old Bev killed her husband, maybe?" Helen sat back in her chair, working over this revelation.

"Don't think it's likely. She moved in without a husband. That was some time ago, probably fifteen, twenty years by now. I'd say this skull has been there for a while longer than that. And that there begs the question even more. What business do those kids have with all this?"

"And the woman with them. You said they were with a woman."

"That's so." Douglas grabbed his empty glass and walked to the refrigerator where he poured another lemonade, then turned and leaned his back against the counter. He looked through the doorway and through the living room window. The Cohosh wave in the slight breeze. He said, "Suppose I should call the cops?"

Helen turned in her seat and looked at her husband. He took a swig of the lemonade and placed the glass on the counter. She thought on the notion, then said, "When they ask how you know all this, what you gonna say?"

"I'd say I saw some shenanigans and went to investigate."

Helen stared at the table. The last thing she wanted was to get caught up with the police. The image of riot police yelling and running with clubs toward her and the school group she was with remained, always, at the edge of her consciousness. It rose now and stared her in the face. "I don't want you talkin' to any police, Douglas. Why don't you tell Faith Bonner what you saw? Suggest she call them."

Faith Bonner lived in the corner house lower on Caroline, the house where Douglas was gardening when he saw the kids walk up the block and around the side of Langston's house. Douglas considered this. "It's a good idea," he said, thinking back to the encounters he had had with police. Some good, if you could call an encounter with police good, and most not so good. Some downright scary. He mulled over his options and asked himself—as he always did in touchy situations involving the law, ethics, and justice—what would Martin do? Douglas always felt good about consulting the 'right man' on tough questions. The 'right man' had answers. Not that Jesus didn't have answers, but Martin was of this earth in Douglas' time and knew the pains of his people, of all the people. And Douglas could say he shook the man's hand. He couldn't say that of Jesus. Jesus was a far-off idea of a man shouted from the pulpit. He had some good ideas, but they were too filtered by parable and ancient concepts. Martin, though, was the right man for the job of examining the inequities of today and throwing the truth, like a pitchfork, at them. Douglas was always assured of getting an answer when he asked tough questions of Martin.

"I'll talk to her tomorrow," he said to Helen and walked with his lemonade to the front porch. Helen followed the man, knowing he'd do the right thing and not get involved with the police.

# THIRTEEN

Katy dropped the four kids off at the trailer park, noting their addresses, and drove back through town, crossing the river, and sat on the bridge behind a line of cars waiting for the light. She pulled out her phone and called Meghan.

"I'm on my way to see you," Katy said. "Can you talk?"

"Twice in one week? You're welcome anytime."

Katy drove west out of town. Meghan's front door was open, the screen door, the only thing between the interior and the insects mowing the meager lawn outside. Drawings covered the kitchen table. Katy marveled at how anyone could spend their days thinking about the details of a building and drawing them out, then sit staring at them all week. She knew Meghan worked out a deal with Marlboro that allowed her to be home when Alex got home from school. The deal mandated she put in time at home.

Meghan turned as Katy walked in. She knew the look on her friend's face. Discovery, mystery, and the need to talk about it.

"I just dropped off four kids who were digging in the cellar of the Caroline house I told you about."

"No one is living there?"

"Apparently not." Katy sat at the table. "That's another thing. But the kids found a skull buried in the cellar."

Meghan swiveled her body toward Katy. "A skull?" she said, astonished.

"Yeah. And my guess is there is a complete skeleton down there. Probably Anna Fitzhugh's."

"The original owner."

"Wife of. First wife of. He married his second wife not four months after Anna disappeared. I'd say he killed her so number two could take over."

"Pretty juicy stuff…coming more than a hundred years after the fact. So, who knows about this?"

"You, me, and the four kids right now. But I think it's time to bring in the police. Could you call Red and ask him what the proper protocol is?"

"He'll just tell you to call the police. But…" Meghan's eyes flashed against Katy's. "Why were you in the house in the first place? And how did the kids know to dig? The police are going to ask what business you all had there?"

"I know. Maybe I'll just forget the police. I need to search that house without having the law come down on me."

"It'll be a crime scene once it's called in. Better do it fast before someone discovers what's down in the basement," Meghan said, then rethought her words. "Of course. I'm not suggesting you do that."

Katy's cheeks rose. "Of course not. So, here's the other thing. I drove over to the house intending to talk to Beverly Langston, the lady I told you about, remember?" Katy moved words through the air rapidly, her eyes lit with excitement and agitation.

"I remem—" Meghan ducked.

"Beverly's no longer living there. The place is empty. There's a 'For Sale' sign out front." Katy drew the sign in the air. The two stared at each other through the sign while Katy continued at full throttle. "So now I'm with no explanation from Beverly. I've got diary entries on my laptop I can't explain, and there's a skull in the basement." Katy looked at Meghan for help, her arms spread to the side. "What the shit?" she said.

Meghan sat looking at her friend, thinking. Katy leaned back, watching Meghan's eyes search empty space. She knew her well enough to know she could count on her for answers. Meghan's reputation for staying cool under pressure was well known. Katy heard the stories about Meghan and the building inspector, her run-in with the builder who shouted at her to get out of his office, the brick mason, the foreman. She knew the stuff of Meghan's tough personality. Now she needed Meghan to help her explain the inexplicable and maybe find some old jewelry.

"The place is for sale, you say?" Meghan said.

"Yeah. One day I'm talking to Beverly, the next it's for sale. Does that make sense?"

"Nothing you've told me makes sense." Meghan stood and walked to the kitchen counter. She picked up her phone and punched in a number.

"Tracy, Meghan. Hi. You busy? Listen, can you tell me about a house for sale? It's on Caroline." Meghan looked at Katy.

"311." Katy had been so wound up about the skeleton she had forgotten about Tracy. Tracy could show her the house now that it's for sale.

"311 Caroline Street," Meghan said. "No. Katy. She's here with me." Meghan glanced at Katy. "I'll fill you in after you look it up. I'm not going to buy it."

"Put her on speaker," Katy said. Meghan laid the phone on the table and sat, rolling up three drawings.

"Here it is," Tracy said. "Four bedrooms, two and a half baths—"

"Tracy, this is Katy. Can you tell me the owner and their address?"

"Hi, Katy. You still seeing Bret?"

"No. He's out of the picture."

"Who dumped who?" Tracy said.

"I did." Katy looked at Meghan and shrugged.

"Then you wouldn't mind giving me his phone number?"

"Tracy," Meghan said, "Look up the owner, please. We've got a skull in the cellar and can't deal with your lack of sex right now."

"Roger that, Mama Bear. Did you say, skull?"

"Yes," Katy said. "I'm about to call the police, but I'd like to call the owner first."

"I'm looking," Tracy said.

Katy and Meghan waited, watching the phone. Meghan knew of Katy's implacable need to dive into historical records—like a sea bird in pursuit of a meal. She seemed to feed off the past. This need of Katy's formed her personality, often getting in the way of the present and her ability to deal with the future. Her ability to plan was dictated by the minutia of the past that floated within her head like dust, soon settling and obstructing any thought of what was occurring today or might occur tomorrow. Now she has a skull thrown into the mix, Meghan thought. Maybe it would be a good idea to call Red. Get a calm and legal perspective on this whole thing.

"Here it is," Tracy said. "It's in a trust. George and Isabelle Tumulty, trustees for the Beverly Langston estate. I really shouldn't give you the number, you know."

"Tracy, I'm not interested in buying the place," Katy said. "I just want to talk to Beverly."

"I only have the Tumulty's number."

"I'll take it. And could you show us the house?"

"I thought you weren't interested in buying."

"I'm not," Katy replied. "I want to look inside. And let Meghan see it." Katy and Meghan exchanged glances. "I want you to see if you can find any hiding places," Katy whispered to Meghan.

"What was that?" Tracy said. "Hiding places?"

Katy grinned. "I want Meghan to use her architectural knowledge. There may be hidden passageways and things."

Tracy thought about hidden passageways for a second and said, "I could show you the house. When do you want to see it? And what about the skull?"

Meghan said, "I'm going to call Red and see what he recommends, but I know what he'll say. The police will have to be called."

Katy said, "Could we see it now? This evening, before it gets dark?"

"I could do that."

"I have nothing else going on tonight." Meghan went to the back door.

"Half an hour?" Katy said to Tracy.

"Sure." Meghan opened the door and called to Alex.

* * *

When two cars drove by, one right after the other, Douglas stood, looking over the hedge. The sun was at the height of the chimneys on the Langston house. He watched as the cars parked in front, then walked to his truck, keeping his eyes on the two cars. No one got out. He ambled to the tailgate, looking through the rear and front windows of his truck. What are they doin'? The view wasn't good. He shifted, now leaning out on the street side of the truck. A car came from behind and turned onto Caroline. He watched. The driver smiled and waved as she passed. A realtor sign on the side. It parked behind the other two cars as their doors opened. "The same woman with the kids earlier," Douglas murmured. "And another with a boy. What do you suppose?"

Tracy walked to the front door, followed by Meghan, Alex, and Katy. Douglas squinted under the shade of the maple tree overhanging the street and the Bonner porch. He lifted his hat and scratched the top of his head. Faith Bonner walked out onto her porch and stood next to the leftmost white column.

"Douglas. What's going on?"

Douglas turned toward the owner of the house on the corner. He knew how exacting she was, how she wished her plants to look, how they shouldn't shade one another or group in such a manner that would interfere with the sightline to other plants. She gleaned her knowledge of plants from the several magazines she would often show him. And he would educate her on the realities of growing and maintaining plants, gently persuading her to change her book notions of proper horticulture. He took a step toward the porch, knowing that Faith Bonner had little patience with idleness. That seemed to be the nature of many of the inhabitants of these three blocks on lower Caroline Street. An oasis of exclusivity on the wrong side of the tracks. Most of the town's elite lived farther north and west. This pocket was oddly out of place. It suited him just fine.

"Curious about the Langston house and what all the activity's about." Douglas stopped at the maple tree and waited for Bonner's reply. He too had little patience for idleness, and Faith knew it. That is one reason she trusted him, she told him early on. "Anyone who works their ass off, no matter what they're doing, is worthy of my praise," Faith told Douglas when she first hired him. He thought that over, studying the woman's eyes, thinking back to when his grandfather told the story about his grandfather, a slave on a plantation in North Carolina. He was considered the best worker on the plantation and the most trustworthy. But he was still a slave on a secluded farm half-hidden at the fork of two rivers. When the war came, he took advantage of the chaos and headed north, away from a life of high praise with no freedom to freedom and a life of brutal insult, disrespect, and contempt. He wondered sometimes what was worse, but he didn't linger on it long. He would rather have a choice—albeit a spiky one—than none.

"I've been wondering that myself," Faith said, walking down the steps and onto the brick sidewalk. She came up to Douglas and looked down the street to the house at 311. "I saw the moving van the other day. Now I see Beverly's kids must have put the place up for sale. We may have new neighbors here soon."

"Maybe so." He was glad she wasn't upset about him not working in her garden.

"That place has been empty for four months. I was wondering when they would get around to selling it." Faith looked up at Douglas. "Of course, they could have given it away. They have more money than they know what to do with."

Douglas smiled, glancing at the grand house behind her. "Mm-hmm," he said. He was thinking of Helen's suggestion. Should he mention the skeleton and ask her to call the police?

"Well, enough fun. Time to get back to work." Faith turned back to the porch.

"You know, there's a skeleton in the cellar over there."

"Say what?" Faith turned and looked at Douglas, then walked back to him. "Skeleton?"

"Uh-huh. I saw it earlier. After some kids and the lady with them left."

"You went in the house? How'd you get in?"

"Window on the side leads to the cellar. They were diggin' it up. I saw the skull. You think we should call the police?"

Faith stood looking at Douglas. "Kids and a lady were digging up a skeleton, you say. And then they left?"

"Couple hours ago. Now there's more visitors."

Faith stood with her hands on her hips, looking down the street at the house with the skeleton. "I say we call the police." She looked up at Douglas, who was watching the house as if it might move off any time. Douglas glanced at Faith. Well, go ahead, call.

Faith turned back to the house and said, "What do you suppose those crackers are doing over there?" Douglas grinned. "Look at the cars they're driving. They aren't serious about buying that place." Douglas glanced up the street at the two compact sedans and SUV, then at his pickup truck and its front bumper as it pouted to the pavement. "Something's not right," Faith said. "I'm calling the police." Faith walked to her porch and climbed up the steps, then turned to Douglas. "Better write the license plate numbers in case they drive off before the police come." She disappeared behind a white column. Douglas turned back to the garden.

\* \* \*

Alex looked up at the ceiling in the hallway. A large chandelier hung down. Pale sunlight splintered by its prisms shown against the wall, spraying stripes of color. The door behind him closed, and the light dimmed. The colors disappeared. He walked into the first room to the left. Behind him, Meghan held a flashlight, inspecting the molding along the top of the ceiling. She dropped the light to the wall and leaned in close, looking at the chair rail trim. Touching it with her fingers, feeling the bumps in the paint. Katy followed Alex, then backed out and said to Meghan, "Remember, we're here to look for hiding places, not old moldings."

Meghan stood. "I can't help it. You'll have to be patient."

Tracy walked to the kitchen and laid her papers on the counter, comparing the interior with the description in the listing. Tracy Fontana was the same age as Meghan and Katy. She and Meghan had been friends since shortly after Meghan moved to town, a year and a half ago. Tracy had met Katy through Meghan sometime later. The three of them were now close, although different in personality. Tracy was the most outgoing of the three, comfortable with her opinions and quick with a retort but lacking in the confidence that Katy and Meghan had.

Katy hurried through the rooms, looking for something that might hint at covering an opening. She inspected the closets and the floors, looking for loose boards. Could there be some hidden nook that hadn't been found before? she wondered. She walked to the second floor, down the central hall to a room on the right, and looked out the window at the sidewalk below. The tree directed a chorus of long shadows against the brick, an evening maestro. The colors along the street were sepia.

Katy opened the window and knelt by it, leaning her arms on the sill. The sounds of deep summer entered the room. She felt a slight breeze on her shoulder and turned.

A carriage made its way toward her, coming slowly up the street. She hesitated, lifting her skirt above her ankles, then stepped off the curb. She hurried to the opposite side of the street. The carriage moved by, its steel-rimmed wheels tapping against the cobble in the same cadence as the tapping of the horse's hooves. It turned up the next street onto dirt, losing its voice. She walked down Main Street, which shared its breadth with both cars and carriages. She adjusted her hat. It was a hot day. A few people were about. She stayed on the west side, in the shade. Across the street, the jingle of a bell, a door opening. Sidney Kaufman's business. Katy looked over. Anna Fitzhugh walked out onto the sidewalk, followed by Jannie Pratt.

"Kate," Anna called and crossed the street, finding shade beneath the awning of a storefront.

"Anna. Jannie. What a pleasant surprise. Are you looking for a new piece of jewelry?"

"No." Anna took Kate by the arm, turning her away from the street. She whispered, "I'm so glad you're out today. Are you busy?"

"I was going to pick up a dress I had altered."

"But then you might come by? For tea?"

"Yes." Kate heard the concern. "Is everything alright, Anna?"

"No. I don't think so. May I accompany you to the shop? I can tell you as we walk."

"Of course. I'm just going to Mary Chaffee's. What's the matter?"

The three women walked to the corner and turned right. Jannie followed behind as Anna confided in Kate. She was familiar with the seamstress, Mary Chaffee. She wanted to say something to Anna but did not interrupt.

"It's Blayden. I believe he's taking my jewelry and having the stones replaced with paste. Jannie discovered it yesterday. She has such good eyes." Anna stopped at Mary Chaffee's doorway. "She noticed a difference in this ring." Anna reached into her purse and removed a small box. She opened it and handed the ring to Kate. Kate peered at the large stone fit snugly into its mounting.

"It looks real to me," Kate said, handing the ring back to Anna.

"But it's not. Sidney looked at it with his magnifying glasses. He said it's a very fine fake."

"But why?" Kate said, pushing the door open. "Mary, it's me, Kate Aldridge."

"Come in, Kate. I'm in the back."

Kate looked at Anna, holding the door for her friend.

Jannie caught Anna's sleeve. "Miss Anna. I don't think I should go in."

Anna and Kate turned to Jannie. Anna's face registered acknowledgment. She nodded to Jannie and said to Kate, "Mary doesn't like Jannie. I'll explain later." Anna turned and walked through the door.

"Hi, Mary. It's Anna. I'm here too."

"Oh. Anna. Please come in."

Anna and Kate walked through the small house to a room at the rear lit by a large window facing south. An older woman sat at a table laid out with material and thin pattern paper with perforated numbers identifying each piece.

"What are you working on?" Kate said.

"It's a princess slip for Mimi Baker," Mary said, putting her scissors down. "I think she will like it, don't you? Here's the picture."

Kate and Anna looked at the picture on the pattern envelope, a full-length petticoat with five different top designs.

"It's lovely," Anna said.

"Mimi wants the low round top embroidered. It will be a little extra." Mary Chaffee walked to an open closet and pulled a dress out, handing it to Anna. "All done. Do you want to try it on?"

Kate took the dress and held it up, turning it before her. "I'm sure it fits, Mary. It looks beautiful. Your work is always perfect." Kate handed the dress to Anna and unlatched her purse.

"Well, thank you. You're a most gracious customer. And your figure is just perfect."

Kate smiled at Mary. "The final price you said was…"

"A dollar eighty-five. A little more than I expected, but…"

"That's fine, Mary," Kate said, removing two bills from her purse. "I would rather pay a little extra for a perfect fit."

Anna stood next to Kate, smiling. She had not used Mary as her seamstress in almost a year. She wanted to compliment Mary on her work also, but she knew if she did, it would not be taken well.

"Thank you," Mary said, accepting the cash.

"Thank you," Kate said. "We must be going now."

"Yes. Do come back," Mary said, looking directly at Anna. Anna increased her smile and turned to the door.

Outside, Jannie stood at the corner of the house, waiting. On the street, Kate folded her dress over three times and held it close.

"It's a beautiful dress," Anna said.

"Now I know why Jannie didn't want to go in," Kate said. "Jannie is making your clothes, isn't she?"

"Yes. Some things. She has a genuine talent," Anna said, coming up alongside Jannie.

"Did she say anything?" Jannie said.

"No," Anna said. "Mary is a very proper person. She would never say anything untoward."

"You know," Kate stopped walking, "how would it be if Jannie were to work with Mary? The two of you could join forces." Kate looked from Anna to Jannie. Jannie bit her bottom lip.

"I don't believe that would work out," Anna said. "Mary is… She has a fear of negroes, I think." Anna looked at her maid. "Don't you think so, Jannie?"

Jannie stared at the ground, then up at Kate. "Maybe she has a fear of me being better than her."

"Yes. That may be true," Anna said.

"Being better and being negro is a potent combination," Kate said. "Come. I'm in need of tea."

Anna laughed. Jannie looked at Kate and the new dress she was holding, her dark hair riding her shoulder, framing her face. She worked the words 'potent combination' around in her head. She had never thought of herself in such a way.

Kate led the way back to Main Street and turned left toward Anna's house. She thought Anna didn't want to lose her maid to perhaps a better-paying position and a more rewarding one as well. Might that have something to do with this? She had a maid, a cook, and a seamstress, all for the cost of a maid. But what was this business with the jewelry? Kate turned to Anna.

"Tell me what you think Blayden is doing with your jewelry."

Anna came up shoulder to shoulder with Kate and leaned her head in. She fingered the two rings on her left hand.

"I dare say, Kate, that something is not right. I'm going home to look at all my jewelry. I think Blayden might be selling the stones—at least one—but I don't know. I just don't know why he would do such a thing. He's a very successful businessman, you know."

"Yes," Kate said, seeing the distress on her friend's face. "I and all of this town know of Blayden's successes."

"My thought is that Sarah Tabor is in the middle of this. It is she who has broken my marriage. Should I ask for a divorce?"

Jannie, two steps behind, listened as Anna explained to Kate her concerns about Blayden. Jannie had her own concerns. She rarely shared them, though. If only she could marry Joshua, she thought. But that won't happen for some time. Not until papa is better, not until his arm is working, until he can be fully employed. And then, maybe never if Joshua marries someone else in the meantime. Jannie looked down at the tips of her shoes. She was grateful for Anna's support, for buying her shoes and offering clothes she no longer wants. Anna is a nice person, but she is needy. She leans heavily.

Jannie looked up and down the street. A man broomed the sidewalk in front of his store. The horse tied at the rail raised its head and sneezed. The man with the broom laughed. Coming up from behind was the sputter of a car. Jannie turned and looked at the driver. He honked and waved at Kate and Anna. To have a car, Jannie thought. Such a wild daydream.

Anna stopped at the end of the block and peered through the window of a pharmacy.

"Shall we stop in?" Anna said to Kate.

Jannie came up behind them. Kate and Anna were looking through the window. A drug store with a counter where drinks and sandwiches were served

"Yes," Kate said. "Let's do." She opened the door and held it for Anna and Jannie. Anna walked in.

Jannie shook her head. "I'm not allowed to sit with y'all."

"Oh," Kate said, still holding the door, looking into Jannie's eyes. "That's right. Anna…"

Jannie stared back, thinking, No. It's not right.

Anna turned around. Someone from inside said, "Close that door. You're letting in the flies." Anna let the door close. The three women stood on the sidewalk outside the store. Kate said to Anna, "We can't sit together. Jannie and us."

Anna looked at Jannie with a frown, then turned to Kate. "I despise these laws." She opened the door and yelled, "You're nothing but a bunch of flies." And slammed the door.

Kate looked at Jannie and said, "Did she tell them?"

Jannie laughed. "I suppose so, Miss Kate."

A block up, Kate stopped everyone at the steam laundry where they stood next to the door and Kate said, "Feel the heat. Imagine what it would be like to work in there."

"I know," Jannie said. "My friend works here. She helps sort the clothes."

"I suppose that's not too bad," Anna said. "Sorting. You just have to decide what goes into two piles: the whites and the colored."

"And the fugitives," Jannie said. "The colored that run."

"The colored that…" Anna looked at Kate. "Of course. I forgot. Hot work."

Jannie gave her a solemn nod. "And noisy too."

"They should move this place across the river," Kate said. "Why couldn't we have a bookstore instead? The town needs a proper bookstore, not a stinky laundry like this."

Jannie followed the two white women down Caroline. When they arrived at 311, Jannie went into the kitchen and made tea. The three of them sat at the dining room table. Jannie had on the bracelet that

Anna had given her. She turned it slowly on her wrist, watching the sapphires pass like lily beetles, as Anna explained to Kate her feelings and suspicions about Blayden and the jewelry. Jannie wanted so much to take the bracelet home with her, but she knew her parents would object. She would not be worthy of such a gift. That is what they would say. You would have to work a lifetime to be able to wear a bracelet like that. So Jannie kept it at Anna's.

"That's when I was at Judson Merrett's," Jannie heard Anna say. "I fear something is amiss…" Jannie had heard all this before, several versions, several times. She didn't understand the complexities of the law, but she knew Anna was concerned for her possessions. Anna had told her about her father and his travels away from home. Whenever he returned, he would bring his daughter a present, a piece of jewelry. It was a way for Anna to remember her father, he would say to her upon his return and then, within days, would disappear again. Now, Anna feared Blayden was doing something with a lawyer that would ultimately deprive her of her jewelry.

"But for what purpose?" Anna asked Kate. Anna had asked Jannie the same question. Jannie couldn't come up with an explanation other than Sarah Tabor. Blayden Fitzhugh was one of the wealthiest men in town. He even owned a car, and the mill had a truck, a truck that Jannie's father once drove. So, what reason would Mr. Fitzhugh have to remove a diamond from a ring and replace it with worthless paste? And return the ring to Anna's jewelry chest?

Jannie's eyes grew wide when she first saw the small chest that Anna kept her jewelry in. Made of walnut and maple, Anna told her. The maple had tiny bird's eyes in it, Anna explained to her. Bird's-eye maple. It was special. It had drawers full of jewelry. Jannie was overcome. Never had she seen such beautiful pieces. Gold and silver, emerald, sapphire, ruby, diamond. Anna explained to her the different stones, but it was the pearls that Jannie most admired. They looked like tiny eggs, she told Anna. Perfectly round. Anna laughed. They were kind of like eggs, Anna said. Oysters laid them within their shell. Jannie tried to envision such a thing. She had helped shuck oysters once but never saw a pearl. How could these tiny eggs come from such a creature? Anna closed the small drawer and locked the cabinet front. Maple panels captured in walnut frames. Even the cabinet was beautiful, Jannie thought, then turned to Anna and said, "Miss Anna, this is a beautiful cabinet with beautiful jewelry, but what if a thief came here? He would see this and know something inside was valuable." "But it's locked," Anna said, holding up the small key. "It would be very easy to break, Miss Anna. You should move your jewelry to a safe place. Where no one would think to look." Anna studied Jannie's eyes, her words, and turned to the cabinet, thinking of the now fake ring. "Perhaps you're right, Jannie. Let me think of a place."

Kate had no suitable answer to Anna's question—what purpose would Blayden have in taking Anna's jewelry? "I think you must be right. Miss Tabor must have something to do with this, Anna."

Anna turned to the window. "Yes." She closed her eyes. "Tell her Jannie. Tell her about when you saw Sarah with Blayden."

Jannie looked up from her thoughts. "Miss Kate," Jannie said, "there was one day in March when Miss Anna was out. I was in the bedroom upstairs where I was sewing. That's when I heard Mr. Fitzhugh and Miss Sarah come in. They came upstairs and went into the bedroom where Miss Anna has her jewelry. I was in the front room at the sewing machine, writing in my diary. I pushed my diary into the drawer on the machine and hid in the closet."

"Did you hear what they were saying, Jannie?" Kate said.

"They were whispering," Anna said to Kate.

"Miss Sarah was whispering," Jannie said. "Mr. Fitzhugh was talking regular. He was showing her some of Anna's clothes. I heard the armoire door squeak."

"Then, perhaps, Sarah had an eye for that ring," Kate said to Anna. "And had Blayden remove the diamond so she could have it set for herself."

"That is certainly an explanation."

"Or…" Kate lingered on the idea, wondering how Anna would take it. "Is it possible that the stone was never real? That you have owned a ring set with glass from the beginning?"

Anna concentrated on the idea, her face hard, glaring at Kate yet not seeing her. Seeing the jeweler who sold her the ring, seeing her father standing next to her in the store. It could not be, she thought. Yet...could it be?

"No," Jannie said. "The diamond was different. It shined different. This ring don't shine like the real diamond."

Anna nodded her head, looking at Jannie. "Jannie can see things I can't see," Anna said, happily wiping away the unsettling feeling that had come over her.

"May I see the ring again?" Kate said.

Anna went to the kitchen where her purse was. "Put it by the window," Jannie said to Kate. Kate walked to the window with the ring. "It looks beautiful. And real."

"To me too," Anna said. "But not to Jannie and not to Sidney. He looked at it carefully and said it was paste for certain."

"What will you do?" Kate said, handing the ring back to Anna.

"I think I must take my jewelry and hide it. Jannie has convinced me."

"You could take it to the bank," Kate said.

"No. Blayden would have access. I must hide it all in the house somewhere. Jannie thinks the cellar. In the boards—"

The front door opened. Anna froze. Jannie went into the hall.

"Mr. Fitzhugh, you're home early," Jannie said. Blayden took his jacket off and handed it to Jannie.

"Just for a moment. Where is Anna?"

"In the dining room."

"Anna." Blayden walked through the doorway and saw Anna and Kate sitting at the table. "Kate, good afternoon. Anna, I have been informed that your mother is sick. Your sister called and said she could not reach you. You should call her immediately."

"Sick?" Anna got up and hurried past Blayden to the kitchen. "Did she say anything else?"

"No." Blayden stood in the hallway, watching Anna reach for the phone. She rang the operator. He turned and took his jacket from Jannie. "Have her call me when she knows something," he said to Jannie. He waved to Kate and walked out the door.

Anna said to the operator: "I need to call my sister in New York. Can you put me through?" She looked down the hall. Blayden was walking to his car. Jannie closed the door. Anna called, "Can you bring me the stool, Jannie? This will take a while."

Kate walked to Anna's side and whispered, "I'll go now but call me."

"I will," Anna said, listening to static.

"He seemed worried…and caring," Kate said. "Blayden. He wants you to call after you hear from Julia."

"Yes. I can't explain." Anna said.

✳ ✳ ✳

The static sounded like birds and the throb of a car engine, then it stopped. Katy looked up at the medallion on the ceiling surrounding the small chandelier. She stood and turned to the window. Outside, she saw a police car as it pulled up behind Tracy's SUV.

"Hey, guys," Katy called, running down the hall to the stairs. "The police are here."

In the cellar, Meghan and Alex stood on dirt, looking up at the beams and joists. Meghan placed her hand on one of the joists. She had to stoop in places in order not to hit her head. Odd, she said to herself.

"The police?" Alex said.

"I guess we better make a hasty retreat," Meghan said, shining her flashlight back along one beam. "Someone must have told them about that skull over there." She and Alex made their way up the narrow stairs. Meghan closed the door behind her. Tracy let the police in the front door. She explained that she was showing the house.

"Have you been in the basement?" one officer said.

"No, not yet."

Katy walked into the hall, followed by Meghan and Alex.

"I was just down there," Meghan said. "A lot of holes in the dirt. Someone seems to have been digging."

"Can you show me the door?" the officer said. "The rest of you stay here. Jenkins will get your information."

Meghan led the officer to the cellar.

In the hallway, the first officer took down everyone's names. A few minutes later, the second officer returned.

"We'll have to ask you all to leave. It looks as if we may have a burial here." Katy envisioned Anna Fitzhugh's corpse lying in the cellar. "None of you have any knowledge of this, I presume." The officer looked at Alex. Alex shook his head.

"I won't be able to show the house, then?" Tracy said, her hand on the front doorknob.

"No. Not for a while, anyway."

Outside, at the curb, Katy said, "How did the police know about this?" Tracy and Meghan shrugged. "I wonder if Justine told her mother or grandmother? They must have called."

Meghan said to Katy, "There's something odd about one of the beams."

"I think the jewelry is hidden down there. I know it is," Katy said.

"How do you know?" Tracy said.

Katy looked at Tracy, then at Meghan. Her eyes were soft, sad. "I just do. I can't explain it." She didn't want to explain it. She knew they would think her sadly unhinged.

Katy turned to Meghan. "I want to talk to the grandmother, Nonna Etta, and I need to call the Tumulty's—Beverly Langston's trustees—but can we call Red? See what he thinks."

Katy stared up at the window overlooking the front yard, the tall oak reaching toward it. Am I inventing all this? she wondered. Have I allowed this history to enter my soul and steer me into absurd corners? I must back away and consider only what I absolutely know. She watched as the two policemen placed tape across the front yard, then walk to the side where the cellar window was. She looked north toward town and felt herself being tugged in the direction of the past. She felt the long dress brush against her ankles and heard the train pull into the new station.

"Katy," Meghan said, putting her hand on Katy's shoulder, drawing her out of her reverie. "What is your objective with this? Where are you going with it?"

Katy looked at Meghan, repeating her words in her mind. "Objective," she said, entering the present.

"Yeah," Meghan said.

"I need an objective. You're right. I just get too caught up with those books in the basement." Meghan nodded. "I have two objectives," Katy said. "One, I want to know as much as I can about Anna Fitzhugh and why she was killed."

"How do you know she was killed?" Tracy said, joining the others.

"I don't. But I'm sure she was."

"Now you're veering off into conjecture," Meghan said.

"OK. This is why I need Red. How can I prove—or not prove—that Anna Fitzhugh was killed by her husband? What evidence do I need? That's objective one. Objective two is to find the jewelry. And objective three is to determine who the rightful owner or owners are."

"That's one more objective than you started with," Meghan pointed out, watching as Alex stood just beyond the tape boundary as the police officers cordoned off the house.

Katy said, "Yeah," wondering what other objectives she should have.

"Alright. Stick to three for now," Meghan said. "Alex and I have to go."

"I'm counting on Red," Katy said.

"I'll call him and get him up to speed."

\* \* \*

Douglas watched the activities at 311 Caroline from down the street. Faith came out on her porch and stood by the white column, her right hand on the black wrought-iron rail at the top.

"Puttin' up the crime tape," Douglas said without turning.

"Wonder who did the crime?" said Faith. "My money's on the blonde."

Douglas turned and looked at Faith. "The realtor?"

"I never did trust realtors. They're always scheming." She laughed.

"Whoever did it, it was a long time ago," Douglas said, ignoring her joke. He opened the truck door and got in. "I'll be back tomorrow," he said. "Just a few more things to do. Don't forget to water." Faith nodded and turned to the door.

Douglas drove home and told Helen that Faith had called the police. Katy drove to Tidewater Trailer Park. Tracy informed her agency that the Caroline house would be off the market for a while. She called the listing agent and informed her as well. Meghan and Alex drove home. Meghan called Red Hamilton and gave him the background on the house. Alex went into his room and started up a game of Minecraft. Officer Bill Forester, after taping the house at 311 Caroline, called his supervisor and gave him the details of what he and his partner found. His supervisor sent two detectives over, then called the realtor, then the home's owners. Faith Bonner went to her refrigerator and poured herself a glass of wine. She took it to the living room and sat in her reading chair where she opened *The Song of Solomon*, setting the bookmark—a plane ticket stub—on the side table and tipped the wine to her lips.

# FOURTEEN

Two grown-ups sat in the living room talking while Justine and Joseph sat on their bed listening. Justine heard Etta tell Katy that the children's mother worked odd hours and that she, Etta, tried to look after the kids when Rachel was at work. Joseph looked at his sister and said, "Are we in trouble?"

"Shh!" Justine said. "No. Katy said she wouldn't tell."

"But she might," Joseph whispered. "Sometimes grown-ups lie." Justine frowned. She knew Joseph was right. She went to the door and set her ear to the door frame.

"I'll see what my cousin can remember," she heard her grandmother say. "But I don't think there was any diary."

Justine went back to the bed and looked out the window at the street. She was thinking of Mrs. Corbin as the frail woman made her way along the path from the river, helped by her two sons. She heard Hauk's words, 'dead soon,' and saw the skull lying in the dirt in the house. Death was just a word a few days ago, but now it took a different form. Justine thought on the word. It had a face, an image she could see, that her mind could conjure. She saw the face of Corinne Corbin and tried to imagine it as a skeleton lying in the dirt. It can't happen, she mouthed, seeing Corinne's smile, hearing her calm and somehow powerful words by the river.

"What?" whispered Joseph. He pushed a toy train across his pillow, its wheels long missing. He wanted to tell someone about the skull he dug up, but Justine said he couldn't. They would get in trouble. He heard Katy. The door opened, closed.

"Justine," Etta called. "Joseph, come out here."

The children appeared in the short hall. Etta motioned them to the sofa.

"What were you thinking, going to the library again? What did I tell you? Justine, you know better. All the way to town. It's dangerous on that road, and there's no telling what kind of people you might meet. Come here." She held out her arms. Justine went to her. Joseph followed. Etta hugged them both.

"Miss Katy is a nice person. You're lucky you found her," Etta said. "She's interested in knowing more about Nonna Jannie. She does research at the library."

"We know," Justine said. "That's why we went to her."

"I know. She told me. I'm proud of you two. But I don't want you going off like that. Alone." Etta looked at the four eyes staring at her. "What would your mama say?" Joseph shrugged. Etta smiled. "Yeah. You're right."

Etta sat with her elbow on the sofa arm. She wondered what Rachel would think of this discovery. Her daughter never believed the story of Nonna Jannie and the jewelry. Should she tell her when she got home later this evening? Or wait until it was more certain? Etta remembered the story growing up. Like her daughter, she professed non-belief when she was younger, but then, as age pushed away her dreams, she decided the story was genuine. It was the urge to believe. Even something so trivial as owning a piece of jewelry and then losing it. The jewelry wasn't important; the story of her ancestor was. Her great-great grandmother. It brought Jannie alive. The story brought her alive. Etta had no picture of the woman, only a story. Yes, she would tell Rachel. Rachel, too, needed something to believe in, she thought.

"Are you going to help her?" Justine said, looking at her grandmother's faraway face. "Katy."

"Katy?" Etta said, then recovered. "Oh, yes. I'm going to call my cousin. Remember Nonna Ivie? She visited a couple years ago. She knows more about Nonna Jannie."

\* \* \*

It was almost dark when Katy drove into the cul-de-sac and parked at Meghan's house. Next to Meghan's Civic was Red Hamilton's Jeep. She walked to the door, laptop under her arm.

"Give me the history first," Red said, knowing how Katy jumped into the middle of an explanation. "From the beginning."

"What beginning? When the house was built, or when Anna was killed?"

"When the two kids came to see you," Meghan said.

"Oh." Katy opened her laptop, then closed it.

"You want some coffee?" Meghan said, sitting at the table.

"No. My brain can't take any more stimulants." She wanted to show Red the diary entries on her computer. She opened the laptop again, then shut it. Red isn't interested in the occult, she told herself. He's a lawyer. Just walk through the sequence of events. "OK," she began. "This all started when two kids walk into my office... Oh, God, I don't have an office. I work beneath two floors of books in a basement filled with old shit that nobody in their right mind should be interested in."

Red looked perplexed.

Meghan said, "Katy, you're dangling. Do you want Red's opinion or not?"

"Sorry. Sorry. Gotta catch up with my brain..."

"No," Meghan said. "You gotta slow your brain down."

"What's wrong with your brain?" Alex said, walking into the kitchen with a book and placing it in front of Katy.

"Alex, Katy's stressed," Meghan said. "We're trying to help unstress her, but your interruption isn't helping."

"Just one question?" Alex said, holding his book up. Katy took the book. "What's the question?"

"See that dragonfly nymph?" Alex pointed to the picture of an evil-looking bug. "It's like a claw. It uses it to catch its food. But I don't know how it works."

"That's called a labium. It's like an arm connected under its head with a jaw at the end. It activates the labium using water pressure built up in its gut to compress the muscles. The nymph can snap that jaw out in front of it in the blink of an eye."

"Yeah. And eat fish that are bigger than it."

"Like you stabbing a fork at a big piece of meat, then taking small bites until you've finished it."

"Question answered?" Red said.

Alex took the book and studied the picture. "Thanks," he said and walked back into the small living room.

Katy leaned over the table with her elbows splayed out.

"She leads a book discussion group," Meghan said to Red.

"I often pick strange topics," Katy explained.

"You have a need to know," Meghan said. "Nothing wrong with that."

Katy smiled and sat up. "Unless you ask how the water got into the gut."

"How?" Red said.

"Through its anus."

"Its anus?" called Alex, jumping up from the sofa.

"Yeah. It's a very utilitarian anus," Katy explained. "It acts like a water jet propelling the nymph through the water when it's not doing other things."

"Cool."

Meghan turned to Red. "That's why Katy has trouble forming relationships."

"Because she talks about dragonfly anuses?"

"That's not fair," Katy said, pouting.

"No. It's not," Red said. "Especially given Meghan's penchant to talk about the beauty of bridge structures."

"I thought you liked bridges," Meghan said, pouting.

"Sure. But I don't possess twenty books on bridge design and talk about them on a first date."

"The truth is out," Katy said with a smirk.

"Not quite twenty," Meghan countered. "And it wasn't a date. You were visiting my office."

"I think I'll go outside." Alex walked to the front door.

"Thanks, Alex," Katy shouted. "You helped me throttle back."

"OK," Meghan said. "Enough prattle. Tell Red what you know. I gave him a broad overview and told him your objectives."

Katy told Red about Justine and Joseph and their quest to find Nonna Jannie's jewelry. Except the jewelry may not be Jannie's. The only information she had was what Etta told her just hours ago. Family lore had it that Anna Fitzhugh (Etta hadn't known her name) had given Jannie some jewelry. But when Anna did not return from her trip to New York, Jannie was let go. That was the last Jannie had seen of her jewelry or her friend, Anna. But, Etta said, Jannie always suspected that the husband had something to do with his wife's disappearance.

"So," said Katy, "I'm curious to know what happened to Anna and what happened to the jewelry. I believe the jewelry is in that house—in the cellar."

Red raised an eyebrow. "How am I to help?"

Katy answered. "Well, you're a lawyer. When I find the jewels, who owns them?"

"When you find the jewels." Red leaned in.

"Yeah." Katy leaned in. "Are you cross-examining me?"

"Have you two found the jewels?" Red turned to Meghan.

"No," Meghan said. "It's a hypothetical." She glanced at Katy and continued. "But you can see Katy is certain."

"How can you be certain, Miss Katy?" Red leaned back, folding his arms over his chest.

"He is crossing me, isn't he?" Katy said to Meghan.

"It's his way of having fun," Meghan said. Red smiled, keeping his eyes on Katy.

"I have Anna's diary if you'd like to read it," Katy said, motioning to her laptop.

"Meghan mentioned that when she briefed me. I can only consider evidence that would be admissible in court. I'm afraid a hundred-year-old diary typed on your laptop doesn't make the cut."

"OK, back to hypothetical. If we find the jewels, who would own them? No. Let's not go there yet. What do I need to prove that Blayden Fitzhugh killed his wife? Well, wait. How can we prove the skeleton is Anna Fitzhugh? Let's start there." Katy waited for Red's reply. He stared with a grin. "What?" she demanded.

"I'm just a lawyer, not a medical expert. Do you have any DNA that could tie the bones to Anna?"

"I got nada."

"Then good luck."

"What if, when we find the jewels, we find fingerprints?"

Red unfolded his arms and stretched them out on the table. "Katy, my lady, you'd have better luck with your first question, determining the ownership of the jewels. Even if you knew for certain that the bones were Anna's, you would have to prove she was killed and then find proof the husband did it."

"What about circumstantial evidence?" Katy wasn't giving up. She slapped her hand on the table and glared at Red.

Red leaned back in his chair and laughed. "Is that a gauntlet you just threw at me?"

"Yes."

"Tell me what you have?"

"Well..." She looked at Meghan.

"It looked like the body was buried beneath the coal bin," Meghan said. "And then covered over with a concrete pad. That's got to have some significance."

"That window was for coal?" Katy said.

"Yes," Meghan said. "There was a coal-fired boiler in that house at one time. The flue went up through the floor and into the chimney on the left side of the house. I could see where the floor was patched. It wasn't uncommon to have a bin put in for the coal. The bin may have been made of wood. But, based on the position of the skull, the pad may have been poured after the body was buried."

"That would be hard to prove, wouldn't it?" Katy said.

Meghan nodded.

"Too bad." Katy stared at the table in front of her. "OK. What about my first question? Who would own the jewelry?"

"I imagine you would have several claimants," Red said. "The owners of the house have a claim for sure. Anna's descendants could make a claim if they can prove the jewelry indeed belonged to her. The husband's descendants could make a case. Jannie's descendants are a long shot."

"What about Beverly Langston?" Meghan asked Katy. "Did you talk to her?"

"No. I talked to her son-in-law, George Tumulty. He said she has Alzheimer's. He and his wife moved her to a home four months ago."

"Did you tell him about the skeleton in his cellar?"

"You kidding? I said I was researching various houses on Caroline Street. But now I have another conundrum. Who did I sit down to tea with the other day?"

"Tea?" Red looked at Meghan.

"I forgot to tell you. Katy went to the house the day before the sale sign went up. A woman invited her in. They talked and sipped tea together."

"She was living in the house?"

"I thought so," Katy said. "But apparently, I was wrong. She was a...trespasser." Katy wanted to say 'ghost,' but she knew Red would raise his eyebrows again.

"She called Katy 'Kate Aldridge.'" Meghan watched Red's eyebrows. "And seemed to know who she was."

"Really!" Red looked at Katy. "How—"

"How would she know my name? In my research, I found that Anna Fitzhugh and Kate Aldridge were good friends. They were written up in the paper. I just have the same name as Anna's friend, but this woman I thought was Beverly acted as if I were Kate Aldridge, a person she knew. My only assumption is that I was talking with Anna Fitzhugh."

"...who would be about one-hundred twenty-five years old if she were alive today," Meghan said.

"But if your intuition is correct, she was killed and buried beneath her house," Red said.

"Yes."

Red sat up, adjusting his chair. "I see why you may be acting a little strange now."

Katy pointed a finger at Red. "Very perspicacious of you, counselor."

"I'm sure there's an explanation."

"There is. And I intend to find it." Katy stood and picked up her laptop. "Sure you don't want to read the diary entries?"

"Maybe another time."

Katy walked through the screen door, leaving only a long shadow on the porch as she descended.

Meghan stood next to Red and kissed him. "What do you think?" she said, looking out the front door as Katy got in her car.

"Pretty intense lady there." He walked to the door and turned. "I like her enthusiasm."

"You're good for tomorrow's canoe trip, right?"

"Not Sunday?"

"Tomorrow now," Meghan said. "We were going to look for jewels, but that will have to wait."

"I'll be here."

"How long do you think before the M.E. has a report on the bones?"

"Who knows? It has to go to Richmond. It'll be at the bottom of the priority list. I'll see if I can get a read on it."

# FIFTEEN

It didn't take long for the local paper to get wind of the discovery at 311 Caroline. Katy read the story online at her desk in the morning. Sometime later, Red called and asked Katy if it would be alright if the police department knew of her research into the house on Caroline.

"Mention nothing about your meetings with any ghosts," Red cautioned. He then called the police chief and told him that Katy could provide historic background on the house that may be of help in identifying the skeleton. In the afternoon, Katy received a call from Detective Townsend. He asked if he could meet with her to discuss the material she had on the owners of the house. She took the rest of the day off to visit with Townsend and then drove to the courthouse to gather more information from the tax records and search for wills that might be on file for Anna and Blayden Fitzhugh. By four in the afternoon, she was tired and ready to lie down and think over the information she had gathered. But she had more questions on the Fitzhugh's and their descendants. Could she locate any of the descendants? She went back to the library and dove into ancestry information, drawing out a genealogical tree. By seven that night, she had had enough. She went home and lay on her sofa for an hour and a half, thinking, dozing, thinking. At nine, Katy's phone rang. It was a reporter. She wanted to know more about the Fitzhugh's. It must be the novelty of this case, Katy thought. Newspapers don't normally get same-day reports from the police department, do they? Katy gave the reporter a quick synopsis of what she knew and referred her to the news articles in the hundred-year-old Free Lance.

\* \* \*

Rachelle took the bus home from the IHOP. It dropped her at the entrance to the trailer park. An entrance that directed visitors down a wide street with a median—the boulevard—that branched off to side streets like tree limbs, leading to more trailers until it dead-ended. Rachelle walked down the boulevard, stepping up on the speed bumps as they lay like flattened snakes every hundred feet or so. Her mind envisioned the snake on Terrell's arm. Disgusting, she said to herself. Everything is disgusting. My life is one disgusting mess. The streetlamps gave off a pitiable amount of light. She passed a washing machine leaning at the curb. No one on the street, but she heard sounds, voices on a side street. She turned her head, searching. There was no one. Near the end of the boulevard, she took a side street and walked it to her trailer, sitting like a shipping container up against the trees. Through the curtained window, she saw a light on. Her mother would be sleeping, she thought, as she made the steps and put the key in the lock. She was tired. She held her purse, oversized for carrying pancakes and other food that no one wanted. When she entered her trailer, Etta woke and sat up. Rachelle went to the refrigerator, pulling the package of food from her purse. She pushed it past the 2-liter Coke and closed the fridge door, took a breath, and turned to her mother. Etta sat on the edge of the sofa and told Rachelle about the article in the paper and the talk she had with Katy the evening before. Rachelle tried to concentrate on what her mother was saying. Her feet hurt. Etta's words competed with the reverberation of orders Rachelle had taken all day and the constant arguing with the cook staff.

"This is the house where Nonna Jannie used to work?" Rachelle looked at her mother with a wary eye. "How do you know?"

"I told you I talked with Katy Aldridge. She works at the library, and she figured it out. Justine and Joseph were the ones who started the ball rolling."

Justine lay in her bed listening to this conversation. She sat up, waking Joseph. There was a silence in the living room, then she heard her mother say, "Steen and Jobo?" Justine got out of bed and walked into the living room. Joseph followed, shuffling his feet.

Rachelle turned and stared at the two small people standing in the hallway.

"I found the skull," Joseph said softly. Justine pulled on his arm.

Etta's face paled. "What?"

Joseph realized his mistake. He looked down at the floor, confirming his guilt. Rachelle had her eyes on her children. "What the hell is going on here?" She swung back to her mother. Etta was still looking at Joseph, wondering what the hell was going on. "Mom, are you listening? What's this all about?"

"I'm not sure I have all the facts, Rachel." Etta sat on the sofa and thought through her conversation with Katy. She looked at Justine's knees and addressed her. "You two were digging in that house, weren't you?"

"We were looking for Nonna Jannie's jewels."

"Was Miss Aldridge helping?"

"No. She saw us and told us to stop because Joseph found the skeleton."

Rachelle's brain worked through this information, her eyes darting back and forth between Joseph, Justine, and Etta. "How'd you get in the house?"

"A window," Joseph said.

"So, this Katy person knows about the jewelry?" Rachelle asked Etta.

"Yes. She said it was written in the paper. In 1910. She knows the names of the people Nonna Jannie worked for and other people.

Rachelle turned to the window and the street beyond. A splash of light from the flood on the pole filtered through the window curtain. "Is Katy looking for the jewelry?"

"I think she was just helping Justine and Joseph find the house," Etta said.

"Where is this house?"

Justine walked toward her mother, hoping her interest was real. "It's at 311 Caroline Street," Justine said. "No one is living in it."

"The police are going to see if they can figure out who the skeleton was," Etta said. "Katy thinks it's Anna Fitzhugh. Nonna Jannie worked for her."

Rachelle continued to stare at the street, then turned. "Is that the article?" She moved to the kitchen table, picking up the newspaper, reading. "It doesn't mention any jewelry."

"No. It just talks about the discovery of a skeleton."

Rachelle reread the brief article. Could it be true? The story about Nonna Jannie? She wasn't interested in a skeleton. Rachelle turned around. "You two go back to bed," she said to Justine. "You better be going too, Mom. It's late."

Etta sighed. "Alright. You all be good. Get some sleep."

Sleep wasn't on Rachelle's mind. She called Terrell and arranged for him to pick her up. "Bring a shovel. And a flashlight."

# SIXTEEN

Saturday morning was overcast. Alex, Meghan, and Red put their canoes in at Ely's Ford. Red provided a running commentary on the Civil War action along this stretch of the Rapidan River. Alex had heard this history before. His interest was fish. The history of the area was interesting, Alex admitted to himself, especially when he could climb on the cannons in the various battlefields. But history had its limits. It was old. It was past. It was not now. He would give an ear to Red, though, and listen as his mother's boyfriend explained the movements of Grant's II Corps under General Hancock, crossing the river at Ely's Ford and marching to Chancellorsville. And farther west, at Germanna Ford, the V Corps under Warren was on their way to Wilderness Tavern. Alex kept his eyes on the lure as it danced at the end of his rod, just above the water.

Katy spent Saturday on her balcony overlooking Alum Spring. She typed her findings, laptop cradled precariously, her feet propped on the railing. There were no direct descendants of Anna Fitzhugh, but she knew that would be the case. She had hoped to find a non-direct descendant. No reward. Anna's sister never married. On Blayden's side, Katy learned Blayden had three children with Sarah. The youngest, born in 1919, was the mother of Stephen Fitzhugh, who, she discovered, lived just fifty miles north. He was the youngest of three in his family. Like his grandfather, he had married twice. Unlike his grandfather, Katy mused, Stephen did not kill his first wife. He simply divorced her. Civilized, Katy thought, running her fingers through her hair, realizing she hadn't showered.

From the cupboard, she took down a box of cereal and filled a bowl, pouring milk over it. She moved to the table, her desk, and pushed aside the laptop. Her phone rang.

"Hi. This is Stephen Fitzhugh. Are you Katy Aldridge?"

She sat up, dropping her spoon on the floor. There was something uncanny about this house and its inhabitants, Katy thought, wondering how Fitzhugh had gotten her number. She asked. He said he had called the newspaper. She didn't believe the newspaper would give out her number. Fitzhugh asked a few mundane questions about the house, then asked if she knew the history of his ancestors who lived in the house? She gave him a quick synopsis of her research, then began asking him questions. What did he know about Anna, Blayden's first wife? Not much, Stephen said. His knowledge of his grandparents, who both died before he was five, was sparse. A few photos in an album. Nothing about Anna other than she was married to Blayden for a couple of years and then disappeared. He remembered his grandfather, Blayden, as a distant man, preoccupied with his work whenever the family visited. His grandmother, Sarah, however, was always engaging and had many stories to tell.

"I was hoping you might provide some detail," Stephen said to Katy. "The reporter said you were a knowledgeable genealogist."

"I'm no genealogist," Katy said. "I'm a research librarian."

Katy had a Master of Library Science degree and worked as a librarian. She expanded upon her duties, stretching them into research, her real love. The library was happy to accept the products of her labors. They hadn't the funds to compensate her for her true worth.

"Close enough," Stephen Fitzhugh said. Katy wasn't sure how to take that remark. Pretty presumptuous, she thought. She was disappointed. She wanted detail from this guy, not the other way around.

"Mr. Fitzhugh, this story of the skeleton in the house is simply a curiosity for me. I'm not employed to do any research on it. I had read the story of Anna Fitzhugh in an old newspaper and provided that to the reporter." Katy waited for Fitzhugh to respond. She was hoping for an opening to ask a follow-up question.

"Call me Stephen. There is a family story about some lost jewelry and a diary. You haven't come across anything, any reports about that, have you?"

Katy walked to the balcony looking out on the creek. Small children played in the shallow water, splashing each other, laughing, running along the bank. So, now we get to the meat, Katy thought to herself. This guy is fishing.

"A Free Lance article mentioned Anna may have had some jewelry with her when she went missing. That's all I know." Fitzhugh didn't respond. Katy waited a few more seconds, then said, "Stephen, you mentioned a diary. Whose diary?" Now Katy was fishing. She waited through the brief silence, then Stephen spoke.

"I was told that Anna used to keep a diary, but it was lost. Listen, Katy, it was nice talking with you. I hoped you may have uncovered some family history of mine. But I guess not. I've always been interested in family lore."

"I'm sorry I couldn't help," Katy said, struggling with herself, wondering if she should ask the one question she really wanted to ask. "One thing, though. You read the article on the skeleton in the cellar. Do you have any idea how it could have gotten there or who it could be?" She waited for Fitzhugh's reply, then looked at her phone. He had disconnected.

She leaned on the railing. He knows. He knows about Anna. She sent a text to Meghan: *Just got a call from Blayden Fitzhugh's grandson. He was fishing for info on the jewelry and diary. He knows more than he's willing to share.* She walked back inside her small apartment to the table and pulled the laptop close, her cereal turning to mush.

* * *

Rachelle was charged with burglary and now languished in a cell at the Rappahannock Regional Jail. She sat with her hands holding her forehead, her elbows on her knees, sobbing in controlled silence, thinking back on her actions. Would she have a job when she got out? Would she ever get out? Where was Terrell? Why did she have anything to do with the man? What would her mother say? Would Steen and Jobo still love her? Goddam, Terrell.

She sat up and dried her eyes, thinking back.

"I'm not going through that little window," Terrell said, holding the shovel handle forward. "This won't make too much noise, and it'll be a lot easier." He jammed the handle into the pane of glass, shattering it, and reached in, unlocking the back door. The two of them walked through the sunroom and kitchen. The half-moon provided enough light for them to make it to the hallway.

"Stairs have to be around here close by," Terrell said, turning on the flashlight, wrapping his hand over the lens. The light panned the walls, then stopped in front of a door. Terrell walked up to it, examining it. He opened it and walked down the narrow stairs. Rachelle followed.

"Shit," he said, standing next to a pile of dirt at the base of the stairs. "This place looks like a construction site."

Rachelle scanned the confined room. The concrete pad beneath the window was broken into pieces and piled in a corner. She walked to the pit beneath the window. Terrell followed, shining the flashlight down. "I guess that's where the skeleton was buried," she said.

"How do we know the police didn't dig up the jewelry already?" Terrell said.

Rachelle turned to Terrell, thinking about that possibility, one she hadn't considered. But now, looking at the condition of the cellar… Could the police have found the jewelry?

"I don't think so," Rachelle said. "Mom showed me the newspaper. It didn't mention jewelry."

"OK. Let's dig." Terrell handed the flashlight to Rachelle and stuck the shovel into the dirt.

"Wait," Rachelle said. "We can't just dig anywhere."

"You got a plan?" Terrell said.

Rachelle shined the light about the walls and floor and stood thinking.

"I'll just dig here while you work on your plan," Terrell said. Rachelle watched as Terrell began digging, then walked to the stairs and sat. "Keep the light on over here," Terrell demanded. "I gotta see."

"Yeah," Rachelle said, pointing the flashlight in his direction. She sat and looked at the pockmarked floor of the cellar. Who would hide their jewelry in the dirt? Rachelle closed her eyes. Tired.

"Hey, you're not holding the light right."

Rachelle blinked her eyes, looking over at Terrell, who had a pile of dirt growing next to his shoe.

"Terrell, there's no jewelry down here. Who in their right mind would bury something they wear every day?" Rachelle stood up and motioned with the flashlight. "They have to be somewhere in the house. Come on. Let's look upstairs."

Terrell pondered her words. "Maybe."

"What do you mean, maybe? Come on."

The cellar got dark. Terrell dropped the shovel and hurried to the stairs.

"What about the attic?" Terrell took the flashlight from Rachelle.

"Is there an attic?"

"Let's see. Sometimes old houses have stairs that go to an attic."

On the second floor, Terrell began searching rooms. Rachelle walked down the center hallway, illuminated by moonlight, to the front of the house. She felt drawn to this spot as she peered through the hall window overlooking the street. The big oak reached its limbs toward her. She put her hand on the window and stared at her reflection, what looked like her reflection in the rippled glass, then stepped back. She frowned. That's not me. She moved her head as if examining herself in a mirror. Terrell called. She turned. He stood at the opposite end of the hall, staring, where reflections of moving lights moved across the wall and ceiling. Rachelle followed the lights with her eyes, then turned back to the window. Terrell ran up, standing next to her. Through the tree branches, they saw a police car.

Terrell grabbed her shoulder. "We gotta get the fuck out of here."

He took the stairs two at a time and was at the rear door by the time Rachelle made the entry to the kitchen. She turned as the front door opened. The bright light caught her eyes. She ran to the rear door and followed Terrell, now beyond the fence. She saw only the top of his head as he ran down across the neighbor's yard toward the street that paralleled the river. A fence slowed her. As she climbed over into the neighbor's yard, she heard the police officer shout after her as he talked to someone on his radio. It was just noise, like the noise of her heart as it pumped in her head and her chest, pushing her on, away from danger. Through the moonlight, she saw tree limbs stretched like arms above her. They were holding up the air. Those arms, she thought. No, they were about to land a blow. All above her were the arms of night. She ran beneath the dead tree, following a brick path to the road. Where was Terrell? Car lights turned and came toward her, fast. She froze, moving back slowly until her feet hit the curb. The car stopped. A police officer stood at his open door, pointing his pistol at her. She raised her arms as she was told. Goddam, Terrell.

\* \* \*

Etta got the call from the jail at two in the morning. Thank God, it's Saturday, she told herself, dressing. She drove to Rachelle's trailer and let herself in. Joseph and Justine were sleeping. She laid down on the sofa, adjusting the pillow, her thoughts on her daughter.

"I'll talk to you in the morning," Etta had told her daughter. "You're a real disappointment to me, you know that?"

"Uh-huh. I'm sorry, Mama."

"I am too.

\* \* \*

In the afternoon, the noise of a party replaced the noise of kids playing in the small stream beyond Katy's balcony. She knew the two guys who lived in the apartment above. They were friendly, not solicitous, which was just fine with her. But they enjoyed the occasional party. And today was another of their parties. The two roommates knocked on Katy's door and invited her up. They told her they were celebrating King Gambrinus, the possible inventor of malt beer.

"I really can't, guys," Katy said. "But thanks. I've got to get some stuff done."

"OK. Come on up if you change your mind."

"You won't be too noisy, will you?" Katy said, knowing the answer.

"No. Just a little."

"Yeah. Thanks."

Katy went back to her research. She had an incomplete record of Jannie Pratt. Unable to access the ancestry site from home—it was only available through the library's server—she searched Professor Stanton's archival resources at the college and other public records. Gotta talk to Etta again, Katy mused as she typed, scanning census data. It was Jannie's husband and her children she was interested in. The 1920 census provided information Katy was looking for. Because of Jannie's name, which was not a common name, at least in the lists of inhabitants for the town, Katy felt confident she had found the children's names for Jannie and Joshua Thomas. There were three: George, Louisa, Martha. Their ages would have been right for a newly married couple of 1912.

The party upstairs was at full throttle. People talking and laughing in the stairwell. Music spilling out the windows and over the balcony, dripping onto Katy's balcony. She leaned back, staring at the ceiling, and decided to drive to town and the library. As she made her way down the stairwell and out to the parking lot, she received more invitations to join the party. How could that many people get into that small apartment? Katy wondered, opening the door to her car.

Entering the library parking lot from behind the building, she heard music coming from the front of the building. She parked, realizing that she forgot there was a concert on the steps of the library today. She sat in her car, thinking, then got out and walked around to the front and sat on the lawn with two-hundred other people. The Believers were performing. She liked bluegrass but preferred jazz, rock, blues. It wasn't music she heard, though. It was the voice of Jannie Pratt. She watched the performers and sighed. I'm obsessed. She got up and walked to her car. And I can't do anything about it. She drove back to her apartment and parked. Music and laughter from the second floor. Katy ran up the stairs and into her apartment. She had forgotten to close the balcony door. The party noise was now pouring down onto her balcony and into the apartment like rain chased by an angry wind.

Standing on the balcony, she stared at a beer bottle hung from a cord. Tied to its neck was a church-key, and a note taped to the bottle. She swung the bottle around and read the note. *Please come to our party, Katy.* She smiled, untied the bottle, and wrote on the note: *No.*

And yanked the cord. The cord disappeared. There was laughter among the music on the upstairs balcony. Katy sat in her chair with her legs propped on the railing. She opened the beer and took a sip. A second bottle appeared, dangling from the cord. A new note: *Please!* Katy untied the bottle and wrote, *I need to think.* She put the second bottle in the refrigerator and returned to the balcony. A third bottle descended. The note read: *We can think for you.* Katy responded: *Who is Jannie Pratt?* She didn't need a third beer. The bottle and her response ascended. The bottle returned with a fresh note: *Come up and we will tell you. No,* was her answer.

She listened to the music and jumbled speech of more than a score of partiers. There was no more beer dangling from cords, no more notes. Alone with her thoughts, she pulled off her sandals and slid her toes along the balusters. What do you know, Jannie Pratt? Kids splashed in the creek. Was this creek here a hundred years ago? she wondered. Might Jannie have played in it?

A voice interrupted her. It came from the lawn directly beneath her balcony. Katy leaned forward and saw a man standing, looking up.

"What light through yonder window breaks?" the man said. "It is the east and Katy is the sun! Arise, fair sun, and join the party. For we have need of thou company." The party on the balcony above Katy's gave their hearty approval.

Katy stood at the railing and smiled at this wayward Romeo. He was not one of the roommates.

"Aye me!" she said. "Why am I so accosted by unwanted beer and fools that parry fancy words?" The balcony above fell silent, listening to the scene in Capulet's Garden.

"It is I, Darren, the farthing fool. I wish only your ear so that I may speak of this Jannie Pratt."

"You have my ear, fair gentleman. Speak the truth or leave with haste. I have no desire for charlatans." Katy took another sip of beer and watched her Romeo. He, too, held a beer. He lifted it to her, nodding.

"I assure you, fairest star in all the heavens, I am no charlatan. I come from good stock—"

"You dally and do procrastinate. I await your knowledge of one Jannie Pratt."

"I have knowledge of many such Pratts, my fair maid—"

"I am not your maid, but Jannie was such. You should know that if you have sipped from the waters of knowledge."

"I have indeed, fair star." Darren raised his beer. "The fullness of this bottle attests to my knowledge. It is but empty. I am filled from the stream of all-knowing."

"And affected by a falseness that the advertising doth convey. What of your answer to my simple question?" Katy was enjoying this tête-à-tête, albeit overheard by a balcony of drunks.

"She speaks, yet she says nothing; what of that?" Darren dropped his empty on the ground and waved to the balcony above. A bottle fell from the sky. Darren caught it and opened it, taking a swig.

"You dare pretend I am not speaking to you?" Katy said, holding her beer toward Darren. "Pretend is not a word I know. It is snow that soon melts and reveals a hard ground. Now speak your words so that I may hear the truth and see with my eyes the lips on your face move."

Darren replied: "I do not pretend, bright angel. It is you who pretends. You have tied in a bundle the fibers of your mind. I must know why this maid, Jannie, steals from you and leaves you forlorn. Some say that ravens foster forlorn children and leave their own to die. Do you seek the raven?"

"I see we have veered from the garden," Katy said. "And into a feast of blood. What is your employment, sir? And what is your purpose? I have no need of ravens."

"My purpose? By love, that first did prompt me to enquire. And now that I gaze in your eyes and see the brightness of your cheek—shaming that of every star—there is conviction in my heart that my purpose was right."

"And your employment?"

Darren finished the last of his beer and called for another. "Another veer. You're driving us into a pragmatic lagoon that may alter the direction of this discourse. Do you truly wish to proceed?"

"I do, fair gentleman. What man art thou that, thus bescreened—maybe not in night—so stumbles on my counsel?"

"I be a simple programmer. I whisper to machines, and they comply to my demands. And you, the star upon my balcony?"

"A simple librarian. No more. But it is my balcony, not yours. Your liberties lack discipline, dear sir." Katy smiled. "Another beer?" She held up her empty beer bottle.

"My liberties and your presumptions are commingled, madam. You there," Darren spoke to the party above, "dangle a beer for the lady." When the beer appeared and Katy untied it, Darren said, "Now that the truth is out, might I prevail upon your good sense to accompany me to the party?"

"What truth? You promised me your knowledge of Jannie Pratt."

"I'm afraid my promises were hollow. I blow air through organ pipes that sometimes make music, yet they are hollow. If promises are musical, can they be bad?"

"Promises are always musical when they are kept."

"Music is best when it is shared. If music is kept and not shared, then it is no longer a promise, it is no longer a truth, it is a sound that no one hears."

Katy leaned on the railing, studying her interlocutor. She smiled at him. He smiled back. "You better come up here and explain that last to me."

"It would be my pleasure, good madam."

"Call me Katy."

"Call me Darren. I'll be right up." The balcony above gave their approval.

Darren arrived with beer in hand. Katy showed him in and sat him on her sofa. He looked around the small room. A bookcase on the wall as you enter and a bookcase against the wall facing the sofa. Books and old photos cluttered the shelves. Behind this wall was a galley kitchen. A small dining area lay off the kitchen and opened to the living room. He saw the kitchen table was also Katy's desk. She had a two-drawer file in the corner. A painting hung on the wall above the sofa. Darren twisted to look at it closer. Abstract. Splashes of colors, shapes.

"Nice," Darren said as Katy sat.

"Local artist. He knew I needed something to liven up my place here."

Darren was not as assured sitting in Katy's apartment as he had seemed on the lawn below. He smiled. "I've never met anyone quite like you. You are unique."

Katy folded her legs beneath her. She grinned, raising an eyebrow.

"Really. I'm telling the truth."

"Oh, I'm sure. But how do you know me to the point of uniqueness? Throwing a few words over the balcony can't be knowing."

Darren studied Katy's face. He noted the smile, the dark brown hair that hung to the side hiding her ears, her prominent brows that set off her brown eyes. He scanned her arms, her legs. Lovely in limbs and lovely in eyes, he thought. Every feature was as if drawn with bold strokes, not tentative, but confident.

"You don't let up, do you?" Darren said, putting his beer bottle on the floor, turning to Katy. "You knew what I meant. Unique in the sense that of the small number of people I've met, you are different." He paused. "I enjoyed our little repartee out there. Why couldn't you have said you enjoyed it as well?"

Katy knew she had erred. She knew Darren was right. Her habit of defending herself from unwanted advances by hurling veiled insults was difficult to control even when offered wanted advances. "You're a quick study, Darren. I'm sorry. I enjoyed the balcony talk, but I invited you in to get to know you. I don't have your ability to know without delving deeper."

Darren blinked, moving his eyes to the floor. I don't know you at all. That's not what I meant, he said to himself. "Maybe we should start over. Darren Vansen." He reached out, extending his hand. Katy shook it.

"Katy Aldridge. Pleased to meet you, Darren."

"So, tell me about Jannie Pratt. Maybe if I enter through the side door, I may come to know better what makes your eyes sparkle and your brain turn."

"I will tell you about Jannie Pratt," Katy said smiling, "if you tell me about your great-grandparents."

Darren tilted his head. "Seems like a strange request, but I accept."

Katy gave Darren the background on Jannie Pratt and her employer, Anna Fitzhugh. She told him about the connection to Justine and Joseph and the discovery of the skeleton. What she wanted to show him was the diary entries on her laptop, but she was reluctant and told him of her research on the Fitzhughs and Kate Aldridge, and her meeting with whom she thought was Beverly Langston.

"That's pretty strange," Darren said. "Are you sure she wasn't Beverly Langston?"

"Yeah. I talked to her son-in-law. He said he and his wife placed her in a home several months back. Apparently, she walks around in a cloud. The woman I talked with at the house seemed pretty lucid."

Darren swiveled his body toward Katy and leaned, staring at her. "Then who could she be?" he whispered.

"Who knows?" Katy shrugged.

"Can we figure it out?"

"We?"

"I like mysteries. I'd love to help you run it down."

"Really?"

"Yeah."

Katy looked over at her laptop sitting on the table. "Alright. Let me show you another mystery. Even more mysterious."

She showed Darren her research and the old newspaper stories she had copied from the microfilm: the Fitzhugh wedding, the Pythian Sister's meeting mentioning Anna and Kate, the story about Anna leaving on a trip to New York to visit her sick mother followed two days later with the story of her disappearance.

"There's one more here on Blayden's arrest for selling liquor," Katy said. "And then no other mention in the newspaper of Blayden or Sarah other than the coverage of their wedding four months after Anna goes missing."

"OK. I think I have the picture. So, what happened to Anna?"

"That's the question, but let me show you one more thing. I have on this machine what appears to be a diary or part of a diary."

Katy and Darren sat shoulder to shoulder staring at the screen, reading what Katy believed to be Anna Fitzhugh's diary. She didn't tell

Darren that. She wanted him to form an independent opinion. When Darren had finished reading the last entry—the fifth time Katy had read it—he turned his head to her and looked into her eyes. He mouthed the word 'wow.' She smiled.

I'd love to kiss you, he thought, but said, "You didn't type this?"

"No."

"You're sure?"

Katy looked at the brown eyes inches from her face, knowing how this evening would end. "I'm positive," she said, but she wasn't positive. Her uncertainty came from having no explanation other than the occult for the diary on her computer.

"I love it. This is my kind of mystery. Now I want to search the house. Can we go?"

"It's a crime scene. The police have it cordoned off. Now…" Katy pushed her chair back and stood. "It's your turn. Sit here with me and tell me about your great-grandfather."

"Why my great-grandfather? Why not grandfather or father? Or me if you want to know about me?" Darren followed Katy the five steps to the sofa.

"I'll tell you that when you have completed your task, cricket."

"Grasshopper," Darren corrected.

"My apologies. Sit. Speak."

Darren was caught, charmed. He sat an arms-length from Katy. "But I'm out of beer, good lady."

"Excuses. We'll get beer at the party when you pass this test."

"Then to my grandfather." Darren adjusted himself on the sofa.

"Great-grandfather," Katy insisted.

"I know nothing about him. I can only go back two generations."

"You're losing points and you haven't even started. OK. Grandfather."

"What about my grandmother?"

"Extra points." Katy went to the sliding door and closed it. The sound of the party weakened. "What was your grandfather's name?"

"Russell, but he went by Bud. Grandmother was Marion. They were both born in Illinois. My grandfather in a small town, Willow Hill. It's about ninety miles from Indianapolis, where my grandmother grew up. When my grandfather was young, he and his brother were given chores they had to complete before they could play."

"How old?"

"Six, Seven, Nine. No fair interrupting."

Katy smiled and nodded.

"They had to weed the garden—the family grew most of the vegetables they needed—clean out the chicken coop, cut the grass and other stuff. Grandpa also raised pigeons. So, the pigeon loft had to be cleaned as well. When the work was done, they took off for the end of Early Street—they lived on Early—where their friend Marty lived. The three of them went to the swimming hole to learn how to swim. It was a small pond. The way you learned to swim was you tied a rope under your arms and then you started out and if you couldn't make it, there was a guy on the other end of the rope to pull you in. They learned to swim dog paddle fashion." Darren sat slumped on the sofa with his feet straight out and crossed. He spoke to his feet as Katy listened. He said, "I know all this because my father told me. I never knew my grandfather—"

"Yes, you did," Katy said. "You knew him through your father."

Darren turned his head. "I suppose. But...I was going to say that I visited the little town several years ago—we would visit almost every summer when I was a kid, visit my aunts and uncles—the pond is gone, filled in. But he and his buddies also fished in the river, the Embarras River. And my grandfather always took his dog with him, a mutt named Black. One day, the two brothers were fishing on the river—more of a good-sized creek—but they were on opposite sides with only one can of worms. Before long, one of them needed a worm. So, the one with the worms tied the can around Black's neck and sent him across the river. Back and forth went Black all afternoon with the can of worms." Darren sat up and smiled to himself, remembering. Katy was fascinated—not so much with the story, but with the fact that Darren could talk about this episode in the life of a person who lived so long ago.

"Tell me some more," Katy said, curling her feet under her and brushing the hair from her cheek.

"Well, how about the circus? That's one of my favorite stories. The biggest thing in the summer was the circus. It was the Hagenbeck-Wallace Circus. Well, a month before the circus came to town—not Willow Hill but Vincennes, which was nearby—posters would go up all over town. Hagenbeck-Wallace Circus! Coming June 21st or whatever. That was the highlight of the summer. So, my grandfather and his brother would stay up all night and wait for the circus to come in. They were just kids—maybe ten, eleven. In those days, these circuses performed in a different town every day. They would load up, unload, dismantle, and go from small town to small town, then set up again.

"Everyone knew when the circus would come in—early in the morning. Kids would go downtown near the freight tracks and the livery stable. The circus train would pull in around two in the morning. It would roll in with all the coaches painted yellow, red, orange, green. There was no mistaking the circus train. It would pull into town on the siding and would unload. The circus carried everything it needed: tents, tools, all the animals, the performers, complete kitchens, Pullmans that the performers slept in.

"What struck my grandfather was that they used all the beautiful performing horses to pull the freight. So, you had all these big wagons loaded down with tents and poles and everything else. They were heavy, big wagons, with wheels on them as tall as my grandfather, painted in fancy colors. What they would do is run these flat cars up on the siding. A winch attached to the flat car held the wagon, letting the rope run out as the heavy wagon ran down the ramp. At the bottom of the ramp, the horses would be led in and hitched to the wagon. They would have four, six horses on one wagon, depending on how heavy it was. And they would pull the wagons out to the circus grounds.

"The train tracks were above the town, so the wagons had to make their way down a hill and into town, then off to the circus grounds. This particular summer, a woman on a black horse bossed the unloading crew. She had a whip in her hand, and she had high black boots and a fancy black outfit with a Mexican hat with balls hanging over the brim. So, this one guy had six horses waiting to be hitched to this wagon. Loaded with canvasses, poles, the works.

"When the team of horses and the wagon started down this grade into town, the wagon bumped into the two rear horses. The driver did not have the brake set right. Now, these were beautiful horses, all white, matched, spectacular show horses. And the wagon bumps into those horses and hits them in the rump. The horses sat down on their haunches. The onlookers stepped back in shock. Were the horses injured? This was not good. What would happen to the act? What would happen to these beautiful horses?

"The lady boss, riding her black stallion, let her whip drop from its loop. It was about as long as this apartment," Darren said, pointing to the far wall beyond the kitchen table. "She cocked her wrist and let that whip run its length and caught the driver around the neck and pulled him right off that wagon in one crack. The kids just stood there in awe. They looked up at that woman on the black horse with their mouths agape. It was just wonderful, he told my dad. He realized much later that the guy was drinking. He wasn't paying attention to what the hell he was doing. The boss lady on the horse, the unloading boss, was responsible for getting everything unloaded quickly and efficiently, with zero danger to the horses and men. She would not put up with that shit. So, she jerked him off that wagon and got someone else up there who could keep the brake on and drive those horses right. Later, the kids saw this woman performing bareback on the same black horse. For the second time that day, they were in awe."

Darren turned to Katy with a smile, pulling himself upright again. Katy's sofa had lost much of its innerspring work, forcing the occupant into a slump and slide. "It occurred to my grandfather much later, when he was working for the government, that the circus was far more efficient than many organizations."

The late afternoon sun threw moving shadows across the room. "I have more circus stories if you want to hear."

"How about later? Have you written any of these stories down?"

"No. But maybe someday."

"Not maybe. Write them down. It's important. Stories like these light up the shadows of history, sometimes even defining the small history that would otherwise be lost."

Darren nodded.

"Let's go to the party." Katy stood.

"Wait. You haven't told me why you wanted me to tell you about my grandfather." Darren got up off the sofa, glancing at the peach coloring on Katy's toenails.

Katy answered, "I'm curious about your curiosity and interest in your past."

"OK. Why is that important to you?"

She gave Darren a sharp frown. "You haven't been listening. These stories add to our cultural history. That's important to me and because you–," she stabbed the air in front of him, "choose to remember your family's stories. They must be important to you, and that tells me something about you."

"I'm still a bit confused."

"You'll get over it." Katy opened the door. The party dripped heavily into the stairway. A jumble of sound echoed off the confining walls. Darren followed Katy. She closed the door and turned.

Darren took her hand and said, "Show me your town. This is too loud and crazy." Katy looked up the stairwell. A few people sat, stood, leaned close to speak above the music coming from the open door above.

"OK." She didn't need convincing. "I'll show you the house on Caroline."

Darren drove. He told Katy how he met her upstairs neighbors. He told her where he worked, an hour north if the traffic was light. Where he went to school. That he majored in English Literature but as a sophomore, his roommate talked him into Business and as a Junior, he changed to Computer Science.

"I may be a chameleon," he said.

They parked on Caroline across from the house with yellow tape. Katy talked about her grandparents and her love of 'small' history.

"Small?" Darren said.

"Small, but only in the sense that all the 'smalls' can add up to make and influence 'big' history," Katy explained, looking out the window at the house where Jannie Pratt worked. "All the tiny tendrils of history that eventually grow and interconnect and form the larger 'told' history, the history we study in school—those tendrils, the lives of everyday people, the small people, that's what I'm talking about. The small history." The willow oak in the front yard overhung the street, reaching to the opposite sidewalk. Katy looked up at its branches. "Do you suppose trees have memories?" she said to herself. Darren looked at her, realizing she was in a zone that did not include him. He interrupted her thought.

"You were talking about small and big history."

Katy took a breath and turned to Darren. "Do you suppose history has a purpose? Is it leading us somewhere?"

Darren was nonplussed. "I don't think I've ever considered the purpose of history."

Katy stared at his dark eyes, sheltered by dark brows. "OK. Let's forget purpose and just tell stories of the past." Katy stipulated they would work their way to the present from as far back as they could remember. Stories filled the car and flowed out the windows onto the shaded street beneath the oak until Katy's phone interrupted the laughter. She pulled the phone from her back pocket.

Etta Tunney was frantic. She told Katy she had talked with everyone she knew, starting with her pastor, but no one had a solution. Katy listened to the woman's voice, wondering what she was talking about.

"Rachel's in jail, Katy. She broke into the house. The police got her. She's charged with breaking and entering. I don't know who else to call."

Katy thought of Red Hamilton, Meghan's boyfriend. Could he call in a favor? Does it work like that? "Have they set bond?" Katy said.

"Yes. Five-thousand dollars. I don't even have fifty. She'll be in jail forever. I didn't think it was a big deal when she called, but the police say it is."

"Surely the judge will be reasonable and have some pity. Does he know she has two small kids?"

"I don't know. I don't know what to do," Etta said just above a whisper, her voice hoarse. Katy knew she had been crying.

"Did she take anything?" Katy thought of the jewelry. Could Rachel have found the jewels?

"No. She just broke a window and looked around. Then the police came, and she ran."

"Let me make a call. I know someone who might be able to help. Can I call you back?"

"Please," Etta said, in a prayerful tone.

Darren followed the half conversation, watching Katy. She put the phone on her lap and looked at him and said, "It's the grandmother of the two kids I was telling you about. Her daughter is in jail. She broke into that house." Katy pointed.

"Wow. So how can you help?"

"I can't, but I may know someone who can."

Katy called Meghan. Meghan, Red, and Alex were on their way home from the canoe trip. Meghan put her phone on speaker and held it toward Red.

"So, the mother is in jail?" Red said.

"Yes, she broke into the house. Five-thousand-dollar bond. They don't have any money. Anything you can do?"

"B&E, Burglary. That's a felony. Did she have a gun?"

"I don't know."

"Does she have a record?"

"I don't know."

"Find out if you can and see if she knows who the arresting officer is, then call me back. I'll be at Meghan's."

Meghan ended the call. Alex leaned forward and said, "Who's in jail?"

"A person Katy knows. She broke into a house." Meghan turned to Red. "It seems something like that would be a misdemeanor. Breaking into an empty house and looking around—probably for the jewelry."

"Seems like it, but that's considered burglary—a felony. Home invasion is a pretty serious crime. Of course, the judge could reduce it to a misdemeanor, depending on circumstances." Red gripped the wheel, thinking back to a time when he and two friends broke the window of a house on Halloween. It was an accident, one that could have been prevented had the perpetrators not been fifteen-year-olds, incapable of thinking through their actions. That didn't prevent the police from arresting them and charging them with a felony. It was only through the intercession of a white lawyer that the charge was reduced. The three kids went home with their parents. "The mother, Rachel, is black, right?"

"I presume so," Meghan said. "Her kids are black."

"There's your answer. They won't let her out on her own recognizance." Red pulled into the cul-de-sac and parked. "She's the wrong color."

\* \* \*

Darren took Katy to dinner in town. She suggested Thai. They stood on the sidewalk outside the restaurant as Katy made a call. She told Red what Etta had told her. That Rachel had never been arrested and didn't have a gun. She doesn't know the name of the arresting officer.

"I'll make some calls," Red told her. "Are you prepared to go down and vouch for her? I may be able to get her released. Where does she work?"

"At an IHOP."

"We'll need them to give her a good reference as well. And her mother."

"I think Etta has talked to them already."

"She's the wrong color, too. But we'll get past that."

# SEVENTEEN

Sunday morning, rain fell from heaven in a rage. Thor is displeased, Katy thought, lying next to Darren in her bed. The past day's revelry on the third floor had been replaced with thunder and the sustained drumming of water. Darren slept, unperturbed by the sounds outside. His breathing was slow, almost silent. Thor had interrupted Katy's musing. Her thoughts were on the day she had found the four kids digging in the cellar. Burglary. And she had joined them. "Christ," Katy said, speaking to the ceiling. "I'm ignorant, so ignorant."

"Ignorant is not how I would describe you," Darren said, rising on one elbow.

"I could be in jail along with Rachel," Katy said, turning her head toward Darren. "I just wasn't caught. I never realized that walking into an empty house was a felony. When I was a kid in Crozet, we would often explore old, abandoned houses. It was just something you did for fun. Ignorance and the law don't mix well." Katy turned back to the ceiling. She knew every crack and paint error, stain, and blemish on it. It formed a map of her thoughts.

Darren studied Katy's hair as it lay across her pillow, falling to the sheet below. Like a waterfall, he thought, listening to the rain beat against the window next to the bed. Is she always this focused on her work, determined...dogged? Won't let go, can't let go. Wanting to know about my grandparents. Why? History. Her brain seems wired to the past. Darren spoke to the silence of the room as the furies outside howled.

"What's this gripping interest with history you have? Where does it come from?"

Katy turned her head away from her thoughts and looked into Darren's eyes. History. What is history? "Yeah," she said, studying Darren's eyebrow, seeing two overlapping eyes, a Picasso in her bed. "I guess it's a way of looking at the world, of trying to make sense of the world. History." Katy raised herself on her elbow. Darren came into focus, two eyes now, and a nose, a chin, a full face. "History is part of being human. It makes us who we are, whether we know it, whether we contemplate it, it's part of us. It defines us. I pursue definition. I need history to do that." She leaned closer to Darren and, smiling, said, "The nature of man and woman is in their history. It's the basis of their stories. It's the foundation of all their fictions. I need to understand the nature of what is human." Darren caught her face and kissed her.

"It's really raining out there," he said. Katy was being too intense. He liked her intensity, her desire to dig deep, to pursue the things she felt strongly about. But it was too early in the morning for this kind of intensity. Darren watched Katy's eyes. "Do you hear the rain?"

She listened. "It really is raining," she said, jumping out of bed and going to the window. "Wow. Look at the creek." Darren came to the window.

"Let's go down there and check it out," he said.

"You want to?" Katy said.

"Yeah." They looked at each other like two kids conspiring to do something they knew to be wrong. "I don't have a change of clothes," Darren said, leaning down at his bare feet.

"You can throw them in the dryer when we get back. Come on, let's go."

They got dressed and ran out into the heavy rain. The creek had risen, overflowing its bank in several places. The little stream tore along, carrying leaves, limbs, trash, and a frog trying desperately to swim to safety. Darren extended a limb, but the frog disappeared beneath the surface before he could get close to it.

"It's out of control," Katy shouted. "I've never seen so much water come through here." Her hair clung close to her face, straight down her forehead. She pushed it aside, hooking it over her ears, but soon it was back. The trees bent and twisted, their limbs chafing each other, groaning. Darren looked up. A large branch broke and fell on the opposite side of the creek.

"We better go back. This is getting dangerous." Katy said, grabbing his arm.

At the kitchen table, Darren sat wrapped in a towel, embarrassed, waiting for his clothes to wash and dry. Katy was at the stove fixing scrambled eggs and hash browns. She glanced over at him. She knew he would have to leave in a few hours.

"The drive up 95 will be a bear in this rain," she said.

"I can wait it out. You could take me to the river."

"Sure. We can do that. Tell me more about your grandparents first." Katy flipped the potatoes with a spatula and reached for a plate.

"More ancestor stories? What is it about the past with you?"

"I'm a sucker for stories with connections to the past, I guess. And it helps me better understand you—here, in the present."

"Hmm. OK. But only if you tell me about your grandparents. I can play that game too." Katy scooped up some potatoes and prepared to toss them at Darren. He held his hands up and said, "Can't I? It's only fair." Katy lowered the potatoes and smiled.

"I guess. Alright, I'll tell you how my grandparents met."

"Great," said Darren, sitting back in his chair, adjusting the towel around his waist.

Katy laid their plates on the table and sat. "They met on a roof."

"A roof?"

"My grandfather was helping his father build a house for a family. This was in Crozet, a little place west of Charlottesville."

"How old was your grandfather?"

"He was about sixteen or seventeen. You see, my great-grandfather was a house builder and this family—my grandmother's family—contacted him, and they agreed to a price. My grandmother and her family lived on the land in a small shack. The new house was being built next to the shack. It was summer. Kids were out of school. And my grandmother wanted to help build the new house. Her mother wasn't sure of the idea, but my grandmother was insistent. She was a year younger than my grandfather. She saw him on the roof working, nailing, and wanted to be up there helping. It was her house too, she told her mother. She should be helping."

"Anyway, my grandmother—her name was Patricia, but she went by Tricia—was eager to meet this boy working on her new house. She climbed onto the roof—it was a shed-style roof, almost flat—and asked to help. My grandfather's father had gone to Charlottesville for materials. Had he known about this, he wouldn't have allowed it. But my grandfather was smitten. His name was Thomas, Tom. He got a hammer, and the two soon-to-be lovers began nailing down the shingles together. Well, it was a hot day. Tom wasn't happy beginning the work on the roof with the sun beating down on his back. He just wanted to get the job done. Tricia wanted to talk—to get to know this guy. The two had met when the housebuilding started, but after that, there was no real opportunity to talk. They glanced at each other over the course of their days until this day. Tom was just happy to be near her now—on top of the roof." Katy took a bite, chewing, looking at Darren. He sat waiting for her to continue. Smitten, he thought. "Did I mention it was a hot day?" Katy said, stabbing a potato.

"You did. Very hot on the roof. Good thing it wasn't tin."

"And sweaty. They didn't have fancy hammers in those days, with formed rubber handles. Just wood. Slippery in sweaty hands." Katy watched Darren's face.

"You're going to tell me Tricia threw her hammer at your grandfather—an accident."

"No."

"He fell off the roof and died—"

"No."

"And now I'm talking to a non-being."

"No, but almost."

Darren looked perplexed and bemused. "On with it, girl. What happened?"

"Tricia and Tom were nailing side by side along the edge of the roof. Fifteen, eighteen feet off the ground. Of course, nailing down a roof wasn't something she did every day. She wasn't proficient at holding a nail between the fingers of her left hand and hammering it with her right hand. But after a while, she felt pretty good about her performance. She got the hang of it as she watched Tom set a nail with a single tap, then hammered it home with a single swat. Not at that level yet, but her confidence was on the rise. Maybe too on the rise. The next nail, she started and hammered in a one-two punch, but she forgot to move her left hand. The hammer crashed down on her thumb on the two-stroke. She dropped the hammer and stood with a scream, holding a bloodied thumb to her chest. She was leaning over with pain, her feet at the roof's edge, her eyes closed. Tom jumped up as she teetered forward, grabbing her by the waist and pulled her from the edge. The two toppled over each other, he holding her so she wouldn't fall flat on the roof. She landed on top of him, tears dripping from her eyes onto his face. She tried to smile through the pain. And he kissed her." Katy leaned toward Darren. "They were married two years later."

Darren smiled. "Nice."

"Yeah." Katy leaned back. "I always liked that story. But it's not finished. After they were married, they built their own house and Tricia was back on the roof nailing. She lost her thumbnail to one roof, but she wouldn't let it intimidate her. The house still stands. In Crozet."

The two sat looking at each other. Katy said, "I want to hear about your grandmother."

"Have to wait till next weekend."

"Is that so? Being a little presumptuous, aren't you?" Katy stood and went to the sink, rinsing her plate.

"Am I? You could come to my place."

"We'll see." Katy turned. "Bring me your plate."

When Darren's clothes were dry, Katy suggested they drive to the trailer park before stopping at the river.

"I want to check on Etta and those kids."

The sun was a gem in the bright sky, free from any clouds. It created tiny copies of itself on every dripping leaf. The air was newly minted. Katy and Darren stood in the parking lot, looking at the mid-morning as if it were painted in place. They stood and turned slowly, staring.

"There are no words..." Katy said, searching.

"Wonder!" Darren turned slowly, his head tilted to the sky, then met Katy's eyes. "Nature shows her power, then shares her beauty."

"Words, but fully inadequate."

"To the river, then."

"Trailer park first."

\* \* \*

Douglas and Helen Freeman stood in their house watching the storm roll through. Douglas walked from room to room, all four, staring at the ceilings with a practiced eye. He listened, his ear close to the walls. Only twice in the years the couple lived in the small house had he found a leak. Both times, water crept in from the roof, making its way onto the ceiling of the spare bedroom. Both times, he climbed a ladder and walked the low-pitch roof to the errant shingles and made repairs. Today, he spied no water infiltrating his home. Helen was relieved. She didn't like the idea of her husband crawling around the roof. When he was younger, it was one thing, but now…he has difficulty walking some days, she said to herself.

She relaxed when Douglas returned to the kitchen, reporting that the house was sound. He repeated this ritual every heavy rain. Douglas searching the house for leaks, searching the walls, the gutters, the grounds to convince himself that his house was secure.

Helen's worries were primarily with her plants, all the different flowers and bushes she planted and nurtured surrounding the house over the years. It seemed in this family of two, Helen was the gardener for her house, while Douglas was the gardener for most of the houses on Caroline Street. He got paid in money. She got paid in satisfaction and the beauty that grew around her. Douglas would argue that he received satisfaction as well, not just payment for his services. He too took pride in the beauty he created, but he admitted it was Helen who was the real artist. She was the one he consulted with before he explained to his clients the plant palette he had in mind for them. Her vision exceeded his, filled in his voids, defining the far contours. Following a first planting, when Douglas' plants had grown and filled in showing their true potential, Helen would accompany him down Caroline Street and review his work. She cast her eyes upon the yards, taking in the scope, the colors, and shapes of his efforts. She would make gentle suggestions. Douglas listened and she would return to her house and marvel at the resplendent beauty of that street, its houses, and their gardens. She didn't visit often—only when Douglas asked—for she believed that grandiosity in great gulps was not good for the soul. Instead, she would sip, then return to her small house among the trees and flowers, leaving Douglas to work among the spectacle. She was immune from magnificence and the pretension that sometimes went with it. Once, she longed for grand spectacle. As she matured, she realized that simple beauty was rare in the affairs of man. Beauty is too often hijacked and made plain and coarse by impostors. She counseled Douglas to garden for simplicity—beauty will come of its own accord.

With the sun peering through dripping leaves, Helen walked to her friend's house four doors down. There, she picked up the week's news, seven newspapers arranged in order. Helen and Roberta sat in Roberta's kitchen. They chatted over coffee, their Sunday ritual, then Helen walked home with the newspapers. She and Douglas sat on the front porch and learned what the world leaders and the local leaders were up to. They read the opinions of various writers, both paid and unpaid, and perused the obituaries to see if anyone they knew had died.

"Here's the story on your skeleton, Douglas," Helen said, folding back the paper.

"Not my skeleton. Does it have a picture?"

"Of course not. It's just a brief article. But it mentions Faith. See, if you had called the police, I bet you would have gotten your name in the paper."

Douglas was reading the sports page. The Nationals were creeping toward first place in their division. He read the stats, but his mind projected the image of Harmon Killebrew wearing the Washington Senators cap. 1959. He and his father sat in the bleachers, squinting toward home plate as Killebrew swung. Everyone in the stadium jumped to their feet, watching as the ball arced high over center field. Douglas stood on his seat reaching into the sky when the ball sailed over him, landing far behind, bouncing among the scrambling fans. Everyone was yelling and waving their arms as Killebrew rounded the bases. Father and son jumped and howled. Douglas smiled at the faraway memory.

"I don't need my name in the paper," he said. "If you do

something famous, then maybe. Besides, you're the one who said I shouldn't call."

\* \* \*

Katy drove into the trailer park, making her way through the potholes, over the many speed bumps, and down the side street that was Greenshadow Lane. Darren stared out the window at the trailers lined up in various states of repair. Joseph saw the car from the window.

"Katy's here!" he shouted, running to the door.

Katy introduced Darren. They sat on the sofa. Etta grabbed a rag and cleaned the table, saying they had just finished lunch. Katy told Etta she hoped Rachel could be released from jail. Her friend, Red Hamilton, was a lawyer. He knew the process.

"Thank you," Etta said. "You're a Godsend. I'm so glad Joseph and Justine met you, Katy."

Justine stood before Katy. "Can little kids get library cards?"

"Of course. You just need to have your mom or Nonna Etta here sign the paperwork."

"Can we go?" Joseph said, jumping off the arm of the sofa. "Can we get a book?"

Etta looked at the two jewel hunters. "I suppose so."

"Today?" Justine said, giving Etta an exaggerated grin.

Darren glanced at Katy. Katy said, "We don't want to take up your time, Etta. We were going to check out the river. I thought we'd come by here first and see if you've heard from your cousin."

"Oh, I forgot…with all that's been going on lately."

"We know the way to the river," Joseph said.

"Joseph, not now," Etta said, looking for her phone. "Let me call her right now. We can all talk to her if you like."

Etta called her cousin Ivie in Pennsylvania. Katy asked if she knew of a diary that Jannie may have had. Ivie didn't think so, but she had some old letters between Jannie and her brother and some poems. She would get them. While Ivie was away from the phone, Katy took out a piece of paper and showed it to Etta. She told Etta she had found that Jannie was married to Joshua Thomas, that she had three children: George, Louisa, and Martha. Etta stared at the chart Katy had drawn. When Ivie returned, Katy asked her if she knew who Jannie's immediate descendants were. Ivie said she couldn't remember, but her grandmother's name was Martha Thomas before she married Charlie Freeman.

Etta, still looking at Katy's chart, said: "And your mother was Elizabeth Anderson before she married John Freeman. I'm looking at a genealogy chart Katy drew. That makes us cousins, Ivie."

Ivie laughed. "I don't need a chart to know that, Etta."

"Nonna Jannie got new shoes," Justine said.

Etta and Katy both turned to Justine. Ivie, listening on the phone, said, "What was that?"

Justine whispered, "Nonna Jannie. She got new shoes."

"What are you talking about, Justine?" Etta said.

Katy's eyes remained on Justine.

"It must have been a dream."

"Oh," said Etta as she turned back to Katy. Katy pulled out of the trance Justine had her in.

"So, if I'm right," Katy said into the phone, "and you two just confirmed it, then Nonna Jannie is Justine and Joseph's great-great-great-great-grandmother. That's four greats."

Justine's eyes widened.

Ivie's voice: "Etta, you told those kids Jannie was their great-great-great-grandmother? You left off a great."

"I suppose I did, cousin. Once you get past the first great, I mean you're just piling on, right?"

Katy frowned.

Joseph said, "That means she was really old, doesn't it?"

Justine touched Etta's hand. "Three times older than you?"

Etta laughed. "No. It has nothing to do with her age, Justine. She died pretty young, didn't she, Ivie?"

"I don't remember her exact age. It was before we were born."

"Is she buried in the house?" Joseph looked at his grandmother.

"No, sweetie." Etta turned to the phone. "Isn't she buried in town here, Ivie? At the Shiloh Cemetery?"

"That's my understanding, but her grave isn't marked. I don't know what happened to the gravestone."

Katy wanted to move on. She asked about the letters. Ivie read, "This is from Carter to Jannie. He signs his letters: 'Your dearest brother.' That's the only way I know he was her brother. I remember my mother telling me and my sister about my grandmother and her family, but I've forgotten most of what she said. I'm afraid I wasn't paying attention in those days. It's only when we get old do we think about these things, then our memories are no good."

Darren watched Katy's face change as she talked and listened to Ivie. Her level of excitement grew, visibly. The genealogy chart proved accurate. Now she listened to Ivie read letters from and to the woman who worked at the mystery house over a hundred years ago. Letters Ivie hadn't read in over fifty years. Katy was fairly bouncing on her seat. Darren felt the sofa rock.

Katy jotted a note on her pad, learning that Jannie's brother, Carter, had moved to Indiana. He wrote to Jannie, telling her about his new life and the farm he hoped to buy. Katy listened, anxious to hear Jannie's letters. Ivie read more. And then there was a letter from Jannie talking about her upcoming wedding to Joshua. It mentioned two rings Anna had bought for her—wedding rings. They were engraved. Katy jumped off the sofa.

"Jackpot," Katy shouted.

"I hadn't heard about any rings," Etta said. "I wonder where they are. Do you know, Ivie?"

"No. All I have is a few letters and some poems Jannie wrote."

"If I'm right, those rings are in the house here in town," Katy said. "Along with other jewelry."

"That *would* be a jackpot," Etta said. "But what I remember is that Jannie had three pieces of jewelry, remember, Ivie?"

"That's right. We were told that Nonna Jannie was given a ring and a bracelet and another piece. I forget what it was, but there were three pieces. And the bracelet was much nicer than the bracelet she owned, the one her father had made for her after his injury, a charm bracelet with two charms."

"The one you gave to Lena?" Etta said.

"Yes. My daughter," Ivie said. Katy's eyes stared hard at the phone. "That was the only piece of jewelry she ever owned, I think. When the mistress died, Jannie wasn't allowed in the house where her jewelry was. That's the story."

"Yes. I think that's right," Etta said.

"Well," Katy leaned toward the phone, "the third piece must have been Joshua's wedding ring. Two wedding rings and a bracelet. Could that be, Ivie?"

"Yes. It's possible."

Katy stood looking at Etta's phone. "Ivie," she said, hearing the word possible. "Would it be possible for you to send Etta copies of those letters? And you mentioned poems that Jannie wrote. Could you send copies of those as well? Just take pictures with your phone. Would that be alright? I'd like to include them in the library archives."

Katy and Darren excused themselves after the call with Ivie. But Joseph wouldn't let them go. "Don't you want to go to the river?" he said.

"Yeah. We can take you." Justine lifted herself onto the balls of her feet.

Etta said, "Only if you're with an adult. You two know you're not to go to the river alone."

"We know," Joseph said.

"Would you like to see the river?" Etta said.

"I didn't think it was this close to you all," Katy said.

"It's real close." Joseph opened the door. "We'll show you."

Etta got up slowly from the table, thinking about the conversation with Ivie, the rings, the suggestion by Katy that she thought the jewelry was in the house still. More than a suggestion. Katy sounded emphatic. Could this story about a long-dead ancestor have any validity?

Joseph was out the door, standing in the wet grass of the backyard.

Etta didn't relish walking through the thick understory of trees and shrubs. "You all go ahead. I'll stay here. Katy, make sure those two hooligans don't get into trouble." Etta knew she could trust Katy. She had talked with the woman for only minutes in the past couple of days, but there was in Katy Aldridge something that truth and trust could not improve upon, Etta felt.

Joseph ran ahead with six years of enthusiasm packed in his slight frame. Katy motioned for Darren to follow him. Justine took Katy's hand and walked beside her, telling Katy about Hauk and his mother, Corinne. How Corinne could draw, and the picture of the Kingfisher. How she thought the Corbin brothers were mean, but they weren't, really. Maybe they were just pretending. Katy listened to her small friend babble on as they made their way through the overgrown, dripping path. At the river, Justine pointed out the tree where Corinne sat with her and Joseph. Katy listened, wondering why this woman, Corinne, was important to Justine.

"Justine, do you and your mom ever come to the river?"

"Here?" said Justine.

"Yeah, here. It's so close to your home."

"No."

"Why not?"

"I don't know."

Justine, Katy noted, simply turned off when her mother was mentioned.

"Your mom is pretty busy working, isn't she?" Katy said.

"Yeah. Let's go down here." Justine tugged on Katy's hand. Katy followed, but within seconds, they heard Joseph call from the path upriver.

"Justine. A snake." Joseph stood motionless on the path, staring at a bright green ribbon entwined in the branches of a gnarly shrub. Darren held Joseph by the shoulder as the two peered at the creature six feet from them. Justine ran toward Joseph with Katy right behind her. "It's just sitting there," Joseph said, pointing as Justine arrived.

"It's so pretty," Justine said, reaching into the branches, grabbing the snake. "A Greensnake. They like to climb trees."

"Justine." Katy's voice an octave higher than necessary as she moved toward the girl with some hesitation. Darren stood frozen, watching with fascination as Justine held the snake behind its head, allowing it to wrap her arm.

"It's not venomous," Justine said, looking at Katy's strained expression.

"How do you know?"

"It's way different from a copperhead."

"True, but…" Katy tried to picture a copperhead snake. She knew it had a distinctive hourglass pattern and was not all green, but there must be other venomous snakes. She took out her phone. "Hold it so I can take a picture. I'm going to find out what it is." She texted Meghan with the attached picture: What kind? "My friend Meghan knows about snakes. Why don't you put it down, Justine? I'm sure your grandmother won't allow you to have it." Katy's phone buzzed. She read the text. "Meghan says it's a Rough Greensnake, it's harmless." She looked at Darren, who still held Joseph, the two of them transfixed—by the snake and by Justine.

"That was close," Katy said. "OK, Justine. Better let it go. Here, let me take a picture of you with the snake."

"I can't keep it?" Justine said, knowing the answer.

"How would you take care of it?" Katy said, realizing that was the wrong thing to say. Never ask a kid a question if you know the answer could lead you deeper into the quagmire you most desire to avoid. "I mean…" Katy's phone buzzed. "It's Meghan. She says her son, Alex, would love to have the snake." Katy looked at Justine. "If you don't want it."

"But I do," Justine said.

Joseph put his hand out to touch the snake. "It looks like the one Terrell has, Justine."

Justine's eyes were fixed on Katy. Katy looked at Darren for help. He shrugged. Great, she thought. "OK, let's bring it back to your grandmother Etta. I'm sure she'll want to care for it. Don't you think?"

Justine examined the snake. She knew what Nonna Etta would say—after she screamed. She looked up at Katy. "Would I be able to see him if I gave it to Alex?"

"I'm sure he would share," Katy said. "Let me call him." Katy called Meghan, telling her Alex could have the snake if he would allow Justine to see it from time to time. Meghan called Alex to the phone. "I'll let Alex talk to Justine," she said to Katy. Katy held her phone toward Justine.

"Hello," Justine said, holding the snake loosely at her waist. The snake nosed at the pocket of her shorts.

Alex said, "Hi. I can take care of your snake. You can see it whenever you want."

"OK. Its name is Pocket. When do you want to get it?"

"I can bring it over later," Katy said.

"What are you going to put it in?" Darren asked Katy.

"You're going to hold it."

"Who's that?" Meghan said.

"Darren, my new boyfriend."

Meghan smiled. New boyfriend. Wonder how long this one will last?

"Hi, Meghan," Darren said.

"Darren. I guess we'll meet when you bring over the snake," Meghan said.

"Pocket," Justine corrected.

Katy suggested to Justine that it might be best to keep Pocket outside while she explained to Etta what was going on.

Etta was happy with the arrangement. She peeked out at Justine holding the snake. "Oh, my word," she said, her hand covering her mouth. "That girl has no fear."

"It's a harmless snake," Katy assured her, marveling at her newfound bravado. She stood at the open door as Etta sat at the table.

"No snake is harmless," Etta told her. "It's the devil. That girl is holding the devil himself. You take it away. Soon."

"We will. We're leaving right now. Would you mind if I took Justine and Joseph with us? They could meet Alex. He's Justine's age."

Etta's eyes fell to the floor, to the sofa leg. It hung above the floor by the thickness of a card deck, less the queen of hearts.

"Rachel will be home soon," Etta said to Katy. "When will you be back?"

"Hour and a half. Is that too long?"

"That's fine. That's probably when she'll be home."

Justine sat in the back seat holding the snake with Joseph helping at a safe distance. She kept up a constant patter as Katy drove to Meghan's house. Darren looked up at the traffic on the interstate as they drove under the overpass. He had hoped to have gotten on the road earlier, but he was infatuated and sensed his life was altered. And now, transporting two kids and a snake to people he knew as voices over a phone. "Not your normal first date," he mumbled to himself.

"What's that?" Katy said, glancing over.

"Just wondering when I might see you again."

"After this weekend, you really want to see me again?"

Darren smiled. "More than ever. I'm curious about the second act."

# EIGHTEEN

Stephen Fitzhugh woke early on Monday. His wife was still sleeping when he slipped a pair of shoes on and walked out the front door to survey his lawns and check on Captain Hickory Run that flowed near the corner of his property. The stream still possessed energy from the corralled rain the day before. Stephen neared its edge and stopped to watch the water course along, then walked back. Tree branches littered his yard, but he had lost no trees in the storm. He was happy about that, having just paid an arborist two-thousand dollars to remove a dead limb that hung close to his house. The man strapped on a pair of climbing spurs, roped the limb, then cut it and lowered it to the ground. He was driving away within an hour. Stephen complained to his neighbor that he'd been ripped off.

"You live in Great Falls, Stephen. What did you expect?" the neighbor said. "If you lived half an hour west, you would have paid half that, maybe a third."

"I may have to switch jobs and become an arborist," Stephen said.

"Is that what your guy called himself?"

"Yeah. Nice new truck, the works. He and another guy."

"Well, I can tell you he wasn't certified. You say he climbed that tree with those telephone pole spikes?"

"Yeah."

"An arborist wouldn't do that. Not to a live tree. Your guy was a chainsaw hack."

"Shit. I paid arborist rates for a hack?"

Stephen came to the front gate and retrieved the newspaper. As he pulled out the Sports section, the Lifestyle section fell to the ground. There, on its front page, was the story of Rachel Parker, in jail for breaking into the house where a skeleton was found. Looking for her great-great-grandmother's jewelry, she told the police.

Stephen rolled up the paper and walked back to the stream. He watched it churn and hop along the bank. He pulled his phone from his breast pocket and held it, watching the fast-moving waters as they washed debris south toward Difficult Run. Searching for jewelry, he mused and then thought back to the call he'd made to Katy Aldridge several days before. What were the chances of finding the jewelry and diary his grandfather once owned? Once, long ago, he had visited the small town with his father. They drove down Caroline Street and stopped at the house where Blayden Fitzhugh and his wife once lived. His father told him, again, the story everyone in the family knew about Blayden and his first wife, Anna, and how she left on a train to visit her mother and was never heard from afterward. She had a collection of jewelry she brought to the marriage and added to liberally after the marriage. And then she disappeared, along with all her jewelry. It was a mystery the family had lived with for over a hundred years. Now, a skeleton is found in the house and the story of the lost jewelry is known everywhere. He was not at all happy that people were looking for *his* jewelry. And he wanted the diary. The diary may confirm a suspicion he had.

Stephen looked down at his phone. The press and others will speculate about the identity of the skeleton, he thought. He and everyone in his family had speculated at one time. Could his grandfather have killed Anna? Blayden Fitzhugh had denied it at the time and forever after. Yet, there were those in the family who had doubts. There was the one time when his grandmother, Sarah, apparently hinted at something sinister in her past. She was a year from her death when she whispered to her daughter: "I have a sadness that twists in my heart, Barbara." But she would not say more other than, "I must bear it alone."

Family lore. How close to the truth is it? Stephen wondered. But he was determined to stop the theft of the jewelry that belonged to him and to read the diary that may hold truths to a story only hinted at. He drew his phone close and made a call to his lawyer. He explained the situation with the house and the jewelry.

"I believe any jewelry that is found in that house is legally mine," Stephen told his lawyer. "Do you agree?"

His lawyer looked at the time displayed on his phone and sighed.

"I think you could make a good argument, yes."

"Then how can I prevent the owner of that house from finding the jewelry and walking away with it? Could you file a restraining order preventing the owner from looking for it?"

"Stephen, I would have to do some research, but I don't believe a judge would issue an injunction that would enjoin the owner from searching for something in his house. However, you could sue the owner for the return of what you believe is your property and enjoin him from disposing or harming it until the rights to it are determined."

"So, I have to sit back and wait, you're saying?"

"Essentially. Stephen, next time you call, can you make it at a reasonable time of day?"

Stephen laughed and thanked the lawyer, then made one more call.

"Hank, it's Stephen. I need you to do some surveillance for me. Can you come by the house this morning? I'll explain."

Hank lifted himself off his pillow and spoke into the phone: "Yes, sir. I'll be there in thirty minutes."

"Make it twenty. It's important."

# NINETEEN

The storm that rolled through town two days before came with high winds and quick water. The winds pushed over trees and ripped limbs from others. Caroline Street, like many in the area, was strewn with downed branches and limbs, roof shingles, and other wet debris left by the storm. The street was loud today. Two chainsaws and a woodchipper defined the din. In front of 311 Caroline, a man in a bucket truck held a screaming chainsaw to a wounded limb. Joseph pointed as the limb attached to a rope was slowly lowered to the ground.

Douglas Freeman walked around the corner of the house, on the opposite side of the street, and stopped. "Same kids," he muttered, putting down his rake. Justine and Joseph followed him with their eyes as he neared them. He stopped, staring at Justine. She stared back at the man. He turned to Joseph, who fidgeted.

"Do you live here?" Justine said, recognizing the man.

"No," Douglas said. "And neither do you. Why are you here?"

"You don't like kids, do you?" said Justine, taking hold of Joseph's hand and backing away.

Douglas blinked and looked at his hands. Dirt stained his palms. *The girl is just like Livia.* He looked back at Justine and knelt before her on one knee. Justine saw his face change. He smiled at her and said, "I do like kids. I just think small kids like you two should be with a parent. It's dangerous out here by yourself." Douglas balanced as best he could on his knee. He had been on his knees all morning.

"We're used to being by ourselves," Joseph said, seeing that the big man wasn't the threat he first appeared.

Douglas stood slowly. "My name's Douglas. What's yours?"

"Joseph."

"Justine."

He put out his hand to shake. How strange, Justine thought. Joseph saw a semblance of a nod from his sister. He reached out and shook Douglas' hand. Justine followed.

"Lotta noise down there at that house." Douglas pointed. "You two know the owners?"

Joseph waited for Justine to answer. He was wary of questions dealing with the house where the skeleton lived. Justine followed Douglas' arm, pointing to Nonna Jannie's house. She saw the dirt on his hand. He worked with plants. She decided he wasn't a bad person.

"Our great-great-grandmother...I mean, great-great-great-great-grandmother used to live there," Justine said. "She was a maid."

Douglas studied the two kids standing on the sidewalk. They wore shorts of similar color but different colored t-shirts. Justine's little toe stuck out from her right tennis shoe. He stared at her, remembering. "Is that right?" he said. "Is she still alive?"

"No. She died a long time ago."

"S'pose so, bein' that great."

The two kids looked up at the man. They didn't respond. Douglas was curious, but he didn't want to spook them. He had read the stories in the paper. The skeleton may be that of Anna Fitzhugh, the reporter wrote. But maybe not.

"What was your great-great-great-great-grandmother's name?"

"Jannie," Justine said.

"The police found a skeleton in the house. It wasn't Jannie, was it?"

"No. It was probably somebody else. They buried Nonna Jannie at a cemetery."

"Look!" Joseph said, pointing toward the house. A man came out of the front door. He walked to a pickup truck parked in the driveway and retrieved a box, then went back into the house.

"Two guys workin' on the house. I saw them drive up earlier with some tools," Douglas said. Justine was going to ask him what he thought the men were doing, but he spoke first.

"Do your mom and dad know you're out here?"

"Our mama's sleeping," Joseph said.

"Sleepin'?"

"She works late," Justine said.

"Uh-huh," Douglas nodded. "So, you're checkin' on the house where Jannie lived. Does your mother know you're checkin'?"

"You ask a lot of questions," Justine said.

Douglas laughed. "I guess I'm curious. I saw y'all at the house a while back. I'm guessin' you're curious too—about the house. What's in it that you're curious about?"

Justine studied Douglas' face. Joseph glanced at Douglas, then at his sister. Will she tell? he wondered.

"Nonna Jannie…" Justine studied Douglas' hands. "Nonna Jannie lost some jewelry in that house." She instantly felt she had made a mistake. She looked at Douglas' eyes.

"I see," he said. "And you think the jewelry is still in the house?"

She listened to his voice, soft, assured. She searched his eyes. Interested. Helping. She nodded.

"I guess that's why you and the boys were diggin' in the cellar."

Justine didn't answer. The men chipping the tree limbs gathered their tools. The street was quiet again. Justine stared at the house, the front door.

"What do you think those men are doing in the house?" Justine said, looking up at Douglas.

"I don't know. They just had a couple tools when they went in."

"I hope they aren't looking for the jewels," Joseph said.

"No. That wouldn't be right, would it? Since they belong to your Nonna Jannie."

The kids nodded in agreement. Justine stood next to the man she now wanted to trust. He could be her grandfather, she thought. She never knew her grandfather. He didn't leave like her father. No, her grandfather left because God wanted him more than anyone on earth. That's what Nonna Etta told her and Joseph. God makes all the important decisions, Nonna Etta said. We make the lesser decisions.

"God introduces us to good people, and we decide to like them or not," Etta had explained. "If God introduces us to bad people, we should reject them if we are wise. If not, we live with the consequences."

"But what if we reject them," Justine had said, "and they hurt us, anyway?"

Etta thought about that question for some time. Her philosophy had always been an optimistic one. She couldn't accept negative outcomes on principle. When they came, which they frequently did in her life, she was forced to abandon principle and accept the outcomes because of her poor judgment and wrong decisions. It was not God, whom she prayed to every day, who was responsible for the bad things that had occurred to her and her family. It was she. She alone made the choice that brought about the bad outcome. Now, she was asked by her precocious granddaughter to explain how a correct choice could cause a bad outcome. She had pondered the question herself and never had a good answer. She'd had many discussions with friends at her church and with the current and previous pastor. Pastor Davis, the current pastor, blamed evil on the devil. Satan was responsible for all the bad that happens on earth, he said. "But God is all-powerful, all-knowing, all everything," she countered. "How could God allow Satan to pull evil over His eyes?"

It was Pastor Jenkins, the previous pastor, who explained that, yes, Jesus allows evil to exist alongside good. He is simply testing us. It is up to us to deal with evil, to counter it the best way we know how. Pastor Jenkins told Etta in the parking lot after her husband's funeral service: it is through prayer that we receive God's grace to take on the evils we encounter, God's grace soaks us in divine comfort and gives us the power and understanding necessary to change evil into something good.

"That is why we are here on earth," Jenkins said. "We are God's soldiers on earth, battling the great Satan."

Etta looked at Pastor Jenkins as her husband's casket was wheeled to the hearse behind him. Her lips quivered, wanting to challenge him, but she dropped her head to the pavement instead and began to cry. He put his arm around her shoulder and said, "You'll be fine, Etta. All things must pass. The sun also rises after it sets."

Etta looked at her granddaughter and said, "Honey girl, sometimes we make the right decisions and bad things still happen. It's the way the world works. The only thing to do is pray to God."

Justine took Douglas' hand and squeezed it. God had introduced her to Douglas. She had not prayed for this to happen, but it did. God was looking after her. Douglas felt the small hand on his and looked down at the person standing beside him. He smiled. Joseph came up and took his other hand. He was startled, a bit mystified by this behavior. He didn't know what to say. The children were looking at the house. They didn't need any words.

Now that the noise from the tree surgeons had stopped, Faith Bonner felt safe to venture out. She stepped onto her porch and surveyed the street. It was late morning. The heat was rising, but it had not reached the level of outright discomfort. Faith enjoyed sitting on her porch in the early morning, beneath the overhanging maple where the abandoned robin's nest sat just above her eye level. She saw it now resting in a fork, unscathed by the storm. It survived, she marveled. How could that be? There must be two natures, Faith thought. One violent but cleansing; the other soft and nurturing, both existing together. She walked to the steps and descended to the sidewalk, still looking up at the nest. Faith wasn't a religious person, although she attended church and volunteered with the food drive. Only a few friends knew her views on God: "I don't believe in God, but I believe in the power of God," she told them. When she turned and glanced down the street, she saw Douglas, two houses up, holding the hands of two small kids. Their backs were to her. She strode down the sidewalk and called, "Douglas."

Douglas and his new friends turned to the voice.

"Mornin', Faith."

"Who are your friends?"

"Justine and Joseph. We've been consultin' on some important issues relative to the house down there." Douglas pointed toward 311.

"Is that so?" Faith came closer. "Do tell." She walked up to Justine and held out her hand. "I'm Faith. You must be Justine." Justine nodded, shaking her hand. "And you must be Joseph." She shook his hand. "Important issues, you say. Anything related to the skeleton the police found at that house?"

"Might," Douglas said.

"You their attorney?" Faith said to Douglas.

"Might be."

"Might you be more specific, counselor?"

"Let me consult with my clients."

"Go right ahead. By all means."

Douglas looked at Justine. "Should we tell Miss Faith about your Nonna Jannie?"

Faith glanced at the girl, waiting for her reply. She glanced at Joseph. Where were their parents?

Justine hesitated. Douglas said, "She's my friend. You can trust Miss Faith."

Justine sucked in her lower lip. "I guess."

"Is Nonna Jannie your grandmother?" Faith said.

"Four greats-grandmother," answered Douglas. "You tell her, Justine."

Justine still wasn't certain of Faith Bonner's motives. She didn't look like the kind of person who would steal someone's jewels. She looked kind of old, maybe real old, had gray hair and wore old people's clothes that didn't fit well. Justine looked at Bonner's feet. She wore slippers. Who wears slippers outside? Even so, she was a friend of Mr. Douglas. Joseph watched his sister's eyes as she sized up this Faith lady. He waited for her reply, confident that his sister would make the right decision.

"Nonna Jannie used to live in that house down there. The lady gave her… She worked for the lady, and the lady gave Nonna Jannie some jewelry. We were trying to find it."

Faith ruminated on this information. "This must have been long ago. So, your fourth-great-grandmother worked for the owner as probably the housekeeper?" Faith looked to Justine for affirmation. Justine nodded. "And the mistress of the house gave her some jewelry. Do I have that straight, Justine?"

"Yes." Justine picked up her right foot and rubbed it against the back of her left calf. She stood like a resting stork.

"So why would the jewelry be in the house? Especially now." Faith gave Douglas a look. Douglas shrugged and looked at Justine.

Justine said, "Nonna Jannie never got the jewelry from the lady."

"I'm confused." Faith glanced at Douglas. To Justine, she said, "What was the lady's name?"

Joseph was ready for this question. He hated being left out. Now that his sister opened the conversation, he figured he was free to contribute. "Anna," he blurted. "That's what Katy said."

"Anna, Katy." Faith put her hand to her forehead. "And Katy is…"

"She works at the library," Joseph said.

"Ah." Faith took a deep breath, then continued her questioning until she thought she had a fair idea of what was going on. At that point, she shifted gears to her real concern.

"May I ask why you two are walking around without your parents?"

"Our mama's sleeping," Joseph said.

"Well, I take naps now and then, but I don't leave my head in the sink," Faith said.

Joseph and Justine squinted at Faith. Douglas tried to help. "She means that it's your mom's responsibility to look after you two, even if she's tired."

Faith discovered that the kids had no father but that their grandmother looked after them at night when their mother was working. "Grandmother, huh," Faith said. After some cajoling, she convinced Justine that it would be alright to come into her house and get a drink and something to eat. Joseph liked the idea. Douglas returned to his gardening across the street.

After more questioning, Faith saw that the children's grandmother went to Shiloh Baptist Church. She made a call to the church and learned Etta's phone number, then called Etta. Etta was pissed. She drove to Caroline Street and parked across from Faith's house. Douglas watched as Etta got out of her car. Her face told stories. She climbed the two steps to Faith's porch and knocked on the door.

"Hell to pay," Douglas said, clipping the encircled roots on a plant he held in his bare hand. He wished he could hear the conversation between the two grandmothers.

Sometime later, Douglas heard Faith's door open and talking on the porch. He raised himself from the bed of flowers, a large meerkat scrutinizing the neighborhood. Justine, Joseph, and Etta crossed the street to Etta's car. Justine waved at Douglas. Etta opened the rear door and said, "Who's that?" Joseph replied it was Douglas, their friend.

"Friend? How many friends do you have in this neighborhood?"

The siblings crawled into the back seat. Etta opened her door and said, "Huh? You know a lot of people in this part of town?"

"No," said Justine.

Etta drove down Caroline, passing a car parked across from 311. She noticed a man sitting behind the wheel with a newspaper. His eyes were on the house across the street until Etta's car interfered with his sightline. He and Etta glanced at each other as Etta passed.

"We're going to have a real talk when we get home, young lady," Etta said.

Justine knew she was in trouble now. 'Young lady' was code. It had nothing to do with being young or being a lady. It had to do with being bad. Nonna Etta said she was worried when she got the phone call from Miss Faith. And Justine knew that worrying your grandmother was worse than doing something bad, especially since this worry was not the first. It could be the baddest thing one could do. She considered the possible punishment. Joseph was still hungry. The cookies Miss Faith gave him were good, but…

"And you, Joseph." Etta leaned over the boy after they entered the trailer. She had come from the bedroom where Justine sat, admonished. "You will be going to first grade in the fall." Etta knew how anxious Joseph was to enter school, to follow his sister, and to gain the elite status of bus rider. "When you're in school, you can't just do whatever you like. School is a special place. It requires special behavior, mature behavior. You know what that means?" Joseph shook his head. "It means you learn to behave like an adult, a grown boy. You don't do dumb things. Understand?"

Joseph nodded. He understood, he thought, but it troubled him because his mother and her boyfriend didn't seem to act like adults. If they were adults, which they looked like, why would Nonna Etta be angry with them all the time and tell them they were being dumb? But he didn't ask that question. He was hungry and saw that Nonna Etta was angry at him and Justine. He sat on the edge of the sofa, tilting it forward, off its rear support, looking toward where Justine was being confined, then leaned forward, allowing the sofa to tilt back. The stacked cereal boxes were gone. His corner of the sofa hung in the air. Joseph sat back down, pressing the wooden foot to the floor. He repeated this several times, his back arched forward, his head almost upside down, watching as the sofa tilted.

Etta sat at the table looking out the window past Joseph, wondering how her life had painted her into this corner. First, her grandchildren walk to town and discover the house where Nonna Jannie worked and unearth a skeleton. Then, her daughter goes to the house—and the police haul her off to jail. Now her grandchildren walk back into town to the same house. To look for the jewelry? No, Justine told her. Just to look at the house. This house, Etta decided, was evil. She didn't want to have anything to do with it.

Joseph took his shoe off and slipped the toe between the sofa foot and the floor. He sat back down. The sofa refused to rock. He looked up at Etta, who continued to stare out the window.

"Nonna Etta," he said softly. "I stopped the sofa." He pointed. Etta looked at Joseph then saw the shoe stuck under the sofa. She smiled. Joseph saw the smile. He knew Nonna Etta couldn't stay angry for long.

"That's good, Joseph. Maybe you could find something other than your shoe to stick there. I always knew you were a smart boy. You'll do good in school." Etta got up from her musings and called to Justine.

It was time for lunch. Etta asked Justine to help Joseph find something to put under the sofa leg while she fixed them lunch. Justine looked at Joseph's repair. She knelt and removed his shoe. Finding nothing suitable, Justine asked if they could go outside and look for a stone. Etta said yes, but don't stray. Brother and sister scoured the yard and the end of the pavement, looking for a stone the thickness of Joseph's shoe. It had to be flat. Flat stones were special—they were skipping stones, Justine explained to Joseph. But Joseph had knowledge of skipping stones. He didn't need his big sister to tell him that. He said, "I know."

They walked down the street. At the corner, they turned around and started back, but not before Joseph caught sight of the Corbin brothers getting into a car. He called to Justine. She turned. Hauk stopped and looked up the street. Justine waved. Hauk and Shahin got in the back seat. The two geologists watched as the car came to the corner and drove toward the park entrance. Justine watched the car turn again and disappear. She and Joseph crossed the street without comment and continued their search for a flat stone. Just as Etta called, Joseph bent down.

"Here's one, Justine," he said.

Justine picked it off his palm. "Let's try."

Inside, Justine handed the stone to Joseph and lifted the sofa. He pushed the stone beneath the leg. The sofa remained steady. They both jumped on the sofa at the same time.

"It works," Joseph shouted.

Etta had little interest in the sofa. Her thoughts were on her daughter. Etta convinced Rachel's supervisor that her daughter was not a bad person. It was against company policy to employ a felon, the supervisor explained. But I'm not a felon, Rachelle countered. Etta put her hand on Rachel's shoulder and looked at the supervisor, a woman in her forties, who clearly enjoyed sampling the food where she worked. "My daughter has not been convicted of a crime. She's only been charged. She's a good employee. You know that. It would be harder for you to hire and train a new person and deal with all the paperwork than to bring Rachelle back, don't you think?" The supervisor thought over Etta's logic, looking at Rachelle, then at her children, who stood beside their mother. She smiled at Rachelle. Rachelle gave her a hug. Etta said, "Thank you," and took her grandkids and daughter home to their trailer.

That was yesterday, just hours after Etta got a call from Katy. "Rachel will be released on her own recognizance. My friend convinced the arresting officer she would not flee. The magistrate agreed to have her released. But she still must go to court and all the hearings and stuff that goes with it." Etta was overjoyed. She hopped in a circle. The trailer rocked. Joseph stood over the toilet, missing his aim. Justine ran from her room looking at her wide-smiling grandmother.

Etta sat at the kitchen table, eating lunch. She was successful in fixing one problem—Rachel's employment—but now she had a new problem. Rachel's hours had been changed. Now she worked the first shift and Etta would be forced to change her working hours or find someone to watch the kids during the day. She chewed on her sandwich, working through her options.

Justine looked up and said, "Nonna Etta, Mrs. Corbin has cancer."

Etta looked at Justine and stopped chewing. Mrs. Corbin. She knew the name because of the stories Justine had told her about the brothers and their antics at school and on the bus. But she had never met the mother or father. From gossip among the neighbors at this end of the street, Etta knew the Corbins were new to the park, having moved in less than a year ago. The father had a good job, apparently. He drove a nice car, and he was often seen wearing a sports jacket as he left for work in the morning. That is all Etta knew of the Corbins.

"Cancer?"

Justine nodded.

"How do you know?" Etta put her sandwich down.

"Hauk told me."

Etta's gaze turned thoughtful. She looked through Justine, thinking. Why had she never walked to the Corbins' street? Just taken a walk around the park and waved at people sitting on their steps or working in their small yards. How thoughtless. How incurious. Etta knew the few neighbors close by Rachel's trailer but knew little beyond their names. Here I sit with my own problems, Etta mulled, when others just a few paces away have it far worse.

"That's sad," Etta said. "I thought you didn't get along with those boys."

"They're OK," Justine replied. "Their mother's name is Corinne. I think it's a nice name, don't you?"

"You met her?" Etta watched as both Justine and Joseph nodded. "Where?"

"At the river," Justine said and immediately realized her mistake. But she barreled on. "She was sitting by the river and Shahin and Hauk were there. She's an artist. She can draw real good."

"Yeah," Joseph said. "She drew a bird with a funny head."

"A kingfisher," Justine said.

Etta studied her two grandkids. Joseph sat low on his chair, his shoulders just above the top of the table. She watched as his sandwich dripped jelly through his fingers. He knows more than I do about what's going on, Etta thought. Justine watched her grandmother's face closely. She isn't mad at us for going to the river, Justine thought.

Etta sat back and glanced toward the window, then set her gaze on the two kids sitting with her. They had walked to the library in town searching for information and then walked to a house where their Nonna Jannie used to work, hoping to find jewelry in the house. Then walked to the river and talked with a neighbor who will probably die. How remarkable is this? Etta mused. How powerful are curiosity and determination? Then she remembered her conversation with Faith Bonner. She sat in Faith's living room—a lovely room, Etta remembered—and listened to Faith talk to her grandchildren, warning them of the dangers they could encounter, alone, on the streets of this town. Etta nodded and said, "Yes, Miss Faith is right," looking at Justine who sat on a couch with brocade pillows, silk peacocks standing proud of the fabric. Curiosity, determination, and danger. Three dials. Etta fixated on the last dial, danger. Justine seems to live with the three dials full open. I worry. The girl has no fears. And she is teaching Joseph. What is driving her? She had no answer.

"Have you seen a kingfisher?" Justine said, interrupting her grandmother's thoughts.

"No. I don't believe I have. What does it look like?"

"Maybe you could take us to the library," Justine suggested. "I could get a bird book."

"Why would you want a bird book?" Etta's mind remained in Faith Bonner's living room with the high ceilings and wide crown molding.

"So, I could show you what a kingfisher looks like," Justine said, a little frustrated.

"Oh. It's a bird. I didn't know."

"Could you?" Joseph said.

"What dear?" Etta stared at the piece of sandwich still in her hand.

"The library," Justine said. "Can you take us there?"

"I think so. Sometime. This isn't a good time right now."

# TWENTY

The faint light from the sconce in the kitchen made its way to the backyard, illuminating a small patch of grass behind two figures. There was no moon, only the light of a million yesterdays. They sat in lawn chairs, close to each other, and talked, a whisper above the crickets. The cicadas were silent, listening as Douglas told Helen about his day. He purposely led with the plants, explaining where he chose to place the salvia. Helen had visited the home on Caroline Street. She knew the yard and had blessed his plans. Helen nodded, invisible to her husband, and replied, "Mmm," every so often. She followed him around the yard in her mind as he walked her through the garden, kneeling before each depression, kneading the soil piled around, then unwrapping the roots, pruning them when necessary so they didn't strangle themselves. "Mm-hmm," she said, swatting at a mosquito as it approached her ear.

"I planted the Silky in the corner. It'll look nice there."

Helen saw Douglas on his knees, pushing the loose soil around the collar of the small dogwood. It backed close to the corner of the cedar fence. "It should be lovely," Helen said, thinking about a dogwood she had planted years before.

"You know those kids I told you about? The ones foolin' around Beverly's house?"

"I remember."

"They were back today. Two of 'em. Brother and sister. Name's Justine and Joseph. Cute kids."

"What were they doin'?"

"Just standin' and watchin'. All three of us stood on the sidewalk outside Faith's house and watched some guys clean up limbs from the storm."

"The three of you?" Helen adjusted herself in the chair, twisting her head toward her husband. The shadow of a head spoke to her.

"Yeah."

"Douglas, stop toyin' with me and tell me what the kids were really doin'."

"Well, seems their great-great-great-great-grandmother used to live in Beverly's house. Long time ago. And she left some jewelry there. And the kids are lookin' for it. That's what they were doin' with the shovels the other day. Diggin' in that cellar."

"That a fact? So, they come by t'ask for your help?"

"Not sure what their plans were. They didn't have any shovels with 'em. They were just lookin' at the house. But…" Douglas swatted away a mosquito. "Damn moeski toes. We gotta go inside." He got up and walked toward the light. Helen followed.

"But, what?" Helen said.

"There was a couple a guys workin' inside the house. The kids were eyein' 'em. Justine said she was worried they might be lookin' for the jewelry."

"How old are these kids?"

"Too young. That's the other thing. Faith come out and talked to 'em and took 'em inside her house. Then some woman come by and picked 'em up."

"Their mother?"

"Don't think so. She was older."

"Faith is probably worried about 'em," Helen said. She and Douglas sat in the small living room looking out at the garden.

"I am too." Douglas looked over at Helen, her face outlined against the wall. "The girl, Justine, reminds me of Livia. I can't get it out of my head, Helen."

Helen dropped her head onto her chest and sighed. "It was a long time ago, Douglas. Let me see…she would be forty-three this year."

They sat quietly, the only sound coming from their slow breathing and the cricket calls in the grass.

"She took my hand. Justine. The boy too. They held my hands, and we watched the house together."

Helen thought about this revelation, concerned. She wasn't sure if she was concerned for Douglas or the kids. "They held your hands?"

"Uh-huh."

Helen didn't reply. She saw her own daughter of six running toward her with a smile as wide as the sky and her arms outstretched. Helen's eyes began to tear. She pulled her glasses off and wiped her eyes with her palms.

"They just walked up and took hold of your hands?"

"Yeah."

"They need a father. Someone they can hold onto and trust."

"And some expensive jewelry they can pawn." Douglas walked to the kitchen, turning on the ceiling light. "You want some lemonade?"

"Jewelry ain't going to do 'em any good," Helen said.

"Might if it pays for some new shoes."

# TWENTY-ONE

Douglas walked into the front yard, three houses south of 311 Caroline, and considered the dogwood he had planted the day before. It was small, not two feet in height. He envisioned it at its full height, sitting at the corner of the fence. It wasn't right, he told himself. Not with the other plants nearby. Plants work together, Douglas knew. They help each other through the troubles of heat and thirst and hungry insects. And unknowing humans. Their roots intertwine with the mycelium in the soil, exchanging nutrients, interconnected, supportive of one another. A gardener had to think like nature and plant accordingly. Might be right now, he thought, but, in several years, look to the future to know today's truth. The truth was, Douglas decided, that the Silky should be moved. He looked slowly across the lawn, the fence, and the vined gate into the rear of the property. A truck drove by and stopped in front of 311, disturbing his thoughts.

Douglas stood on the sidewalk, looking north. Two men, the same two from the day before, got out of the truck and walked to the door. They carried tool cases. A car turned and slowly came up the street, parking across from 311. Curious, Douglas thought. He ambled down the sidewalk until he came to the man in the car. The man turned. An open newspaper lay across the steering wheel.

"Nice day," Douglas said. He didn't like it when strangers appeared on his street. But he would be nice, he told himself. He knew Helen would question him when he told her about his day.

"Uh-huh," said the man in the car.

"You waitin' for somebody?"

"Just sitting here minding my business." The man folded his newspaper and placed it on the seat beside him.

"And what business would that be?" Douglas squeezed his hands, feeling the small hands he held the day before.

"That would be my business and not yours." The man opened his door and stepped out. He walked toward Douglas, staring at him. Douglas sized him. An inch taller, early forties maybe, muscular, tanned, jaw set with a menacing frown. "I'll ask you to move on, old man. I'm not bothering you or anyone else on this street."

Douglas stood firm. "Nor I," he said. "Just bein' neighborly. I see you have a curiosity about that house over there." Douglas nodded toward 311.

The man kept his eyes on Douglas and said, "Maybe. You know something about it?"

"Know the owner. Nice old lady. Story is she killed her husband and buried him in the cellar."

"I read something in the paper about that." The man's expression changed. He put his hands in his pockets and turned half toward the house. "I was reading about it just now."

"Is that a fact? Word gets out, don't it?"

"Except the story says that a woman may have been buried there, not a man. Where did you hear about this story?"

"My grandmother used to live in that house. Used to work for the lady who owned it."

"Your grandmother? And the lady killed her husband?"

"Nope. Another owner. Those guys in the house over there, they're lookin' for evidence."

"Evidence? What kind of evidence?"

"Evidence of murder, of course. I told you they found a skeleton in the cellar."

"Yeah, yeah. But I'm a bit confused. Those guys aren't the police, are they?"

"Plainclothes. They don't want to tip off the suspect."

The man looked at Douglas with a twisted face. "How do you know all this?"

"My nephew's in the police department."

Dumfounded, the man turned away and stepped back into his car. "Have a nice day," Douglas said, and walked back to his Silky Dogwood. "Yeah," Douglas heard the man say in a tone that betrayed his confusion.

Near lunch, when Douglas was about to get in his truck and join Helen, he saw the two men step from the house and walk to their truck. They too were going to lunch, Douglas thought. He hurried down the sidewalk toward them. The man in the car watched Douglas approach the two men. He strained to hear and thought of getting out of his car and approaching as well but decided against it. That's not what Mr. Fitzhugh ordered him to do. He sat back and watched the three men talking. Soon, Douglas walked away. The truck drove toward town, followed by the man in the car.

✳ ✳ ✳

Through her bedroom window could be heard the sound of Alum Spring hopping over rocks, sliding toward the river. A breeze whispered through the tall trees beneath a dark sky. Katy lay in a tumble, tossing her head to the side, her eyelids closed, her eyes moving, watching beneath, hearing the voices of her dream. The sounds in her head echoed through the house, down the steps, and across the memories of a century. Time, Katy's high school history teacher told the class, is dimensionless, an invented concept. Without memory, there is no time, there is no knowledge, there is no God. Katy sat in the class and wrote in her notebook: Time is a concept. It's as real as the color red, the red of a strawberry. If you were colorblind, it would have no meaning. Time is a color we see with our memory. Katy laid her pen down. The pen lifted from her desk, ignorant of gravity, and dropped to the floor with a loud thud.

Katy drew in her breath with a start and opened her eyes. In a burst, she was out of bed, running to the kitchen table and her laptop. The apartment remained dark except for the glow of the screen as she typed.

The house stood back from the street, even with its neighbor to the right. To its left, an open lot, where I walked to the rear of this house on Main Street. There, a garden of wildflowers and small bushes with bright white flowers presented itself. A man knelt, tending the plants as I walked toward the back door. He

179

rose and greeted me and said Anna was waiting for me. He smiled, brushing particles of dirt from his calloused hands. I had never seen him before, though he seemed to know me. And then I saw Anna by the window. She motioned for me to come in. The gardener nodded his head toward me and said, "Have a nice day, Kate." I opened the back door and went in. Anna was making tea in the kitchen. She smiled but said nothing. I sat at the table looking out the window to where the gardener was working. Anna came to the table with our tea. She was beautiful in her summer dress. Dark brown hair that came to her shoulder, sliding past her cheek as she leaned with the tea. She smiled. Her eyes played upon me like brown pebbles washed over in a shallow stream. She placed the cup and saucer on the table, then turned and hurried to the hall. The front door opened. It was Jannie. She and Anna talked in the open doorway. The sun, falling through late afternoon, played shadows upon the floor behind their silhouetted forms. I could not hear what they said, but the smile on Jannie's face told me of her happiness. Anna, too, smiled. She held Jannie's hands, a charm bracelet with three charms, hanging like bright droplets. An embrace of friendship, and then Jannie was gone. The door closed. But where was Anna?

I sat looking down the empty hall. I held the teacup in my hands. It was empty. I stood in the drawing room. The long evening light poured into the room. There were voices upstairs. A man and a woman. I walked up to the bedroom. It was Blayden with a woman. Her back was to me. Anna? A different dress. The hair was Anna's. She turned to Blayden. Sarah. They stood beside a jewelry cabinet sitting atop an inlaid table. The two cabinet doors were wide to the side, their drawers open.

Sarah pointed to the empty drawers. Her eyes showed anger. "Gone. All of it," she said. "She knows what plans we have for her sparkly wealth."

Blayden looked distraught, but his voice was resolute when he told Sarah that their plans were secure.

"She does not know of our enterprise," he said, taking hold of her shoulders. Sarah twisted free and went to the window. "No," she said firmly. She told Blayden he had been careless. "Anna knows about me. I have kept my distance all this time, but you have been the fool."

"I don't care about that. She doesn't know about your father's ethanol operation or my plans to expand it. I will divorce her, and she will be gone."

"She will be gone and so will her jewelry," Sarah said, turning to Blayden. Blayden took his vest off. He laid it across the bed and rolled up his sleeves. He told Sarah that the jewelry had to be in the house somewhere. They should start looking for it. "But what if she took it with her?" Sarah said. Blayden searched the wardrobe. "You said she keeps a diary," Sarah said. "Maybe the location of the jewelry is in the diary." Sarah stepped to the small closet at the corner of the room and opened the door. Towels and sheets lay on the shallow shelves. She shoved her hands beneath the linens while I sat beneath the oak tree in the front yard, waiting.

I didn't know what I was waiting for, but I felt it necessary to wait. The street had recently been paved. I heard the clop of the horse's hooves before I saw the buggy. Jannie and Anna sat behind the driver with two suitcases between them. When the buggy stopped in front of the house, Anna got out and paid the driver. She was wearing a new dress that Jannie had made. And, catching the last rays of the evening sun, her wedding ring and diamond engagement ring. Jannie stepped down and pulled the suitcases to the curb. Her charm bracelet dangled three charms. The suitcases had leather handles with brass catches and locks. I picked up one, Jannie the other, and the three of us walked to the door and entered.

We heard noises from the floor above, then the sound of someone descending the stairs. Anna called out to Blayden, who appeared at the other end of the hall. He stood staring, his sleeves rolled to his elbows, hands on his hips. He asked why she was home. "She should be on the train," he said. His voice held a tone of anger, but then he looked up, up the staircase where Sarah stood, her eyes narrowed. Blayden looked back at Anna and walked forward, speaking in a low, conciliatory tone. "If you have decided not to go to New York, then I must speak with you about something of great importance," he said. Anna looked at Blayden with concern. She turned to Jannie. The two women exchanged glances. Blayden told Jannie she was not needed. She should go home. Anna spoke: "Blayden, the train is late leaving Richmond. It will make the station in two hours. I must be on it." "And you will," he answered. "Now, go, Jannie. You are no longer needed." Blayden opened the door. "No," Anna said, walking up to Blayden. "She will stay."

In the kitchen, Blayden stood in awkward silence. Anna sat at the table, crying. She demanded to know why Blayden wanted her jewelry. Blayden turned and shouted, saying that it was his right to possess all that was hers. He moved to the table and sat beside Anna and said in a low, calm voice: "You will have all the jewelry you wish, but right now I need your jewelry."

Anna rubbed her eyes and set her jaw. "No," she said. "You are asking me to lose part of myself. That I cannot do, and certainly not if you refuse to tell me why you want them."

Blayden considered her statement. Sarah appeared in the hall, then stepped into the kitchen. Blayden looked up. Anna turned. Her eyes, her entire face, changed. I saw the eyes of a wolf staring. I watched as Anna rose from her chair and said, "You. You are not welcome in this house."

Sarah stood in the doorway next to Jannie. Jannie's face was tight with anger. Her fists clenched, but she was silent. Sarah took a step past her as if she weren't there. "Tell her, Blayden. Tell her why we need her jewelry."

"We?" Anna was incredulous. "You two..." Anna looked about, searching for words that would help her deflect the power of this woman in her house.

"Anna," Blayden said in an even tone. "I have two bank loans keeping my business afloat. These last couple of years have not been good for the building trades, my buyers. But I have hope in a new enterprise, one selling distilled liquor throughout the state—"

Anna interrupted him. "That is illegal. You know that, Blayden. We have discussed this."

"I know you—" Blayden began.

"Why is she here? Why must I endure her presence?"

Blayden sat with his elbow on the table, his head tilted. His eyes moved to Sarah. He sighed and said, "Sarah is my partner, and her—"

Sarah came forward and said, "That's enough, Blayden. This has gone too far." She walked up to Anna and said, "Tell us where you hid the jewelry. Now."

Anna approached to within inches of Sarah.

"You have no right to be in my house. Get out." Anna shoved Sarah, who stepped back, catching her fall. The two women stared, each furious at the other. Sarah turned, running past Jannie into the hall and the front door. She stooped down and unlatched a suitcase. Anna, right behind her, pushed Sarah away, shouting, "Get away from my things. Get away. Get away."

"They're in here, Blayden," Sarah said, scrambling to her feet. "In these cases, for certain."

Blayden had followed the women. He picked Anna up, pushing her to the side, then brought both suitcases to the kitchen where he laid them on the table. Anna and Sarah followed. Blayden opened the two suitcases and dumped their contents.

Anna's clothes lay on the table, the floor, a chair. She stood in horror, unable to speak. Sarah pushed her aside.

"Miss Anna," Jannie said, grabbing Sarah by the waist and pulling her away from the table. Sarah took hold of Jannie's wrist, twisting her skin, breaking the charm bracelet, and hurling the bracelet against the window. Jannie held her wrist as if it were broken and went to retrieve the bracelet while Sarah went through Anna's clothes, searching for the jewelry.

"It's not here," she said finally, looking up at Blayden. He stood with his arms folded, watching Sarah pick through his wife's clothing. Jannie turned back, grabbing Sarah by the wrist. Blayden said, "That's enough, Jannie," and pulled her away from

Sarah, then picked her up by the waist. Ignoring her struggles, he carried her down the hall. "Get out of this house and never come back," he said, and pushed her out the door.

Anna's eyes flared. She rushed at Sarah, yanking her hair, pulling her to the floor. Sarah screamed. Blayden grabbed Anna by the waist and pulled her away from Sarah. Anna's grip on Sarah's hair was absolute. Blayden dragged both women across the floor, reaching with one hand to break Anna's grasp on Sarah. "Let go!" he said to Anna.

"You will never get my jewelry. You will never find it," Anna yelled. Sarah had regained her balance and was standing, leaning toward Anna, who held firmly to Sarah's hair. Sarah grabbed Anna's hand and peeled away her fingers while Blayden struggled to control Anna, who squirmed and kicked at him.

"The bank vault," Blayden said, letting Anna go. He walked over to the phone on the wall and picked up the receiver. Sarah struggled to remove Anna's hand from her hair. Anna now had both hands clenched onto Sarah's hair. Sarah said, "No, don't call." She punched Anna in the gut. Anna fell. Sarah kicked her, then ran to Blayden. "You ask about jewelry and the whole town will know," she said to Blayden.

"I was calling Robert," Blayden said, placing the receiver back on the hook.

Sarah stood by his shoulder. "Go to the bank in the morning," she said. "Talk to him in person."

Anna lay on the floor now, breathing steadily. She raised herself and looked at Sarah and Blayden. She smiled.

Sarah turned to Blayden. "The jewelry isn't at the bank," she said, running her fingers through her hair. "She's hidden it somewhere."

Sarah walked to Anna and grabbed her arm. Anna swung her free arm at Sarah, hitting her in the side. Sarah bent over but held fast to Anna's arm. Anna shoved her away. Sarah fell but stood almost immediately. Blayden watched from his perch by the phone, seemingly in thought. Anna went to her clothes and began repacking. "I'm leaving," she said. "When I get back, I want a divorce. Whatever you two are doing, I will not be party to it."

Sarah glared at Blayden. She clenched her teeth and said to him, "You're just going to allow her to leave?"

"What do you want me to do?" he said.

Sarah went to the table and shoved the remaining clothes to the floor. "Make her tell us where she hid her jewelry," she shrieked. Anna pushed Sarah away from the table. Blayden came up behind Anna and held her by the waist. "That's enough," he said. Sarah turned and grabbed Anna by the neck. The two women glared at each other, Anna's mouth wide, gasping for breath as she raised her foot and kicked Sarah. Sarah fell back, dropping her hands from Anna's throat. Blayden loosened his grip on Anna. She bent her neck forward and bit Blayden on the arm. Blayden yelled, dropping his arm but keeping Anna immobile with his other arm.

Sarah stood at the sink holding a knife. Blayden shouted, "No." Anna didn't see the knife. She struggled against Blayden, who suddenly let her go, but Sarah stepped around Blayden's outstretched arm and shoved the knife into Anna's ribs. The handle broke off. Sarah held it, examining it curiously as Blayden caught his wife and dragged her to a chair by the table. Anna looked at him with her mouth open. Her right hand fumbled at her breast, searching for the thing that would end her life. But it was well hidden within the blood and fabric of her dress. Her fingers probed as Blayden called to her. She struggled for breath, then her arm fell to her side. She was dead, and I couldn't do anything for her. I just stood in the kitchen and watched. I felt helpless and looked out the window at the garden. Such a beautiful garden.

Behind me, I heard thumping noises. I stood on the landing to the cellar. Sarah was pulling Anna down the stairs. Anna's head banged against each stair tread as Sarah hauled her by the feet. In the cellar, Blayden was digging. A grave for his wife. I turned my head and saw the train coming from the south. Sarah stood on the platform with two suitcases. The train whistle woke me.

Katy sat at her laptop and read the last several sentences, then closed it. She leaned on the table, holding her head in her hands.

Outside, the morning sky began to bleed through the dark. Soon, it would reveal to be overcast, threatening rain.

In the basement library, it was dark. The library was closed this early in the morning. Katy stared at her computer screen, the only light on in the room, then walked to the microfilm cabinet. Two articles on Henry Tabor, father of Sarah Tabor. She pulled two reels from the cabinet and threaded the first on the reader. The black letters of the old newspaper scrolled by. She slowed the machine and crawled it to the page.

"He's making ethanol," Katy whispered. "For cars." The article discussed Tabor's plans to provide ethanol filling stations in the state, taking advantage of the Free Alcohol Bill passed in 1906, removing the tax on ethanol. Katy walked to her computer and searched for early car engines. She found that the 1908 Model T had an adjustable carburetor. The car could run on ethanol or gasoline.

"Flex-fuel," she whispered, walking back to the microfilm reader. The second article, written a year later, expanded on the first, stating that Tabor had perfected a way to increase the overall percentage of ethanol by reducing the water content of the product using a mineral called zeolite.

"What the hell is zeolite?" Katy began to type, then paused and looked up at the dark ceiling, then down at the computer screen. 6:24 AM. Why am I doing this? she asked herself. Chasing rabbits. For what purpose? She put her thumb in her mouth and bit down, then typed: Prohibition in Virginia. Thousands of hits.

"Gahhhh!" she screamed. She picked up her phone and texted Darren. "Thinking about you." She looked at the screen, waiting, then put the phone down. Twenty seconds and her phone beeped. "On Metro with thousand other people. This weekend?" Katy typed: "Yes. With just me." She leaned back in her chair and smiled. A chance to be normal, she hoped.

# TWENTY-TWO

The black wrought-iron fence met the white brick wall with more than trepidation. English ivy clung to the top of the wall, lying like an obese snake wearing its garish morning pajamas. It was on its way to swallowing the wrought iron.

Douglas cut back the ravenous green vine where the fence and wall met while the white brick house sat behind in silence, confident in its gardener. From his vantage, Douglas could watch the cars round the corner past Faith Bonner's house and make their way up Caroline. The number of vehicles traveling this street was few. And Douglas knew when one didn't belong. Today, the one trespasser that had frequented the street was missing, along with the truck and its two occupants who were being surveilled. But now, a new car. Douglas dropped his shears and walked along the fence to the gate and the brick sidewalk. He peered down the street, following the car. It stopped in front of 311. Douglas thought of Joseph and Justine. What would they think? He walked down the sidewalk to the cross street and watched. A woman got out of the car and reached into the back seat. A sign. For Sale.

Douglas watched the woman struggle with the unwilling sign, then turned back to his favorite house on the street. He didn't know its history, but he liked it for its mass and its clean lines, the big magnolia, and the other trees along the north side. It was a house built in 1764, at least that was what the black numbers high at the corner of the house showed. With those numbers and the heft of the structure and its beautiful garden, Douglas knew this house was important. It had endurance. Endurance and character. Everything Douglas believed in.

Twelve years earlier than the house's construction, Roger Dixon, a young lawyer from nearby Culpeper, bought three-hundred thirty acres along the river just south of and adjoining the sixty-four lots that made up the original town. A ferry at the mouth of a small stream and a couple of farms were the only signs of European civilization.

Dixon planned to divide some of the land along the river into lots—forty in all—and make a handsome profit. He advertised in the Virginia Gazette and built himself and his family a large house on the street. Dixon's plan, however, proved to be a no-go from the start, and even after persuading the House of Burgesses in Williamsburg to extend the town boundary to include his new lots, Dixon's real estate venture remained static. He was undeterred, committed to developing the lower end of Caroline Street. He borrowed money and built two more houses on the street, seed houses, hoping to attract new residents: prominent, wealthy owners like the ones buying at the north end of the new town where his friend, Fielding Lewis, was selling lots. His brother, John Dixon, bought four lots, and a few friends bought lots, but Dixon's hoped-for windfall was not to be.

Roger Dixon persuaded his brother to build a fine house up the street from his, but that was the practical end of Dixon's career as a land developer. The house Dixon built on the street was destroyed, probably by fire. However, the house his brother built and never lived in still stood. Douglas sat on its front steps drinking water from his plastic jug, thinking over his plan to revitalize the azalea bed and boxwoods now that the ivy had been reprimanded.

What would Roger Dixon think of his beloved neighborhood today? That is a question without a sure answer, but one imagines the man whom Dixon Street is named for, the street crossing Caroline just south of where Douglas sat, would approve.

Two cars approached from the west on Dixon and turned north on Caroline, passing in front of Douglas. He knew the cars, the ones Faith Bonner implied, were not worthy of this street. Douglas walked to the sidewalk. Three women got out of the cars and walked to the front door of 311 and entered the house. The same three as before. No kid this time. Douglas removed his gloves, laying them over the wrought-iron fence, and strolled up the street.

Tracy followed Meghan and Katy down the central hall. "Charlene called me this morning and said it was back on the market. She knew I had people who might be interested. Of course, I didn't tell her you didn't want to buy it."

Katy wasn't listening. Her mind was on the cellar. Meghan had told her there was something odd about the joists and now she would see if that oddity held a secret. Katy made the steps as Tracy continued talking behind her. At the bottom of the steps, she turned on the light and looked around the small cellar. Meghan walked up behind Katy with a flashlight.

"Over here," Meghan said, handing the light to Katy, pointing to the overhead framing. Tracy stood by the landing and watched when her phone rang. She pulled it from her purse and looked at the screen. "Charlene," she said. "Hi, Charlene."

"Right here," Meghan said, reaching between two joists. She put her hand on the end of a beam and pulled with her fingers. "Not budging. See this piece, Katy? It looks like it's a continuation of this beam on the other side of the summer beam. But it isn't. It's not end-grain."

"OK. I'm not sure what you just said, but what does it take to get it out?"

"I need a hammer, something with a claw," Meghan said. "Or I could screw a hook into it, maybe—"

"Hey, guys…" Tracy said. "That was Charlene. The house has a prospective buyer. There's an offer on this place."

"Already?" Katy said. "It just went back on the market."

"It did. But I guess the buyer was already plugged in—"

"An offer without walking through the house?" Meghan pressed her fingers against the joists.

"Seems odd, but yes," Tracy replied.

"Hello? Anyone home?" The three women stopped and listened. A voice from upstairs. Katy looked at Tracy. Tracy shrugged and walked back up the stairs.

"Just what we need," Katy whispered. "So how do you propose we get this piece of wood out of here?" Katy jiggled the flashlight.

"I have some tools in my car back at work."

"I'll take you now. We'll leave Tracy here."

At the top of the stairs, Tracy talked with Douglas, explaining to him that the house already had an offer. He said he wasn't interested in buying the house. He couldn't believe she would think a person like him could afford such a place. But he didn't tell her that. He just looked down at the dirt on his hands and knees and shook his head.

"Then why are you here?" Tracy said. Meghan and Katy came up behind and looked at Douglas.

Katy scrutinized his face, his hands. "You look…" she whispered to herself.

"Well. To tell you the truth, I'm lookin' after this house for some friends of mine. Two kids whose great-great-great-grandmother used to live here."

Katy came forward. "You know Justine and Joseph?"

"Uh-huh. That's right. You do too, I guess."

"How are you related to them?"

"Just a friend. But I've been watchin' different people come and go from this house the past couple weeks. It seems to me they're all after the same thing."

The three women stared at Douglas, waiting for him to tell them what everyone was after. Katy turned to Tracy. "Who put an offer on this house?"

"Charlene didn't say."

"Call her and ask, would you? If I'm right…" She turned back to Douglas. "I'm Katy Aldridge. These are my friends." Katy introduced Tracy and Meghan. "And you are?"

"Douglas Freeman. I do the gardening at most of these houses on this street."

"You probably knew Beverly Langston then," Katy said.

"Yes. I worked on her garden. It's a shame her kids let it go like this."

Tracy interrupted. "Charlene said it's a Stephen Fitzhugh."

"I knew it," Katy said. "Douglas, do you have a hammer?"

"Sure."

"Can you get it and come down to the cellar with us?" Douglas nodded and backed out the door. Katy knew Tracy was skittish about this visit to begin with. Now that the house had a buyer, she would not be comfortable loitering about. She put her hand on Tracy's wrist. "Just a couple more minutes. Meghan thinks she may have found an anomaly in the structure—"

"Why do you two always talk like lawyers?" Tracy said, annoyed, watching Douglas saunter down the brick sidewalk. "I don't like it. I could lose my license. And what's his business here?"

190

"I don't talk like a lawyer, do I?" Meghan said, looking at Tracy then at Katy.

"You won't lose anything," Katy said. "Stephen Fitzhugh's grandfather killed Anna and now he's after the jewelry. Meghan thinks the jewelry is downstairs. We have to find it before he does."

"The grandfather?" Tracy tilted her head.

"The grandson. Stephen Fitzhugh. The man who wants to buy this house." Katy looked out the door. "Douglas is coming with a hammer. Good." She turned back. Tracy's face registered a look of profound bewilderment. "I'll explain later," Katy said.

"Hammer," Douglas said. Meghan took it from him and walked to the stairs. The others followed. Tracy turned at the end of the hall and ran back to the front door, closing it. She followed Douglas down the narrow stairs.

Douglas ducked beneath the joists, craning his neck as he watched Meghan use the hammer to pry a foot-long piece of oak from between two joists. It sat on the main support beam that ran the width of the house, revealing a pocket where a box sat. Katy handed the flashlight to Douglas. She reached up and grabbed the box. Her hands trembled as she brought it from above to her chest, studying the lid as if gazing at a newborn, unable to comprehend just what she was holding. Douglas stood next to her, the light in his hand washing across Katy's hands. Meghan and Tracy came in close. Four people standing in the cellar of an old house peering at a box. Tracy put her arm on Douglas' shoulder, moving him aside just enough so she could get a better look. He didn't feel her touch. His thoughts were of the two kids he wished were here now.

Meghan said, "Open it, for Christ's sake, Katy. You're killing me."

Katy looked at her friend, then pried the lid up on its two brass hinges. Inside was a small book. Katy's hand shook as she lifted it out. Beneath the book was a brown envelope with the word Jannie printed in black letters. Katy closed the lid.

"Let's go upstairs where we can see better. I need to put this down. My heart is pounding out of its cage." She pushed through her companions. The others followed in silence. The simple plank stairs spoke as Katy lifted the past into the present. In the front hall, she sat with her back against the wall, the box in her lap. She took a deep breath, then put the box on the floor and took the envelope out. Douglas, Meghan, and Tracy sat around the box like kids about to play a game of Jax. In her lap lay the diary. No one spoke. No one moved forward to examine the contents of the box. Six eyes followed the motions of Katy as she opened the small envelope and emptied it into her hand. Two silver rings and a bracelet with red stones fell into her palm. She picked up the smaller ring.

"J & J inscribed in this," Katy said. Looking at the larger ring, she noted it too, was inscribed with J & J. She placed the larger ring over the smaller. "Jannie and Joshua." She held her hand out to Douglas, then picked up the diary and opened it. "Pass the jewelry box around," she said, flipping the pages of the diary. At the last entry was a photo, a bookmark. "Anna and Jannie," she whispered, examining the photo. "I think it was taken out front. Look, there's the big oak— but smaller." She handed the picture around.

Tracy peered inside the box. She put her hand in and scooped out several pieces. "Oh my gosh." She dropped the jewels back into the box and looked around at the others, holding out the box as if making an offering to the gods. Douglas took the box. Meghan collected the two wedding bands and the bracelet and replaced them in their envelope. Katy stared at the diary, reading. Douglas handed the box to Meghan.

"There must be thousands of dollars' worth of jewelry in here," Meghan said, picking out a necklace and holding it up to the light of the transom window above the door.

Katy turned to the last pages of the diary. "There's an inventory of everything that is in that box. Right here." She held the diary up, showing everyone the pages.

"What are you going to do with this?" Douglas said.

Katy and Tracy looked at Meghan. Douglas addressed her, "It looks like you might have the answer."

Meghan laughed. "I suppose you want me to call Red."

Katy nodded, holding the diary close.

Douglas got up off the floor and stood by the door. "What's in that book you're readin'?" he asked Katy.

She looked up at him, then stood. Meghan and Tracy stood. The four of them standing in the dark hall, their faces lit by the transom window.

"It's a diary Anna Fitzhugh kept. She mentions Jannie Pratt, Justine and Joseph's 4th-great-grandmother. I wonder what will happen to this stuff?" Katy looked at Meghan and said, "We need to let Red know what we found and see what the law requires."

"Or not tell anyone," Tracy said. Everyone turned to Tracy.

"Did I hear you right?" Meghan said, thinking the same thing.

Katy looked up at Douglas, then at Tracy and Meghan. What are the chances of this find staying secret? she wondered. None.

Tracy said, "I didn't mean it. I was just trying to be bold like you two."

Douglas stood with his arms crossed, listening to this conversation. He wished Helen could be here with him. She'll be asking him questions past when the owls snore. His eyes fell to the floor and the plaster just above the floor molding. Holes drilled every foot or so along the wall, then poorly patched. He turned to the other wall and leaned down. Same. Small patches all along the bottom of the wall.

"What do you suppose was goin' on here?" Douglas said, bending down and touching the wall behind him. Meghan stretched her neck and looked along the wall.

"Those weren't here the last time we came," Tracy said. Meghan inspected the wall more with the flashlight, tapping her knuckles on the plaster. Katy walked into the parlor just off the hall.

"Same in here as well," Katy said.

"There were two guys here last week," Douglas said. "I talked to them. They said they were spraying for insects."

"Insects?" Tracy's voice rose an octave. She pulled out her phone and called Charlene, the agent.

"I don't think so," Katy said, walking back into the hall.

"I agree," Meghan said. "They were looking for the jewelry. They had a small inspection camera, I'll bet."

"Yes," Katy said. "Beverly Langston's crew. They were looking everywhere but where the jewelry was. Come in here." Katy backed

193

into the parlor. "There's more light. Everybody." She motioned to Tracy, still on the phone. Katy came up to her and whispered, "No insects."

Tracy ended the call and stood with the others as Katy explained what she wanted to do. The late morning light from the front window shone across the dark pine floors. Katy held the jewelry box under her arm. Her thumb held her place in the diary.

"I don't know what is going to happen to this stuff," Katy said. "Probably some kind of court case once word gets out we found it. In this diary is a list of the jewelry. I want to lay out the jewelry and check off each item as listed. That way, we will have four independent confirmations of what we found, and no one can say that we took anything." Katy looked around the room. Everyone nodded.

"Sure," said Douglas, curious to see the full contents of the box. "It would be mighty nice if Justine could get the two rings and the bracelet. Or her mom."

Katy turned to Douglas. Her cheeks filled. She was now certain of her appraisal of this gardener. Katy said, "I agree. But—"

"But," Meghan said, "the law may have something to say about it." Douglas said, "Mm-hmm."

"OK." Katy sat on the floor and spilled the jewelry out. The sun caught the many gems as they fell to the floor, tiny cut-pebbles captured in gold. "Let's sort." She sat cross-legged with the diary in her lap and called off each broach, ring, necklace, earring set, while Meghan and Tracy searched the jeweled floor and set aside the find.

Douglas put his hammer on the floor and sat with his back to the window against the wall. His lower back ached and his neck creaked as he moved it from side to side. He watched as these three girls knelt on the floor at 311 Caroline Street sorting through a cache of jewelry. How odd, he thought. Sitting in a vacant house with three white women. Downright dangerous. Should he leave? His back hurt, but otherwise, he felt comfortable here. Sitting in this empty room. He looked at the ceiling, the plaster medallion above the chandelier, the fireplace along the wall, the bookcases built into the far wall, the blue and white wallpaper with flourishes of gold. Douglas had known the owner, Mrs. Langston, for years. He had pulled weeds in her backyard and planted alumroot and lizard's tail and summer phlox in their right places so they would get the right amount of sun, and if their toes needed to be wet, they would be properly wetted. But never in those years had Mrs. Langston invited Douglas into her house. Never had she offered him a drink. Never had she thanked him for doing more than she agreed to pay him for. But that was alright, Douglas told himself. That was just life among those who had no color, who could elocute and negotiate among the well-off. Douglas didn't work for them. He worked for the plants, for their undemanding beauty. And now, sitting in Mrs. Langston's front parlor for the first time, looking at another kind of beauty, the beauty of stones set in silver and gold by long-forgotten artists, Douglas felt good, maybe hopeful. He looked down at his fingers and squeezed them. He felt little fingers fill his hand. Livia, he said to himself. Justine. Joseph.

"OK," Katy said. "That's 71 of 73 items on Anna's list. The two missing are her engagement ring, which she describes as a 'diamond surrounded by six rubies' and her wedding band."

"And you know where they went," Meghan said.

"I know," Tracy said, raising her hand. "She was wearing them."

"I'm sure," Katy said, reviewing the list she photographed with her phone. "Before we go, I want to take a picture of these all laid out here on the floor. And then get a picture of the pages in Anna's diary."

"What do you want me to do?" Douglas said.

"You're a witness," Meghan said. "We all are. My boyfriend is a lawyer in town. I expect that once this gets out, there will be different people coming forward to claim it. Lawyers will be involved."

Douglas stood up. "I was thinking about what Tracy said." Tracy turned. Meghan and Katy looked at Douglas. They all knew what he was talking about. Douglas looked at each pair of eyes, staring, waiting for him to continue. "What if…" Douglas stopped and raised his hat, rubbing his hands through his hair. "I gotta go now. I'm usually workin' somewhere on this street during the day if you need me. It was nice meetin' y'all."

"Nice meeting you too, Douglas," Katy said. "Can I get your phone number in case we need to get ahold of you later?"

Douglas walked down the sidewalk back to his 1764 home and its languid ivy fence. Meghan called Red Hamilton and told him what they had found. "Who do we hand it over to? Just walk into the police station?" she said.

"No. Bring it over to the office. I'll prepare some papers for the court. I take it you all were just walking through the house and this stuff suddenly appeared."

"Pretty much," Meghan said, standing in the open front door, watching Douglas disappear. "It just fell into our hands—with a gentle nudge."

"You might want to polish your story," Red said. Meghan turned back to the parlor, where Katy held her phone over the diary as Tracy held it to the floor, turning the pages.

"We'll be there in a few minutes," Meghan told Red.

* * *

Anna Fitzhugh's diary covered the kitchen table. Katy stood arranging the freshly-printed pages in order, speaking to the phone lying on the table. "You're still coming down Saturday, aren't you?" she said, double-checking the dates printed to the left of each entry.

"I was thinking I would come down Friday night," Darren said. "If that's alright."

"For sure. See you then."

"Wait. You didn't tell me what you found in the diary. Any confirmation that Blayden intended to kill Anna?"

"Not so far. I haven't read the whole thing. I'll tell you Friday."

"You're stressed. I can tell by your voice."

"Just... Not stressed. Maybe excited? Gotta go. Friday."

Katy took the photo images of the diary to the balcony and sat in her chair, putting her feet on the railing. Her curiosity had complete control of her. What would she learn? She held each page in her left hand, close to her eyes, chewing the nails off her right.

Later that night, she gathered the pages and placed them on the kitchen table, then went to the sofa and laid down.

"How can it be?" she asked herself. Katy looked at the ceiling as she searched her brain for an explanation. Nothing was adequate. The diary itself held little in the way of explanation for what had occurred to Anna Fitzhugh. Anna's entries were less than informative as to what led to her death. Katy's research at the library was more enlightening, providing insight into the work that Henry Tabor, Sarah's father, did and his possible connection to Blayden. Tabor owned distilling equipment, Katy thought. He produced ethanol as fuel for the hungry automobiles that became more and more affordable to the masses. Was he hoping to expand that business? Is that why he needed money? Was Blayden hoping to cash in on the temperance movement in Virginia and neighboring states and sell whiskey to the many who would ignore the laws? He would need money to acquire the illegal alcohol and transport it. Would he get the alcohol from Henry Tabor, his future father-in-law? Was he using his lumber and molding business as a front for this new illicit business? All these questions were on her mind as she read through the diary. And one other question: Were the entries on her laptop also entries in the actual diary? She now had her answer. They were.

Katy closed her eyes. Her phone rang. She got up and went to the table. The reporter.

"Why do reporters always call late at night?" she said.

"Sorry, Katy. I was just wondering if you know anything more about the skeleton that was discovered at the house on Caroline. The police have nothing new to pass on."

Katy stood with the phone to her ear. She walked over to the sofa and sat, wondering whether to tell this woman about her find. Red held the jewelry and diary in a safe in his office. He told Meghan and Katy that he would file an interpleader. Katy knew there were at least two parties who would claim ownership: the Tumultys, who represented Beverly Langston, the current owner of the house, and the Fitzhughs, descendants of Blayden Fitzhugh. Those two parties, Red had explained, would be named in an interpleader, a legal procedure that would begin a court action to determine who the rightful owner was. But Katy told Red she wanted Etta Tunney, Jannie Pratt's descendant, to be named as well. There were three pieces of jewelry in the box—marked as Jannie's—that should go to Etta, Katy argued. Meghan sat next to Katy in Red's office. She saw in her boyfriend's eyes the look of disappointment as he stared at Katy. "OK," he said. "I can add her as well. There will be three claimants: the Langston estate, Stephen Fitzhugh, and Etta claiming Jannie's three items." He caught Katy's eyes. "But don't get your hopes up." Katy nodded and said thanks.

The reporter sensed in the long silence that Katy had additional information. She said, "You know, I don't get to write too many really interesting stories. My normal beat is the local political scene covering stuff like council meetings. I got this story because no one else was available and I had my stuff covered—"

"Yesterday, I asked a realtor to take me and a friend through the house. I'm researching it as part of my work at the library—"

"Did you find something?"

"Yes. We found the lost jewelry."

"You found it? Really? Where is it? What did you find?"

"It's in a safe. There was a diary with the jewels. It will be up to the court to decide who takes ownership."

"So, you think the jewelry and diary belonged to Anna Fitzhugh?"

"That's my assumption, but they could have belonged to later owners as well."

"Do you also assume the skeleton that was unearthed was Anna?"

"I don't know, but it's probably a good guess, wouldn't you think?"

A pause. Katy heard the reporter tapping on her keyboard.

"So, the jewelry. Was it in something? How did you find the jewelry?"

"It was stuck in the joists in the cellar. In a box, along with the diary."

"Why do you suppose none of the owners, including Anna's husband, ever found it?"

"Because Anna was good at hiding things, I guess. Or possibly Jannie hid it."

"Jannie? Who's Jannie?"

"She was Anna's maid. They were close," Katy said, remembering the picture of Jannie and Anna standing in front of the house on Caroline Street.

"How do you know that? Did you read the diary? Is there evidence in the diary that Blayden killed his wife?" Katy bit her lip. "Surely, you read it, or at least some of it," the reporter said.

"When I found it, I flipped through it, but I didn't read the whole thing. A list of the jewelry is on the last two pages. The list and what's in the box correspond. Everything but Anna's wedding ring and her engagement ring were in the box."

"Wow. How much jewelry was in the box? What kind?"

"All kinds. Seventy-one pieces. And three other pieces marked for Jannie. All of it beautiful."

"Jannie had her jewelry in the box?"

"Yes. It was in a separate envelope marked 'Jannie'."

Katy was tiring of these questions. She told the reporter about the two engraved wedding bands meant for Jannie and her fiancé, Joshua. "That's all I know," she said.

In the morning, she was still on the sofa. The balcony door was open. Mosquitoes explored her ears, waking her.

* * *

The phone rang. Douglas, sitting in his Adirondack chair on the porch, turned his ear to the screen door. Helen turned. They looked at each other.

"Who could that be?" Douglas said. "Nobody calls us."

Helen got up and walked to the kitchen. A minute later, she opened the screen and hurried past Douglas. "What?" he said. "Who was that?"

"Roberta. She said there's a story in the paper."

Douglas watched his wife disappear among the flowers, her head just visible as she stepped through the clematis-covered arbor. "Story," he said, his arms stretched out on the arms of the chair. He shifted his weight, wondering how he was going to get out of the chair now that he had committed himself. He loved the chair, but as he aged, he found that the laid-back design was too embracive. He let his feet ponder the wood porch as his mind pondered the story he told Helen the night before.

"You were in that house with three white girls?" Helen said, incredulous.

"Yep." Douglas showed her every tooth in his head.

199

"I don't believe it. You just walked up and invited yourself in."

"That's right. I had to see what was goin' on. So—"

"And they just let you in?"

"Are you gonna let me tell the story or not? How come you're so interested in what the girls thought of me?"

"Because...it just seems strange. You bein' a big black man and them bein' white girls." Helen searched Douglas' face for an answer to a question that astronomers might ponder. Why do planets stay in their orbits? Has something to do with the sun, she thinks.

"Guess things have changed a bit," Douglas responded. He had considered the scene in the house rather strange as well, but this was his time to swell. Helen looked at his dark, round eyes and smiled. "So, anyway, Katy asked me for a hammer."

"Katy! You're on a first-name basis now?"

"Yeah. It's me and Katy and Meghan and Tracy. Tracy's the realtor. She was showin' the other two around the house when I come up."

"Why did Katy need a hammer?"

"Meghan needed it to get the jewelry box. It was down in the cellar."

"You went in the cellar with the girls?"

"Course."

"My."

"So, then we all come back up and set on the floor and counted the jewels. You should have seen all them jewels. Pretty little things all settin' there on the floor like they'd never been lost. Katy took a picture with her phone." Douglas looked over at Helen. She was staring out at the flowers. He was about to ask if she was listening to him when she spoke.

"What did they look like?" she said, turning to Douglas. Douglas pondered her question. He was about to say they looked like jewelry when she added: "What color was their hair?"

"The girls?"

"Yeah."

Douglas frowned. "Well, Tracy's hair is blonde and the other two have dark hair. Why you interested in these girls?"

"Just am. What were they wearin'?" Helen sat in her chair looking at her flowers. Douglas followed her gaze to the Black Cohosh, bending with the breeze. He thought.

"You know, I'm not exactly sure. I think they were wearin' shorts. Maybe Tracy was wearin' a dress. Yeah. She was."

"Was it nice? What color was it?" Helen said, still gazing at the tall flowers rising above their neighbors. Douglas now knew where Helen's questions were coming from. He sat back in the chair and looked up at the darkening sky. He wasn't sure what color Tracy's dress was. His memory for colors began and ended with petals and leaves and soils. What people were wearing, the colors and patterns of their dress, held little significance for him. But he knew it was significant to Helen. She would want an answer.

"It was the color of bluets, the sky-blue ones."

"That's pretty," she said, and changed the direction of her inquiry. "Katy sounds like the ringleader of this gang of yours."

"Yeah. She and Meghan. But I guess Katy's runnin' the show."

Helen wanted to know what kind of jewelry they had found. Did they try any on? Were there bracelets? Helen had always longed for a bracelet but couldn't afford such luxury. Douglas could answer only a few of her questions. He hadn't looked that closely, he told Helen.

"I bet those girls did," Helen said.

"They didn't seem all that interested in the jewelry. They just counted it. Katy was more interested in the diary, I think."

Helen followed a hummingbird as it flew through the flowers, sampling this one, hovering before that one, moving to another, then sipping. Did it have favorites? Were its taste buds attuned to where it could tell flower from flower with its eyes closed? She knew a couple of girls who kept diaries when she was young, but she never understood the appeal. Diaries were supposed to be secret. If you can't share your thoughts, then why write them down? It seemed like you were talking to yourself. For what purpose?

"What did the diary say?"

Douglas said he didn't know.

"It's in the paper," Helen said, walking up the stone path to the porch. "Katy's in the paper. She's tellin' about the jewelry, just like you said." Helen waved the newspaper. "Here, read it."

Douglas took the paper and looked up at his wife, who stood close to his chair, breathing hard.

"You run all the way?"

"Sorta."

"You needed the paper to tell you I wasn't lyin'?"

"No. But…things in the paper are more true it seems. Don't it?"

"Maybe." Douglas thought on it, then opened the paper and read the brief article. The reporter quoted sections of an old paper from 1910. "How can things be more true? I'd say true is as true as you get."

"The more people know about somethin', the more true it is. That's all I was sayin'."

Douglas folded back the section of the paper to its first page. "You didn't bring the whole paper, just this one section," he said.

"I didn't want to ruin our Sunday. I'll get the whole week in due time."

Douglas said, "Mmm." He checked the obits. No one he knew. A young woman dead from cancer. Corinne Corbin. "Always sad when young people die," he said. Helen looked at him, glancing at the section he was reading. She nodded, transported to a time long before.

Douglas looked out on the flowers. Two hummingbirds were buzzing each other. He shouted at them. "Hey, there's plenty out there for the both of you."

\*\*\*

Tiny lights floated in the night air. The small yard behind the trailer glowed with a winking luminescence. Justine and Joseph ran across the wet grass with plastic peanut butter jars. Their bare feet slid as they turned toward their here-I-am-now-I'm-gone prey. A brief but violent scrape of metal pierced the dark. The kids hesitated, then went on capturing. They knew the sound. A car's underbelly bottoming on a speed bump as it raced from the trailer park on its way to freedom.

Inside the trailer, Etta sat with her daughter. She knew a different person sat across from her. Since being released from jail, Rachel's demeanor had changed. She had abandoned her combative ways and was no longer the churlish daughter she had been since she was a teen. Etta found it remarkable and attributed Rachel's transformation to her stay behind bars and the consequences of her actions, still not played out. Etta was hopeful but careful not to push the girl for fear she might nudge her from the line she was on.

"Since you're off Tuesday night, I thought you could go with us to the funeral," Etta said.

"But I don't know that woman, Mama."

"I know. I didn't know her either, but she was a neighbor, and Justine and Joseph knew her. It's paying your respects. That's all."

"I still don't know how Steen and Jobo knew her. I thought Steen didn't like the brothers."

"She didn't, but she said when she got to know them, they weren't bad kids. My guess is they were angry at the world because God was going to take their mother from them."

"It is sad," Rachelle said. "I guess I can go. What do you wear to a funeral?"

"Something nice, like church."

The back door opened. Justine and Joseph appeared with two jars filled with excited insects.

Rachelle looked over. "Oh, no, not inside."

Justine held her jar tight to her chest and looked at her mother with upturned eyes. "We just want to keep them till tomorrow. They won't get out. See, we punched holes in the lid so they can breathe, but they can't get out."

Etta put her hand on her daughter's arm and smiled at her. She would prefer the insects remain in their domain, outside, but she had felt the hard edge of her daughter's existence soften. She wished for its continuance. "OK," Rachelle said. "But just for tonight."

Etta breathed in. She has changed, Etta thought. Something good from something bad. "Your Mama's going with us to Mrs. Corbin's funeral. We'll all pay our respects to the family. It's what people do."

"We know," said Joseph, holding his jar up close, watching the fireflies crawl up the sides.

Justine came up to her mother. "You would have liked her, Mama. She was a real nice lady."

"What did you talk about?" Rachelle said, pulling Justine to her.

"She showed us her drawings."

"She's not afraid of snakes," Joseph said.

"We talked about Nonna Jannie and the jewels. She said she didn't have a father. Like us," Justine said.

Rachelle mused on that. The image of their father appeared, then washed away like smoke in a fair breeze. "Nonna Jannie's jewels. I think that's just a fable, Mama."

"I don't think so," Etta said. "It's been in the family for more than a century, so there's got to be some truth in it."

"Some, maybe. But if they ever existed, they would be long gone by now."

"Katy doesn't think so. She thinks the jewelry is still in the house. When we talked to Aunt Ivie, she read some of Nonna Jannie's letters, and one of them mentioned two wedding rings. Katy was excited."

"Who is this Katy?" Rachelle said, making a face.

"She's the librarian—"

"I know all that. You told me. Why is she so interested in our Nonna Jannie?"

"I don't know. I guess—"

"I know," Justine said. "Because we asked her at the library. Joseph and I asked her to help us find the house. She likes to help people."

"Uh-huh," Rachelle said. "I don't know. I never met anyone who just likes to help people. They always want something."

"That's not true," Etta countered. "I know good people who don't ask for anything."

"Why don't they teach you to swim, then?" Rachelle gave her mother a stern look. Etta thought back on her comment days before when she declared herself unable to swim. A comment attached to no context that Rachelle had somehow divined. She returned her daughter's look with one of wonderment.

"It isn't your fault, Mama, that you never learned to swim. You were never given a chance. And now it's me and Steen and Jobo without a chance. We inherit our problems, and they grow. It's like inheriting the night, never getting to see the morning."

Etta's eyes grew moist. She went to her daughter and hugged her, then turned to the door.

"You kids should be getting to bed," Etta said. "I have to get to bed myself." She looked at her daughter. "You be good." Justine and Joseph stood by the sofa holding their jars of fireflies, watching their grandmother. "You too." She pointed at the insect hunters.

"See you tomorrow," Rachelle said.

Etta opened the door, then turned back. "There are some people—" she began, but her phone interrupted her. Etta dug in her purse and pulled it out, looking at the screen.

"Who could this be at this time of night? Hello?" Etta listened. Rachelle saw Etta's expression change from annoyance to delight. "OK," she said and put her phone back in her purse.

"Who was it?" Rachelle said.

"Katy."

Justine and Joseph turned their gaze from the insect jars back to their grandmother. "She said she found Nonna Jannie's jewelry in the house." Justine jumped up and screamed. She ran to Etta and hugged her. Joseph followed. Rachelle's mouth hung open. Etta said, "There's lots of jewelry, but there are three pieces that were in an envelope marked 'Jannie.' Two wedding rings and a bracelet. She said there was an article in the newspaper."

"Is she going to give them to us?" Rachelle said.

"She doesn't have them. A lawyer has everything, including a diary that Anna Fitzhugh kept."

"But shouldn't we go to the lawyer?" Rachelle said. "It's our Nonna Jannie. It's her jewelry."

"We'll have to wait. It's the same lawyer who helped get you out of jail. We'll just have to wait." Etta turned to the door and said, "All these years. It's like Nonna Jannie is back."

# TWENTY-THREE

"That's a nice church," Joseph said as the car pulled into the parking lot. He held his hands on the side of the door, peering over the window frame at the tall white steeple. The low angle of the sun gave the steeple a bright yellow hue, leaving the rest of the building painted with the muted light of the evening sky. A spiritual massif reaching through the clouds searching for warmth. Joseph turned to Justine. She looked out the other side of the car at the people walking into the church. Faint sounds of music came from the open double doors.

Rachelle opened the passenger door and stood by the car. Justine got out and looked up at her mother, who stared at the church. Rachelle sighed.

Justine said, "What's wrong, Mama?"

Rachelle didn't change her gaze. "Nothing."

Etta and Joseph walked around the car. "Are you OK?" Etta said.

"Yeah. I'm always uncomfortable at church."

Etta tugged her daughter's arm. "Maybe you should go more often. Come on. We don't want to be late."

"This isn't exactly church," Rachelle said. "It's a funeral, which makes it even more uncomfortable."

"Hush now," Etta said in a low tone. "Let's be respectful."

There was a short line near the door where people waited to sign a guest book. Justine stood close to her mother, taking in the unfamiliar surroundings, the unfamiliar people in their nice clothes, the somber murmurs, and the music that seemed to float in the air just above her feet. She looked down at her shoe, lifting it behind her calf, then placed it back on the floor.

Etta and Rachelle signed the book. They walked up the aisle toward the sanctuary where a casket lay. Joseph stood next to Justine, trying to look around the adults who filled the aisle. Justine saw Hauk and Shahin talking with people who stood in line. Was that their father? Justine looked at the man's face. He was shaking another man's hand, smiling. Why would he be smiling? He couldn't be their father if he was smiling, she thought. His wife was dead. She looked at Shahin and Hauk. Hauk saw her. He held his hand up next to his face and smiled at her. She smiled and slowly raised her hand in reply. Why is he smiling? She turned her gaze away. Joseph pulled on Etta's hand.

"Why can't we sit down, Nonna?" he whispered.

"We're waiting to see Mrs. Corbin and say some words to Mr. Corbin."

"But Mrs. Corbin's dead."

"She's lying in the casket there, sweetie. Stay with me."

Justine looked to the side opposite the casket, at the source of the music. Standing on a raised platform were five musicians: guitarist, bass player, trumpeter, drummer, a woman humming into a microphone. The trumpeter whispered into his instrument. The drummer painted his cymbal with a brush, tapping it, then deadening the sound with his hand.

As they approached the casket, Rachelle motioned for her mother to come forward. Etta held Joseph's hand and walked to the casket. Rachelle and Justine followed. Corinne Corbin lay with her hands folded across her waist. She's sleeping, Joseph thought as he peered above the casket on his toes. Justine glanced at the person she recently sat with at the river, then looked away. She saw a kingfisher land on the edge of the casket and cock its head. It, too, was smiling. Justine closed her eyes. Her eyelids dampened. She rubbed them with her fists. Shahin was talking, then Hauk's voice. Her eyes opened. Etta shook a man's hand.

"Aaron Corbin," the man said to Etta. "So nice of you to come."

"This is my daughter—" Etta said.

"I'm Rachel. These are my children, Justine and Joseph."

"Ah, yes. My boys told me about you two. You are the intrepid jewel hunters. It's a pleasure."

"We're so sorry for your loss," Rachel said to Aaron.

"We are too." Aaron held his sons close to his side. He introduced Shahin and Hauk. "But we knew it was coming," he said. "Corinne prepared us for her leaving. She was our strength throughout her sickness. We know she is in a better place. She will be with us forever in our thoughts, though." He looked at his sons, who were looking up at him as he spoke.

Justine looked at Hauk. He smiled. She smiled and followed her mother. They were introduced to Corinne's mother and brother. Justine looked back at Hauk. He stood next to Shahin, who looked at the floor as his father talked to a man. Behind, the five musicians scattered sweet sounds among the pews like seeds in a bare meadow.

Everyone took their seats. The Reverend Jackson Lewis stood before the little church and spoke.

"Welcome, my friends," he said, standing above and to the side of the casket, holding his arms out in greeting. "Thank you for coming out this evening to honor our sister Corinne. I see familiar faces, and I see new faces. Welcome to you all."

The church was full, sitting at attention. The musicians stood to the side and listened as Reverend Lewis spoke. Justine looked up at the stained-glass window behind the pastor. Changing light shone through it from the low clouds that drifted across the sky. Blues and golds and a ruby red flickered, dancing in anticipation. Justine thought the window was speaking to her. Was it Corinne? She kept her eyes on the window, remembering the woman by the river.

"The person we honor tonight, Corinne Corbin, mother to Shahin and Hauk and wife to brother Aaron, made it very clear to me she did not want this service to be a maudlin affair. She intended this gathering to be a happy affair, a celebration. Not only did she pass these words on to me and Aaron, but she also stipulated the program down to the smallest detail. So, let me tell you all how this evening will proceed. I am going to say a few words of remembrance, and then I will stand aside and let Aaron say a few words. If anyone of you would like to come forward, we welcome your words as well. Finally, Shahin and Hauk will read a note from their mother, a note she wrote for this occasion.

"We will then walk outside with the casket, accompanied by our jazz friends here, and listen—and sing, if you like—to the songs Corinne has selected. And then we will come back and go downstairs where we have some nice food laid out for you. And the band will provide music throughout." Reverend Lewis looked at his parishioners, holding his arms out. "Are we good?"

'Amen' and 'Bless Corinne' came from the seated gathering. Joseph looked around. Etta put her hand on his arm.

"Let us pray," Lewis said, bowing his head. Rachel listened as the reverend talked about Corinne and how she helped the church, how her spirit always lifted those who worked with her. Aaron spoke of his wife. Rachel saw the hurt in his eyes and the forced smile on his lips.

"I know Corinne wanted this to be a celebration. That's the word she used," Aaron said. "But I can't help but feel sad...that I will not see her again, that our boys...will not..." He stopped and lowered his head, then looked up and said, "I promised. I promised her, and I always keep my promises. We are not saying goodbye, my friends. We have our memories. Our memories are our lives and our history. They can bring the past into the present. Corinne is here in this church tonight. She will always be with us, and she will be singing, 'Sun showers it might rain; Sun will shine again. Dark clouds of sorrow will soon be a sunny tomorrow, while sunflowers raise their little eyes up to the flamin' skies.'"

Aaron spoke of his wife's love of nature, the beauty that nature gave to all without hesitation or qualification. It was, he felt, the same with Corinne. "She was the sun and the gentle rain and the bright flowers in between—all day, every day. Her face, her words will be in every tree and leaf I see from now until I meet her again in another place." He paused, looking out at the small church, then nodded to his sons.

Justine and Joseph watched as Shahin and Hauk walked up next to their mother's casket and spoke into the microphone. They each had a piece of paper they read from. Justine noted the self-confidence the two of them had standing before the congregation. Was it the same bravado they possessed on the bus earlier in the year, on those snowy days when the bus windows spewed cold air over the seats and everyone pedaled their legs to keep warm? When the Corbin brothers challenged anyone who glanced their way, was it then that they knew their mother was dying? Now they stand in a church among friends.

They aren't crying, not sad like their father. They're brave, like their mother, Justine thought. She listened to Hauk as he read from the paper.

"Grace is my favorite word," he said, then looked up. "This is my mom talking. 'Grace' was her favorite word." He looked down at the paper. "Because it means so many beautiful things. It is a hummingbird floating over a flower, a descending leaf in autumn, and the sound of snow falling in a forest, and the voice of your favorite singer, and the smile on the face of your lover, and the weight of a newborn baby in your hands. It is honor and dignity and elegance. But it is also the voice of God telling you that all will be right. It is all the blessings you and I have been given. You all have been the grace in my life, and I thank you. I thank..."

Rachel listened to the words Hauk spoke, the words of his mother, and contemplated her own life, wondering if a speck of grace existed hidden somewhere in the corners of her being. Did she have time to work on grace? It would be a challenge. She looked up. Aaron stood next to his sons, listening, as Hauk spoke for his mother. She would take the challenge, she said to herself.

Six men lifted the casket and walked through the double door to the rear of the church and into the cemetery. Speakers placed outside spoke the sounds of the band playing "A Place in the Sun," followed by "Really Gonna Miss You" and "Take My Hand, Precious Lord." There was just enough light left in the sky to throw faint shadows amid the gravestones, something that Corinne had planned. She never enjoyed walking through a cemetery at midday in the open sun. If there were trees with shade, that was fine, but the best time to visit the departed, she said, was early morning or just above dusk when the long light washed across the quiet earth.

The congregation followed the casket and stood around while Reverend Lewis said a last prayer and then the band played "To My Old Brown Earth." And when everyone returned to the church, the singer began singing "Unforgettable."

Aaron Corbin walked alongside Rachel and Etta and said, "I picked out this song. Corinne gave me permission. It was one of our favorites, especially the version with Natalie singing along with her late father."

Rachel looked at Aaron. She saw he was talking to her. He wore a blue blazer and an open collar. The sadness that shone in his eyes when he spoke was gone. He was smiling. A relieved kind of smile.

"I like that song too," Rachel said. "But I don't know the others. Corinne sounds like an amazing woman." Rachel's words echoed in her head. She wanted to reach up and catch them and put them in a box. What a fool, she thought. I am so ignorant.

Hauk and Shahin followed their father. Justine turned around and caught Hauk's eyes. She turned back, walking next to Etta.

Aaron said, "She had a broad taste in music. More so than I do. She educated me in so many ways."

"You've lived in the neighborhood for a while now, and I never met her." Rachel recovered herself. "I'm so sorry." Etta turned and spoke. "I am too. I don't live in your neighborhood, but I visit Rachel and the kids almost every day. It's so sad the way we live our lives, always rushing here and there, never taking time to visit."

"I agree," Aaron said. "We moved in because we couldn't afford the payments on our house with all the medical bills. But we never got to know our neighbors in the trailer park. Of course, most of them are pretty old. They might not want our company."

Etta and Rachel laughed. "They are," Rachel said. "I think the trailer park must be a magnet for old people."

Etta put her hand up. "Now, let's not get carried away here."

"You're not that old, Mama."

"Thanks." Etta made a face.

"Have you all lived there long?" Aaron said.

"A couple years," Rachel said. "My job doesn't allow me to save much, so I guess we'll be there for a while. Do you work in town?"

Etta smiled to herself, hearing Rachel's words.

"I work at Cannes Bistro. I'm the manager there."

"At Cannes? That's a real nice restaurant."

Reverend Lewis came up. "Excuse me, Aaron. There's someone I'd like you to meet."

Rachel turned to Etta as Aaron walked off. "He's in the same business I'm in," she said, her voice low.

"Restaurant business, yes. But I dare say there is a big difference between your IHOP and his restaurant."

"Sure. But…maybe I could get a job…"

"Always scheming, Rachel."

They made their way downstairs to the basement room, where food was staged along one wall. Opposite, the band was setting up. A wall of glass gave a view of the wide lawn sloping away and a near patio area. The open doors invited people to sit or wander the grounds.

"Not scheming," Rachel said. "Just saying."

"Remember, you have a preliminary hearing coming up soon. You gotta work on cleaning up your act before you take to a new stage."

"Yeah. I hear you." But Rachel was optimistic. She allowed herself to scheme.

Justine walked over to Hauk, who was standing by the cookies. "I found a Greensnake at the river," she said.

"A Greensnake? What kind is that?"

"Rough Greensnake. It's all green. They like to stay in trees. I gave it to a friend. He's keeping it for me."

"Maybe you could show it to me sometime."

# TWENTY-FOUR

When Darren arrived Friday evening, Katy told him they were going to dinner with Meghan and Red. The restaurant was in an old bank building. Both Katy and Meghan had wanted to try it after hearing Red's words of praise.

People talked on the sidewalk and stone steps as they waited for a table. After introductions, Red said they had reservations, but it would be a few more minutes. Darren asked about Red's work as a prosecutor. Meghan described their trip on the river the previous weekend. Katy stared down the street, listening to this chatter without taking it in. Her mind was elsewhere.

When their table was called, Katy sat and said, "Let's talk about the jewelry and the diary."

"Shouldn't we order first?" Red scanned his menu.

"I like this place," Meghan said, twisting in her seat. "They did a nice job fixing it up, don't you think?"

"How old is it?" Darren watched two diners eating within the open bank vault.

"Goes back to the 1820s," Red said.

"So, it was here in the Civil War."

Meghan looked at Red. He had put down his menu. She knew they were in for a treatise. He caught Meghan's eye and smiled, then turned to Darren.

"The town went back and forth between occupiers during the Civil War. It was a dizzy and destructive time, but this bank survived pretty much unscathed. It was a Union headquarters at one time. Are you interested in the war?"

"Yeah. I—"

Katy looked at her menu, hands in her lap, knowing she must wait until the war was over. There was of it, a disruptive power that was difficult to deal with.

"Well, you live in this town long enough, and the war will inevitably settle on you like a fog," Red said. "You can't help but be touched by its long reach. This building is famous for several reasons, but for me, it's most famous for being the place where John Washington lived before the Civil War. Washington was a slave who worked for the family who managed this bank. In April 1862, Union forces, led by General Rufus King, entered the town. King used this bank as his headquarters for a while." Red looked across the table at Darren. "In this building," he said, stabbing his finger at the table. "Maybe laying out maps on a table like this right here." He stabbed the table again. "The same building John Washington lived in as a boy."

Darren waited for him to continue, but Red turned to Meghan. He, too, could get caught up in his passions, not unlike Meghan or Katy. He knew this about himself and, since meeting Meghan, used her to gauge his enthusiasm for a subject that might put off some people. Meghan had heard the stories of Red's family, their roots in these parts going back before the war, their lives through Reconstruction, into the new century of enforced segregation and Jim Crow up through mid-century and the civil rights movement. Red knew the stories. He knew where the truths were buried and where the lies flourished like weeds. Meghan turned to Darren. His eyes were on Red, waiting. She leaned in and said to her boyfriend, "Well, finish the story."

"Washington was determined to be a free man. When the Union forces arrived on the northern banks of the river, he was working at the Shakespeare Hotel. It was down on Caroline." Red pointed toward the door.

Katy glanced in the direction Red was pointing and gave a small sigh. She knew the compelling story of John Washington, having read his memoir, but her thoughts were on Jannie Pratt and the two concentric rings engraved 'J&J.' It was Jannie Pratt and her jewelry she wanted to discuss with Red. She had suggested to Meghan that they go out to dinner together just for that purpose. She glanced at Darren. Maybe not those exact words. It would be fun to try out the new restaurant, and I want to run some things by Red. Darren was engaged in Red's account. But what about her story? What about

Jannie's story? She picked up a spoon, clenching it.

"The Union commander demanded the unconditional surrender of the town. The mayor was opposed to any surrender, saying many Confederate troops remained in town ready to defend it. 'Is that so?' the commander said. 'You either surrender and stop burning everything of value, or we will fire on your town.' Any remaining Confederate soldiers quickly disappeared while the white patrons in the hotel took little time to run home and pack their things. And the manager of the Shakespeare? He handed John Washington a roll of bills and told him to pay the servants and lock the place up." Red scanned the table. "What's that tell you about the character of this man? What the manager and others thought of him—to trust him with that money and the responsibility to secure the owner's property. That's exactly what Washington did. He paid the staff and closed the hotel, then walked back to this bank where his old mistress still lived. Washington said there wasn't a white person to be seen—only the coloreds were on the streets. His mistress was hurriedly packing. She wanted John to accompany her. He said he would but had to deliver the hotel keys to the proprietor's wife first.

"Well, it didn't take Washington and his cousin and another friend long to run to the river and investigate their chances. They saw soldiers on the other side who asked if they wanted to be free. Hell yes, they wanted to be free. So, they crossed over and entered the Union camp. Washington later returned to town. General King asked him to work in the mess kitchen. This he did. After accompanying King on campaigns to the west, he moved north to DC and later wrote about his life as a slave." Red paused. "That's a quick snippet from the history of this place." He saw the server approach. "One other snippet. The church across the street. It took a beating the following December when Union forces pummeled the town from the heights across the river, then fought their way through these streets. And later, the church was a Union hospital during the Battle of the Wilderness." Darren's eyes showed a level of interest Red appreciated. "We can move on to that battle if you like once we order."

"Can we skip that battle?" Katy leaned her head in. "At least until we discuss a little issue I have."

\*\*\*

The back door opened. Joseph called from the bathroom, "I'm coming." Rachel looked up from the table at someone she knew but never wanted to see again. Terrell and a friend entered the back door. Her face dropped, her eyes burned. Justine, pulling her plate from the microwave, placed it on the table next to her mother.

"Why are you here? Get out immediately," Rachel said. She put her hand over her phone and pulled it to her lap.

"Now, don't be like that, Rachelle. We're just here for a friendly visit."

"My name's not Rachelle." She stood up and glared at the two intruders. "And I want you out of here. Now!"

"Not Rachelle!" Terrell lifted his brows. His buddy, taller and wider than Terrell, stood motionless, looking around. "Hah! And I suppose not jewelry either. Huh, bitch?"

"What are you talking about?"

"I heard about the jewelry. And half the people in this town who can read." Terrell looked at his friend and laughed. His friend smiled and cracked his knuckle.

"Well, you heard wrong because you belong to the half who can't read. I don't have any jewelry."

"Mama…" Joseph moved toward the sofa.

"It's alright, baby. They're leaving right now," Rachel said, not taking her eyes off Terrell. Justine stood close to her mother, looking between Terrell and his friend. She spied the snake on Terrell's left arm. Coiled with its tongue probing the air. DTOM printed beneath. It didn't look like a real snake, she decided. The markings weren't right. It was more like a cartoon.

\*\*\*

"I don't want Stephen Fitzhugh to get the jewelry." Katy began. She held her fork close to her cheek, steam rising from the food. Her eyes moved from friend to friend at the table, then at the chicken on her fork.

"Are you going to eat that?" Darren said. Katy put the food in her mouth.

"What is it about Fitzhugh you don't like?" Meghan asked Katy.

Katy chewed and swallowed quickly. "Two things: He's an ass and his grandfather…" She paused, "was instrumental in Anna's death. I did a little research on Stephen Fitzhugh. He owns a big trash company and buildings at Tyson's Corner and land all over. A house in Great Falls and another in Loudon County somewhere and another in the Caribbean."

"So, he's got money. That doesn't make him an ass," Darren said.

"It just makes him more of an ass," Katy said. "When I talked to him on the phone—he called me, remember?—he came across as an ass, fishing for information on his grandfather. He knows everything I dug up and much more."

"Do you think he'll get the jewelry?" Meghan asked Red.

"Probably, unless you can prove he doesn't deserve it. And being an ass won't cut it."

Darren said, "Is there a way to prove Blayden killed Anna? Proof after a hundred years would be difficult."

"Is there anything new from the medical examiner?" Katy asked Red.

"Only preliminary. A woman was killed—the M.E. confirmed the bones were from a female. Killed with the knife found on the ground next to her."

"So, there's no question it was murder," Katy said. "Bones found in the house where Blayden continued to live for two years after his wife disappeared. That's circumstantial, but pretty good circumstantial, wouldn't you think?"

"Not good enough," Red said. "Proof the bones are Anna's would help. And, although the M.E. believes it was the knife that killed her, who's saying she didn't kill herself? You need more evidence, Katy."

"Kill herself?" Katy twisted her face in disbelief, staring at Red.

"Well?"

She glanced at the white tablecloth. Bleached white, she thought. Like a flattened bone in the sun. Anna wouldn't commit suicide. Especially with a knife to her chest like the Samurai. "Anyway, the women cut their throat—not their gut—with a ceremonial knife," she said to the tablecloth.

"What?" Meghan and Darren said almost simultaneously.

Katy looked up. "Sorry. I was thinking about suicide."

"Not yours, I hope," Darren said. Katy smiled, shaking her head.

Meghan lifted her fork to Katy. "You said you thought Blayden needed money to fund his liquor scheme. And Sarah's father was in on it somehow. Maybe there's an old article about that scheme that would provide a motive."

"Yeah, motive," Katy said. "If there was evidence—an article that talks about Blayden being involved in a new business…" Katy's eyes went wide. "Or maybe a deed of trust. Maybe Blayden took out a loan, put up his property as collateral. It could prove he needed money, thus the jewelry."

"I love your intensity, Katy. The two of you are twins." Red looked from Katy to Meghan. "Your determination lights your eyes like fireflies in the night. But even if you found evidence of Blayden needing money for some business adventure, it's still circumstantial."

\* \* \*

Rachel glared at her ex-boyfriend. He moved closer. Justine moved back, away from the table. She wasn't sure how this row with Terrell would turn out, but she wanted to remain as neutral as possible. She and Joseph never had direct experience of the confrontations between her mother and Terrell. They always took place behind closed doors or outside. But this flare-up felt different— and was different in that she and Joseph were so close. Terrell leaned toward Rachel and said, "What's your new name, then?"

Rachel didn't move. She stared at her plate—a hot dog and some sauerkraut—then looked at her phone. "It's Rachel."

"Fuck. That's not new." He glanced at her plate. "You gonna feed us? It's the sociable thing to do, you know."

"You think it's sociable to walk into someone's home without their permission and make demands? Get out."

"Well, that's not sociable." Terrell laughed, looking at his friend, whose eyes betrayed a reluctance to be in this place. "Speaking of which, I haven't properly introduced Tread here. Tread, say something to Bitch. That's her new name."

"Nice to meet you," Tread said. He smiled. Rachel studied his face, the face of a child lost. She smiled back at the big package, standing like a stuffed bear before her. Putting a hand to her face, she tried to stifle the laughter that welled within, the absurdity of the thing.

"Oh. You think it's funny?" Terrell took Rachel by the arm and forced her to look at him. Joseph yelled, "Take your hands off my mama." Terrell glared at Joseph and let Rachel go.

"Alright then, let's get down to business. Everybody have a seat," Terrell said, pulling out a chair and sitting. "This looks good." He pulled Justine's plate to him, picked up the hot dog, and took a bite. "Sit, sit," he demanded.

\* \* \*

"You know," Darren spoke. "I was thinking. If Blayden buried Anna's body under the house, wouldn't it smell something awful? People walking by would know something was not right. Wouldn't they?"

Katy said, "That's a good point. How would he have pulled that off with no one asking questions? And how could he have lived in the house at all?"

"Don't look at me," Red said. "I'm no cadaver expert, but I would think the corpse would put off a foul odor for some time."

"It was found beneath the concrete slab," Katy said. "If Blayden poured the slab right after he buried her, maybe that would affect the smell."

"Maybe," Meghan said. "But that would only work, I would think, if he buried her in the concrete." Her mind shifted. She looked at Katy. "That house is sitting on two different foundations. Brick and stone. Easily seen in the cellar. The older house was torn down or burnt and then the newer brick foundation went up alongside the older stone, providing support for the new 1908 house. So—"

"Wait." Katy sat up, staring at Meghan. "I forgot all about that older house. The tax records showed a house was built on that lot in 1887. But I guess something happened to it. That means that the skeleton could have been buried before the newer house went up. Oh my gosh. That's...." To Red, she said, "That's significant. It could destroy my whole theory."

"Your theory that Blayden killed Anna. Maybe. But the M.E. said that the knife found appeared to be the murder weapon. There are marks on one of her ribs. If you could tie the knife to Blayden." Red paused. "No. That's not enough."

"It was a kitchen knife, don't you think?" Meghan said.

"Yes," Katy answered automatically, staring hard at her plate, not seeing it. She looked up at Red and said, "I can't prove anything, can I?"

He gave her a crooked smile.

Katy changed directions, her eyes still on Red. "So, I couldn't find any will filed at the courthouse for Anna, but I'm wondering if she may have filed it somewhere else. If she stipulated in a will that her jewelry was to go to someone other than her husband, that would count for something, right?"

"Yes, a will would clear up a lot as far as ownership."

"There has to be an alternative outcome to Stephen Fitzhugh getting the jewelry." Katy stared at Red. "And the diary."

"Katy, I just think it goes to Fitzhugh. Unless you have evidence that the grandfather killed Anna, then the law is pretty clear."

"Blayden didn't kill Anna," Katy said. Red and Meghan both tilted at her words. Darren looked up.

"What?" Meghan said.

"Sarah stabbed her. With one of Anna's kitchen knives."

"And you know this how?" Darren said.

Katy and Meghan stared at each other. Katy looked down at the tablecloth and said, "I just do. I was there." The table went silent. Katy looked up. "I know. You now know I've dropped off the deep end. But it's the truth. I believe it to be the truth."

Red broke his look and sat back in his chair. Intensity gone awry. "I believe you, Katy. I believe a great wrong was done over a hundred years ago, but today we can't prove it, given the little available evidence. Whether Stephen Fitzhugh is entitled to this treasure or the owners of the home, that's for the judge to decide now."

"Well, what about Etta and Rachel? What's the law say about them? They better get the rings and the bracelet that were in the envelope. They're descendants of Jannie."

"Does the diary stipulate those items are for Jannie?" Red said. "More so, since you said Anna had no will—"

"The diary says that Anna had given a bracelet and two rings to Jannie. And the envelope with the three pieces in it has Jannie's name on it."

"The question is: is the diary a legal document, a legal stand-in for a will?" Red waited for Katy's reply.

Darren put his hand up. "I'm not a legal expert, but I am thinking not."

"You're thinking correct," Red said. "The diary does not uphold the authority that a will does. Virginia law allows either a handwritten will—but it must be written from start to finish in the testator's handwriting—it can't be dictated by somebody else, and it must be signed by the testator, and somebody must attest that it's the testators handwriting. Or...the other way is to have a lawyer draw it up, and have it witnessed. The theory behind this and the reason the diary doesn't rise to that level is to prevent fraud. Who knows that Anna wrote the diary? Jannie could have written it... Yeah, I see your look. But this is the law looking at the diary, not you."

"OK, but—" Katy began.

"And..." Red pointed at her. "Who knows whether the jewelry belonged to Anna? Does she have the right to dispose of it as she wishes?"

"Of course, it was Anna's," Katy said, even more annoyed.

"Just saying." Red put up his hands in surrender.

"Why did she hide the jewelry?" Darren asked Katy.

Katy shot a stare at him. To keep Blayden from getting it. But that wasn't in the diary. How did Katy know that? She rummaged through her mind, unable to defend her dreams.

"She was well off, right?" Meghan said. Katy nodded. "Well...and she had a lot of jewelry—"

"Seventy-three pieces, according to the diary," Katy said.

"So, is any self-respecting woman going to keep her valuable jewelry in a jewelry box where everyone can see it? My guess is no. The jewelry box holds pieces that aren't valuable, costume jewelry, things that would throw off a thief. And the real stuff would be hidden somewhere—or stuck in a safe deposit box." Meghan lifted her dark eyebrows at Katy. Katy saw the intense green eyes of her friend. She dwelled on her words. Words similar to ones she heard in the vault of her mind.

Katy said, "You're saying that Anna hid the jewelry not from Blayden but as a natural desire to keep it safe from thieves?"

"Especially if she was well-known in town as a wearer of expensive jewelry," Meghan said.

Darren aimed his wine glass at Meghan. "If that were the case, Blayden would have known her hiding place, I would have thought."

"Yes," Katy said with conviction. The image of a skeleton lying in the dirt.

***

"What is this shit?" Terrell pushed half a hot dog at the pile of sauerkraut on Rachel's plate.

"It's sauerkraut, you idiot." Rachel, Terrell, and Tread sat at the table. Justine stood by her mother while Joseph sat on the sofa arm, watching.

"I like sauerkraut," Joseph said.

Terrell looked at Rachel. "Bring me the jewelry."

"I told you I don't have it. The court has it. Didn't you read the article?"

"Tread read it." Terrell turned to Tread. "What did it say?"

"Said...I don't remember all, but there were three pieces of jewelry for Jannie..."

"And Jannie is your grandmother, right?" Terrell addressed Rachel.

"No."

Justine's eyes were on her mother's phone. She wanted to call Nonna Etta or the police. Terrell was a bully and a gangster. Nonna Etta was right.

"No? That's what you told me when we went hunting for it in the house."

"And you should be in jail right now for breaking and entering."

"I didn't get caught."

"And who the hell is this, Tread?" Rachel pointed to the big man sitting next to Terrell. "What kind of name is Tread?"

"Tread here is my new assistant. He's good at treading water."

"You better be," Rachel said, looking at Tread. "Because he's gonna throw you in the deep end whenever he feels like it."

Justine reached out and grabbed Rachel's phone. Terrell slapped his hand down over her hand and the phone, staring at Justine. Justine winced and pulled back.

"Don't you ever…" Rachel grabbed Terrell's arm, "…touch my daughter."

She leaned and jammed her elbow to the side of Terrell's face. He reared back and stood, pushing Rachel away, grabbing her phone. From his camo pant leg, he drew out a knife and stabbed the phone tight to the table. Its display lit momentarily, then died.

"Now then. Where were we?"

Everyone stared at the knife standing upright on the table. Terrell sat back down and picked up the remaining half of Justine's hot dog. He stuffed it in his mouth, chewing, looking hard at Rachel. He reached up for Rachel's arm and pulled her down into her chair. "The jewelry," he said.

"Blayden knew where Anna kept her jewelry up to the point when he stole one of her rings, a diamond," Katy said. "Jannie realized that the stone had been replaced with a piece of glass, a very good fake that fooled Anna."

Everyone had their eyes on Katy, who stared at her napkin.

"That wasn't in the diary, Katy," Meghan said. "At least not in the version you sent me and Red."

"No. It wasn't." Katy looked up at Meghan. "I was just testing you all."

Red glanced at Meghan, then at Darren. "Dessert?"

"Not for me," Darren said, swallowing the last of his wine.

"Katy," Meghan said. "I think you've invested too much of

yourself into this jewelry business. You may want to step back and take a breath."

Katy looked at her friend and frowned. She knew Meghan was right. She had had this thought herself on several occasions. But she wasn't willing to admit it. She wasn't ready to admit that she had gone past reality into fantasy and was now trapped within that world. Somehow this situation differed from past research she had done, where she reached back into history and constructed a framework of the truth from the few facts available today. Enough of a framework to give substance to a long-forgotten time and place. And, if the facts were compelling, Katy would take them further and construct a fiction around the facts, a story that clothed the simple framework and made it come alive in Katy's mind. It was a fun exercise, and then she went on to other research, other projects.

Now, it was as if the story were reaching forward in time, reaching out to Katy, not the other way around. How could she let go if she had no grip on the past? The past had taken hold of her and wasn't letting go.

"I know you're right," Katy said to Meghan. "But something is drawing me into these past events that I cannot control. There's no explanation for it. So, will you indulge me for a few minutes? I'd like to tell you what my mind knows of these events from the past. Then you tell me if my mind has tilted." Katy looked around the table. Her friends were quiet. They nodded. They all thought she was acting strange, but they agreed to listen.

"OK," Katy said.

Meghan interrupted. "Before you begin, what do you mean your mind knows? Is that different from saying you know?"

"Yes, I think so. It's confusing, but...have you ever had a dream that was so real it scared you? The dream itself may not have been scary, but the realness of it was truly real." Katy studied her subjects. "No? OK, forget it. I don't know what I meant when I said my mind knows. It's just something I feel."

"We're listening," Meghan said. "Tell us."

The two women became close friends over the past year. It was as Red had pointed out, they were like sisters. The two of them could often read each other's minds. Now, though, Meghan struggled to understand what her best friend was experiencing. They were similar in their approach to their work and their determination to do it well. Life was best when it was a game, when a challenge existed that required the better part of thought and action to accomplish it. When the results of your actions and calculations and decisions lay right in front of you at the end of the day. Tiny pieces you constructed from the hard pebbles lying about and the soft intuitions that dropped from a supple mind. You could see these pieces move into a persuasive position and give rise to substance. You, the creator, the accomplisher. It was as close to God as you could get. It was exhilarating.

Meghan created structures, homes, businesses, tree forts for her son, Alex. Katy created histories from a disconnection of documented facets, information that lay strewn and disorganized. It was through her efforts and insights that these shards sometimes came together to form a coherent interpretation of happenings.

Meghan thought of Katy. Had she entered one of Meghan's buildings, one sketched on paper without walls to lean against, and gotten lost? Meghan wondered. And listened.

\* \* \*

"I told you," Rachel said, "I don't have the jewelry."

Terrell clamped his hands against Rachel's cheek and turned her face to his, staring into her eyes, inches from her face. She grabbed Terrell's hands and tried to pull them away, but he pressed harder, squeezing her head and face. "I know you're lying," Terrell said calmly.

Justine yelled, "Stop hurting her." She jumped at Terrell, who put out his hand and shoved Justine back toward the sofa. Joseph slowed her motion, catching her by the shoulders, but was thrown back against the sofa himself. Justine turned and helped Joseph up.

Rachel used the distraction, shoving her palm at Terrell's nose. He leaned back and screamed, pulling his hands to his face.

Tread, now standing by the rear door, came forward, moving first toward Terrell, then toward Rachel. His movements showed he wasn't sure whom he should approach. He halted, standing close to the table with his hands dangling. He said, "You OK, boss?" His boss looked at him through teared-up eyes. Blood ran from his nose down across his lips to his chin, where it dripped to his shirt front.

Joseph, kneeling on the sofa, held onto Justine's back, looking over her shoulder, his mouth wide. He didn't know his mother was so strong. Justine stood watching the bully cover his face with his hands as Rachel left her seat and backed away. Her eyes never left Terrell. The rage and pain he felt acted to clench his teeth. He stared hard at Rachel. She saw the eyes of an animal. The fear she felt seconds before now multiplied itself. She had her back to the front door, which was locked. It would take time to gather her children and unlock it. Her eyes moved to the knife standing tall in the middle of the table, pinning her phone down. Terrell watched her eyes move to the knife. Blood dripped from the palms of his hands into his lap. The throbbing in his nose and head slowed. Rachel knew she had to act. "Let me get you a towel," she said, turning to the sink.

"No!" yelled Terrell. He stood suddenly and reached for his knife, yanking it from the table. Rachel's phone remained on its tip. Terrell tore it loose and threw it to the floor.

✳ ✳ ✳

"A few weeks ago, a couple of small kids asked me to find a house for them. They wandered into my dungeon in the basement. Cute kids. They were looking for jewelry. I searched through some files and gave them the address. It piqued my curiosity. After a little more research, I drove to the house, hoping to talk with the owner, Beverly Langston. I walked around the back of the house. A woman—elderly—invited me in. I thought I was talking with Beverly. We had tea. The conversation was cryptic. I wanted to know about the house. Beverly—I'll call her that—told me I already knew everything about the house. I asked a few more questions, then said I had to go, and we parted. That was the last I ever saw of the woman. A normal occurrence on an otherwise normal day." Katy paused and looked around at her listeners. "You following?"

"We're with you," Meghan said. "And I have no explanation who this mystery woman may have been or why she was in that house." Meghan looked at Red. "Do you?"

"None. But there is an explanation. I'm sure."

"I'm going with ghost," Darren said.

"So, that's oddity number one," Katy continued. "A couple days later, I find on my laptop what looked like entries in a diary. Anna's, I thought at the time, and now know for sure. On my laptop. No one had access but me."

"Was it plugged into the internet?" Darren said.

"Well, yeah. I have Wi-Fi."

"So, someone could have hacked your computer and planted the diary."

Katy took a deep breath. "I suppose. But how would they know what to type? We found the actual diary after the entries appeared on my laptop. It's been missing for over a century."

"Unless someone made a copy," Darren said. "And it was handed down through the generations."

"A copy?" Katy frowned. "That's possible, I guess, but improbable," she said.

"Just considering different explanations. The laws of quantum mechanics may be at play here."

Katy gave Darren a look of disdain.

"So, I have on my laptop some entries—not all—of Anna's diary. Word for word." Katy scanned her audience, stopping at Darren. "Can quantum mechanics explain that?"

"There may be an element of uncertainty, but…" The stare from Katy was enough to halt Darren's words. He now knew with certainty that his amusements were not hers.

Meghan knew the same long before. She struggled to make an informed reply to Katy's quandary but had no words. Katy's wine glass stood before her, full. She had her eyes on Meghan, waiting for a reply. Meghan opened her mouth, hesitated. Katy said, "Nothing can explain that, can it?"

Meghan said, "No. Nothing that has any meaning in the world we live in."

"Then, either we are blind to the possibilities of this world, or I set foot in a different world."

\* \* \*

Rachel backed to the sofa, waving her kids toward the front door. Terrell pushed the chair aside, sending it skittering across the floor, and moved toward Rachel. Justine and Joseph huddled together by the door.

"Get out," Rachel yelled, pointing to the door, then putting up her hands against Terrell's advance. He held the knife by his side in his left hand, stepping slowly toward Rachel, who was now backed against the corner of the sofa. She could run to the rear of the trailer—with nowhere to go—or move toward the door where her children stood motionless. She chose to remain where she was and fight. Justine watched Terrell with a mixture of fascination and horror. Without her fully realizing, her hand reached for the door—but she remained immobile. She would not leave her mother. Rachel pointed to the door as Terrell came up to her. "Go," she said more calmly now. "Leave this house and never come back."

Tread stayed by the table, watching his boss inch closer to Rachel. He stood close to the rear door with his hand still on the table, unable to release it, focusing his eyes on Terrell's knife.

Rachel reached for Terrell's left arm, aiming her knee at his groin. He stepped aside, grabbing her shoulder, and spun her around, raising the knife to her neck.

Justine cried, "No!" rushing toward Terrell. He elbowed her with his knife arm. As Rachel struggled to release Terrell's right arm from around her neck, Joseph grabbed Terrell, biting into his arm. Terrell yelled out and lifted Joseph in the air. Joseph let go, falling, as Terrell swung his arm down, swiping Joseph's head with the knife. The blade slashed Joseph's forehead, cutting across his eyebrow and right cheek.

Joseph dropped to the floor, screaming. Blood flowed down his face. Justine fell to his side, holding his head. Rachel shoved Terrell back against the table. She was crying as she ran to the sink and grabbed a towel. Tread opened the back door and looked at Terrell, who stood dumb and perplexed next to the sofa.

"Boss," Tread said. Terrell looked up at Tread and the open door. He stepped over Justine and exited the trailer.

Rachel wrapped Joseph's head in the towel and looked over at her phone on the floor. "Justine, go to Hauk and Shahin's. Tell their father it's an emergency. We need to go to the hospital."

Rachel remembered the kind face of Aaron Corbin. They talked for some minutes at Corinne's funeral as Justine, Joseph, Shahin, and Hauk sat eating in the church basement. Aaron knew Rachel worked odd hours and that Etta watched the kids when she could. He knew this because Corinne had told him about her brief conversation with Justine and Joseph at the river. She was thinking about the future. She knew her husband would have no one to look after the boys when she died. At one time, when she was working, they could afford a sitter. Then, when she became ill, she looked after Hauk and Shahin. But now, she told her husband, he would be on his own. Perhaps the grandmother, Etta, would be willing to look after the kids. Visit them. Introduce yourself. Make the case. Be gentle but be persistent. You don't want to be stuck in this trailer forever. Standing in the church, Aaron felt blessed by circumstance. Surely, Corinne had spoken to God. He made the proposal…and sweetened it, asking Rachel if she would be interested in working at his restaurant. He needed a hostess. Rachel grinned with delight. Etta was intrigued. He offered to pay her to watch the kids during the day in the summer and after school when it was in session.

Justine stared at her mother's face, wet with fear and concern. She jumped up and grabbed the front door, pulling the latch, swinging the door open, and ran down the steps to the street. Terrell was backing his car into the street. She ran past the car and yelled, "Gangster. Coward gangster." And continued running until she arrived at the Corbin trailer.

Joseph cried, his knees on the floor, head bent in pain. Rachel could see that the knife had not harmed his eye. She stanched the blood, soothing him, then got up and opened the freezer. She placed a frozen bag of spinach on Joseph's face and told him to hold it there. The cut was deep on his cheek, but less so as the cutline ran over his brow and forehead. "You'll need stitches," she said as she wetted a new towel, wrapping it around the spinach, then pressing it against his face. The floor where he lay was infused with clay and decayed iron. His shirt would be stained forever, as also his memories—oxidized with the rust of anguish and anger. He looked up at his mother with his good eye.

"I bit him on the snake. If I have poison, maybe he'll die."

Rachel began crying, looking down at the boy's head patched with spinach-wrapping. "You don't have poison, Joseph, but you are my hero."

\* \* \*

Katy's phone chirped. She reached for her purse.

"It's Tracy," she said, studying the screen. The other three watched as she read the text. "The offer on 311 Caroline has been withdrawn. Stephen Fitzhugh is no longer interested in buying it." She stared at the screen, then dropped it in her purse. "Who knew?"

Meghan said, "He was going to buy the place to have free access to the jewelry. Does that make sense?"

"Either there's something very valuable in that cache of jewels you all found—," Darren began.

"Or there's something in the diary," Katy said. "Something that Stephen believes might implicate his grandfather of murder."

"I read nothing that would," Meghan said.

"There isn't anything. He didn't kill her. Sarah killed her. Sarah killed Anna."

Meghan touched Red's hand beneath the table. Darren watched Katy's head bow down, her eyes closed.

"Excuse me." A man came up to their table. "Hi, Red. I hope you and your guests are enjoying your meal."

"Aaron. Yes, the food is excellent as always." Red introduced Aaron Corbin, the manager. "I'm sorry to hear about your wife," Red said.

Aaron gave a hurt smile and said, "Thank you. It's been difficult, but we will survive." He looked at Katy and her wineglass. "May I get you a different wine? It seems you aren't fond of the one we have poured for you."

Katy blushed. "Oh, no. It's fine. I guess I've been talking too much." She reached for the wine and took a sip. "Enjoying the company, the food, the surroundings...and not paying attention to the wine." She smiled. "I get preoccupied sometimes."

Aaron backed away. "Enjoy, then. Please let me know if I can bring you anything."

"Nice man," Katy said, turning to Red as Aaron walked into the kitchen. "What happened to his wife?"

"Breast cancer," Meghan said. "I met her once, briefly, when Red and I were at Market Square. As soon as she spoke, you knew what kind of person she was. Special. So sad."

Everyone nodded.

Red said, "She would come in here occasionally. We would talk about the war and what effect it had on her ancestors. Her family goes way back. Some lived down on Sophia Street."

\* \* \*

Justine opened the door to her trailer. Rachel, standing next to Joseph sitting on a chair, turned, and looked at her daughter, then past her, out the door. Her eyes searched for the man who would take them to the hospital. The man who had offered her a job, and now, she was asking a favor of. She wanted that job. She would take it, but first, could he take her son to the emergency room? What would he think of her? Needy, asking for favors. But it was he who was needy also, wasn't it? Aaron had asked if Etta could watch the kids. Maybe he won't feel put out by this request, especially after he sees Joseph's face. Rachel looked past Justine, her eyes searching the empty evening.

"No one was home," Justine said. Rachel's face fell. She thought, her eyes on Joseph, who held frozen spinach against his face, blood dripping down his arm to his elbow onto his shorts. She looked out across the street. Francine. "Go over to Francine and ask her if she could take us to the hospital. It's an emergency."

Justine stepped off the canted porch. Rachel watched as her young daughter knocked on the door. Francine lived with her dog, alone. One of the original residents of the trailer park, she made it her business to know everyone else's business and had an intimate knowledge of Rachel's. The porch light came on. Rachel saw Francine's face as she talked to Justine. Francine looked up and peered through the dusk at Rachel standing on her unlit porch, a silhouette standing in the doorway.

"Can't you get your mother to take you?" Francine yelled at Rachel.

"My phone's broken and it would take too long. Joseph is bleeding badly. I can pay you."

"Oh, Christ," Francine said, looking down at Justine standing on the step below her. "You people are hopeless. Let me get my purse and keys."

Rachel helped Joseph into the back seat while Justine sat in the front.

Francine turned. "Don't get any blood on my seats, you hear me?"

"No. We won't." Rachel held the towel and spinach pack to Joseph's head.

"How did he get cut? Playing with a knife, I suppose. You got no business leaving your kids alone like that." Francine looked in the rearview mirror at Rachel.

Rachel saw Francine's wrinkled face. "No, ma'am. I'm hoping to get a new job—"

"A new job? You need a new boyfriend. Terrell is bad business. I saw him over there a bit ago. Why couldn't he have taken you to the hospital?"

"Because he…" Rachel considered her reply, 'Because he was the one who hurt Joseph and then ran away,' then abandoned it. "He… It was just bad timing."

"Bad timing? Shit, it was bad timing that you ever came to the trailer park."

"What's that supposed to mean?" Rachel spoke with growing anger but then pulled back, realizing her circumstances. "I mean, it was just an unfortunate accident. I appreciate you taking us. I'm hoping to earn enough to have a car soon."

"Is that so? Well, maybe you can earn enough to find a new place to live. You need to live with your own people. It's not right mixing people up. It doesn't matter who's in charge of the government. They're all racists."

"Excuse me," Rachel said, re-wrapping Joseph's head. "Racist?"

Justine listened to the woman who loved to call the police but complained that the police never did what she truly wanted them to do: rid the park of the people who didn't fit her notion of proper.

"That's right," Francine said. "Racists, every one of them, it seems. Oh, there's some who abide by the Bible, but most are heathens."

Rachel was truly confused now. Her former self would challenge Francine and start a verbal battle that she would not hesitate to intensify. She sat back, cradling Joseph's head. "Heathens?" Rachel said. "Racists?"

"Two Corinthians," Francine said. "Do not be mismatched with unbelievers. What partnership is there between righteousness and lawlessness? What fellowship is there between lightness and darkness? You don't know your Bible, do you? You're all heathens."

Rachel looked at the lights along the road leading up to the emergency entrance. Would they let her in? she worried. She had no insurance. But they had to. Wasn't it the law?

"And racists," Rachel replied to Francine.

"That's right. Good. You're learning. We're almost here. You can call your mother when you get inside."

"Thank you, Francine. I really—"

"Next time? No next time."

Rachel gave Francine a disgusted look. I never said, 'Next time.' She opened the door and helped Joseph out. Justine stood waiting.

"One other thing," Francine said, leaning over the back seat. "I lost my garden shovel. The little one I always keep in my bucket. I know one of you took it." She looked at Justine. "I want it back by tomorrow." Justine slammed the door. "I mean it!" Francine yelled into the empty car.

\* \* \*

Darren drove the car down one-way streets and asked Katy if she was always so caught up in the lives of the people she researches.

Katy turned to him. "Caught up?"

"Yeah."

She didn't respond. Darren had asked Katy this question before—in different ways. Her answers seemed to satisfy him, but the question resurfaced. "I mean, involved. It's as if you have a personal connection to these people. Even though they're long gone."

"Yeah. You're right." Katy eyes were on the taillights of the car ahead, out of focus, mesmerized by her thoughts. She blinked and said, "You ever body surf at the beach?"

"Sure."

"It's like watching a wave come in from far out and then when it gets close… The wave came from the past—who knows when or how it was created—but it moves into the present and you can see it coming and it's a big one and you want to ride it. You know it's going to give you a rush. You're jumping in the shallows, your head bobbing just above the water, watching, and you swim out to meet it, then turn at the right time. Timing is critical. And then you feel the wave's power. It begins to scoop. You're swimming through the trough and the wave lifts you, like a thermal lifts a hawk, and you're moving with it and it flings you forward. You're flying on the crest." Katy paused, looking out the window. "That's how I feel reading about people from the past. They come into my life like a wave, and if the wave is right and the timing is right, then I ride their lives as long as I can. I read all I can about their lives and then my imagination starts paddling. I'm on a high and I ride it for all its worth."

Darren took the turn, glancing over at Katy, wondering about this strange woman.

"People are different," Katy said, going on a different tack. "Some people hang their story out the window for all to know; others hide it in a box that only they can open and view and share if they desire."

Darren listened without comment, driving slowly through the streets of the small town, extending the drive back to Katy's apartment. Katy watched the lights illuminating the buildings, shadows of their true selves as seen in the light of day. "It's interesting to read about important people," Katy continued. "People who have a sense of their importance as their lives unfold. Usually, there's a lot of documentation available to construct a fair picture of who they were. But with ordinary people, like you or me, we don't leave behind much evidence of our existence. And after we're gone, any evidence that existed is probably gone as well. So, the puzzle of their lives becomes overwhelming. That's when I stay up late and invent stories. I guess that makes me a romantic in some sense."

✳ ✳ ✳

On the way home, Etta didn't know whether to be angry or relieved. So, she was both. She berated Rachel for thinking that Terrell was a good person. She praised her and her children for standing up to Terrell. And she scolded herself for not having the back door lock fixed. Rachel ignored her mother and asked about Francine. How could Etta ever think Francine was a good person?

"Francine? But she drove you to the hospital," Etta said. "That's good, isn't it?"

"She's a bigot, Mama. She's a racist." Rachel looked into the mirror and caught Etta's eye. Joseph slept. Justine thought about the word 'bigot.' It was the sound of an animal, she determined, like 'ribbit' and 'cricket.' Francine making bigot sounds. Her mind's eye saw a big frog with Francine's face.

"Mama," Rachel continued, "She doesn't even know what racist means, but she spouts hatred like a geyser."

"Oh. I guess I didn't notice. We talk about gardening."

"She was raving, talking about the Bible and how I need to live with my own people and—"

"Raving?"

"Maybe that's why I don't go to church."

Etta raised an eyebrow and saw Rachel sigh in the mirror. "She said you should live with your own people?"

"She wants us to move out of the park."

"Well, she has suggested that Terrell was no good. You know my views there."

"And she said something about a missing shovel. She knows one of us took it. What's that about?"

Justine turned. "I think Joseph and I borrowed it. We needed it to dig for the jewels."

Rachel had her hand on Joseph's chest, feeling his breathing. "Do you think we'll get any jewelry?"

\* \* \*

Darren's breathing was slow, soft, steady, sounding of deep sleep. Katy stared at the wall and the faint shadows that appeared, then were gone. She dressed hurriedly and left the apartment. To think and to attempt to reach for the past.

The cool breeze of the open window blew past Katy's ear, lifting her hair, swirling it about her neck and face. It felt good, the night air. It woke her more fully. She breathed in then exhaled long, staring out at the dark street, now turning onto Caroline and parking a block from her destination. It would be early light in another three hours. The moon was quartered, sharing its light with a sleeping street. Katy walked to the rear—as she had done several weeks before when she had met someone she thought was Beverly Langston. Standing at the door to the sunroom, she took hold of the handle and jiggled it, then stepped back, peering into the windows, seeing nothing. She walked to the small ground-level window leading to the cellar, now repaired. She returned to the sunroom door and sat, pulling her legs up to her chest, leaning her chin on her knees.

"Speak to me, Jannie. Anna. What happened to you? Tell me. Tell me your stories. I need to know."

The house was silent. Katy stared across the yard at the dead tree in the distance. Its bare limbs reached out, unmoving. Dead, she thought. Dead but still here. Standing among the living. Taking in the present, embracing the soil with its roots, sharing its bark with the birds and insects. She put her hands on the flagstone and pushed herself up, staring at the tree. The silent, dead tree.

# TWENTY-FIVE

Helen watched from the back window as rain fell through the tall trees. Flowers bowed in reverence, thankful for sustenance, their toes parched from weeks of heat. Douglas stood motionless, staring at the roof from within his hooded rain jacket. His shorts splotched wet. Helen looked at his legs, thinner than when she married him more than half a century ago, she thought. But still sturdy. He walked to the edge of the house, studying the downspout. Helen followed his movement until he disappeared around the side. She moved to the front room and looked out the window. Douglas came into view, his eyes high on the roof. Helen walked into the bedroom and looked up into the corner where water had once damaged the plaster. There was no sign of any wet area. She walked back to the living room. Douglas was at the front door, moving beyond the porch to the other side of the house. She went to the kitchen and opened the door. Rain from the gutter dripped over the edge, forming a curtain through which she saw an out-of-focus Douglas, like a ghost, making his way to the door.

"Too much rain, too fast," Douglas said, standing under the roof overhang and pulling off his jacket. Helen handed him a towel. "Why can't the laws of nature be more even, consistent?" He handed the rain jacket to Helen and swiped at his legs with the towel.

Helen took the wet towel as Douglas stepped into the kitchen. "You're a grump," Helen said. "What're you talkin' about? I thought laws were supposed to be consistent."

"Alright, fair then." Douglas grabbed the towel back and dried his face.

"What about your feet?" Helen pointed. Douglas looked at his feet. He lifted each and wiped them dry. "Is rain a law of nature?" Helen said.

"Well, rain is natural and so it should obey nature's laws, right?"

"What are the laws of nature, anyway?"

Douglas sat, looking out the front window. The view was one of grays. Laws of nature, he pondered. "I once asked that very question in Vietnam. Don't recall getting a straight answer. I don't know, and I don't think nature knows what its laws are sometimes. That's the problem."

Helen sat down beside Douglas. "You're being a grump. I think you're mad because you can't be outside playin' in the dirt."

"Humph!" He watched as the rain slowed, then stopped. Branches dripped. Water droplets lined the gutter above the window like birds on a wire, resting upside down. Clouds lay low, weary. The sun pushed through and slowly pulled them aside.

"Look at that," Helen said. "Nature always comes back to beauty." She pointed to the rainbow above the trees. "Now I can go to Roberta's and get the newspaper."

"It's not Sunday," Douglas said, seeing the arc of colors in the sky.

"She called when you were out. There's an article on the jewelry people." Douglas gave her a questioning look. "Better get my boots on first."

"The jewelry people?"

"Uh-huh."

He watched Helen walk down the stone path to the street and adjusted himself in his chair, then looked over where his accordion sat. He got up and fitted the instrument to his shoulders, then sat on the edge of his chair and pulled open the bellows. Several holes were patched with tape. He sang: 'Baby, please don't go/ Baby, please don't go/ You know I love you so/ I beg you all night long/ Baby, please don't go.'

And then: 'Got to find me a way/ To take me back to yesterday/ How can I ever hope to forget you?'

Douglas put the accordion down and stood. "I gotta see a man about a horse."

When he returned to the living room, the front door opened.

"Here it is," Helen said, holding the newspaper up.

"What does it say?"

"We can read it together." Helen leaned down, removing her boots. Her excitement bubbled in her throat. "Let's sit outside."

"You sound like you're about to open the big Christmas present."

"Well, I'm curious. And you were part of it."

"Part of it, huh? I was just standin' on the street watchin' the jewelry people go by."

"Yeah." Helen sat in her chair on the porch and opened the paper. "Court rules on ownership of jewelry," Helen read. "Here it is." Douglas took his seat next to Helen and listened as she read.

∗ ∗ ∗

Judge Garner sat behind his bench, scanning his courtroom. He enjoyed and relished the opportunity to look out on all those who came to listen and learn, seated on sturdy oak pews not unlike those in a church. This was his church, he often thought, but never verbalized. The story of hidden jewelry had drawn to his courtroom curious onlookers and the press. He smiled.

At the desks in front sat the claimants with their respective lawyers. Etta and Red at one table. At the other, longer table, sat the other two claimants and their lawyers. Garner asked the lawyers to come forward.

"Gentlemen," Judge Garner said, "I want to wrap this up with no delay and with the utmost decorum. I've looked over the papers filed in this case and understand the issues involved. So, there is no need to belabor anything. I appreciate you sticking to the points at issue."

Katy sat with Joseph and Justine just behind the railing within a long reach of Red and Etta. She had her eyes on Stephen and Darcy Fitzhugh. Darcy was considerably younger than her husband. She wore a floral dress and heels. On her right hand, partially blocked by her body, Katy noticed a ring.

Etta looked up at the judge. Next to him sat the box with the jewelry. It wasn't large, about the size of a shoebox, she thought.

Justine bent forward and looked around Joseph at Katy. She whispered, "What are they talking about?"

Katy shook her head. "I don't know."

Judge Garner sat back. "Alright, let's proceed."

Katy leaned across the railing and whispered to Red. "What was that about?"

"The judge wanted to get a feel for how this was going to play out." He turned to the front, waving her off.

Judge Garner spoke: "Let me set the stage. We have here a case of missing property. A box of jewelry and a diary missing for over a hundred years. The question is, who is entitled to the property found in the house at 311 Caroline Street, here in the city?"

Garner turned to Stephen Fitzhugh's lawyer. "Mr. Sorenson, why don't you begin?"

Sorenson argued that the jewelry was never lost. The original owner, Anna Fitzhugh, knew where the box was. She was hiding the jewelry for safekeeping. But her husband, Blayden Fitzhugh, was unaware of its exact location. He had full knowledge of her collection of jewelry.

"Indeed, what remained of it has been handed down." Sorenson turned to Darcy Fitzhugh. "This beautiful ring my client is wearing belonged to Anna Fitzhugh." Sorenson gestured for Darcy to raise her hand for the judge.

Katy stared at the ring. Anna's engagement ring. Those are rubies around it. She leaned forward, whispering to Red, staring at Darcy's hand, now resting on the table. Red heard 'engagement ring' as he flapped his hand under the table at her.

Sorenson continued, "Upon his wife's disappearance and later declaration of her death, Blayden had every intention of locating the jewelry. However, he never found it." Sorenson expanded this argument with several nuances, raising the eyebrow of Judge Garner, and sat down.

"It's Anna's engagement ring," Katy whispered to Red. "She would have worn it when she left for New York on the train. So how did Darcy get it?"

Joseph squinted at the judge out of one eye. His face was bandaged in half with seventeen stitches hidden beneath. He listened to the talk, trying to understand.

Beverly Langston's lawyer argued that Blayden Fitzhugh had "full control and dominion" of his property and could have turned the house upside-down to find the jewelry.

"But he didn't," Early said, looking over at the empty jury box as if this were a murder trial. "In fact," the lawyer concluded, "whatever was left when Mr. Fitzhugh sold the residence was meant to be conveyed. Judge, I know that Stephen Fitzhugh believes his grandfather's first wife, Anna Fitzhugh, owned the jewelry in that box sitting to your left. And that the diary found in the box corroborates her ownership and, thus, his ownership. However, there is nothing in the diary that definitively ties it to Anna Fitzhugh other than names of people she may—or may not—have been associated with. The fact is that we do not know if the diary was Anna Fitzhugh's. It could very well be someone else's diary altogether."

Judge Garner's eyebrows stretched skyward as Stephen Fitzhugh shouldered his lawyer, whispering in his ear. Garner said, "Mr. Early, I have read this diary. You'll have to do better than that to convince me it was not written by Anna Fitzhugh."

"Judge," Sorenson said, "we anticipated this line of attack and have handwriting analysis that supports the fact that Anna wrote the diary. My client has letters written by Anna to her husband, Blayden. We compared those with a sample page of the diary the court provided. The handwriting is the same." Sorenson rose. "May I offer this analysis to the court?"

Judge Garner nodded, motioning the lawyer forward. "You have a copy for the Langston estate?"

"I do."

While Mr. Early and his clients read the analysis, Katy said to Red, "How could he make such an argument? That the diary wasn't Anna's. That's ludicrous."

"He was reaching for air, hoping the judge would see it as firm ground."

Mr. Early granted the legitimacy of the handwriting analysis but doubled back on his argument that Blayden abandoned the jewelry when he sold the house.

Judge Garner listened to the two lawyers exchange fine points in their arguments. He then turned to Red.

"Mr. Hamilton, may we hear from you regarding Ms. Tunney's desires?"

Red stood and gave a brief history of Jannie Pratt's background and employ with Anna Fitzhugh, as best Katy had gleaned from her research. He repeated what everyone already knew about the three pieces of jewelry in the envelope, including their mention in the diary.

"Regardless of what the law has to say about ownership, ethically, the three pieces of jewelry should go to Etta as Jannie's heir," Red said, putting his hand on Etta's shoulder.

Justine listened to Red, watching the judge's eye and head movements. She liked the judge and thought he was fair. She had never been in a courtroom before. She knew her mother would soon have to appear before a judge. Maybe it would be Judge Garner.

"I have heard your arguments," Garner said. "Let me begin by dispelling a myth about lost or mislaid property. 'Finders keepers' is not a legal concept. The finder of lost property has rights to that property only when the true owner cannot be identified, that is, the finder's title to the property may be forfeited if the legitimate owner comes forward. If that owner is no longer living, then the title passes to the executor of the estate and the heirs in accordance with the will of the original owner." Judge Garner paused, scanning his audience, then continued. "One other thing. When the legitimate owner is in possession of property in their own home, it cannot be said to be legally lost. The fact that the owner cannot locate it within his or her own home does not make it lost. If, on the other hand, the owner knowingly abandons the property, then the property becomes ownerless, and the first finder may claim title to it.

Judge Garner looked over his courtroom. "In this case, I believe the jewelry had not been abandoned. Stephen Fitzhugh, as the heir to Blayden's property, is entitled to the box and its contents found in the house Blayden once owned."

Garner looked at Mr. Early, Langston's attorney. "If Beverly Langston's trustees wish to contest this ruling, they may request that the Virginia Supreme Court accept an appeal."

"Now," Garner said, reaching for the box on his bench. "There remains the issue of the envelope." He opened the box and removed the small envelope and diary.

"Within this box, which contains seventy-one pieces of jewelry, is this envelope and diary." He held them up. "Written on the envelope is the name 'Jannie.' And in the envelope, we have three items." Garner produced the rings and bracelet for everyone to see.

"Jannie Pratt was Anna Fitzhugh's maid, as Mr. Hamilton has said.

242

"Anna mentions Jannie several times in her diary. She says she intends to give Jannie these two rings—engraved with 'J&J' on each—and this bracelet. A later entry states Jannie kept her jewelry in this box for safekeeping. I believe the fact that the envelope with Jannie's name on it containing these items and existing separate from the rest of the jewelry gives credence to the fact of Anna's intent. They belong to Jannie Pratt."

Garner paused and looked at Etta then addressed his courtroom. "Anna Fitzhugh had no will of which we are aware. The diary, although interesting, cannot legally convey those items to Jannie Pratt or her heirs. Thus, as a matter of law, all the pieces in this box belong to Mr. Fitzhugh."

Garner motioned to Stephen. "Mr. Fitzhugh, I hope you will consider giving the three pieces of jewelry in this envelope to Etta Tunney here." Garner nodded toward Etta.

Stephen Fitzhugh said something to his lawyer. Katy, straining to hear, leaned far forward, losing her balance, and grabbed the railing. Fitzhugh glanced at her, then turned to Judge Garner.

"Your honor, may I say something?" Stephen said.

"Go ahead."

Sorenson whispered to his client.

Stephen said, "Your honor, I haven't seen what's in that box. I understand what you're saying about the maid. Let me take this home and look it over. I'll decide then whether those three things should go to these people here."

Garner gave Fitzhugh a stiff gaze, then said, "That is your prerogative, Mr. Fitzhugh. I believe we are finished. Mr. Sorenson, the property." Garner pushed the jewelry box to the corner of the bench. "Court is adjourned."

Katy got up and went over to the desk where Stephen and his wife were just getting up.

"Mr. Fitzhugh," Katy said. "I'm Katy Aldridge. We talked on the phone a while back."

"Yes. You're the one who found the jewelry."

"That's right," Katy said, eyeing the ring on Darcy's finger. A diamond surrounded by six small rubies. "You own a large and successful business, along with several properties. I dare say the three items meant for Jannie Pratt hold little real value and no sentimental value for you. I hope you will do the right thing and pass them onto Etta over there and her grandchildren." Katy looked back at Etta. "It would mean a lot to them."

Stephen narrowed his eyes. "As I said, I'll consider it."

"Thank you," she said and looked at Darcy, who was reaching for the box in Sorenson's hand. "That's a beautiful ring," Katy said to Darcy. She stared at the preoccupied woman for a second, then turned and walked to Red and Etta. "We're done here."

"What did he say?" Etta said.

"He would consider it," Katy said. The asshole. "Anna died in that house and Blayden took her rings from the body. She's wearing one of them." Katy nodded toward Darcy, who was examining a necklace draped over her palm.

Red said, "Probably."

Katy looked up at him, her brows twisted in a scowl.

A young woman carrying a notepad came up. She introduced herself as the reporter Katy had talked with on the phone. She wanted to know what Katy had said to Fitzhugh. Katy told her. As the reporter turned to the Fitzhughs, Katy grabbed her by the arm. "Ask him why his wife's ring..." Red put his hand on Katy's shoulder. Katy flinched and turned to the door. She thought back to the argument Mr. Early put forth. That the jewelry could have been anyone's, not necessarily Anna's. Had that argument any traction, Judge Garner's ruling may have gone the other way. The Langston estate would have taken possession of the jewels. Would they have been more willing to hand over Jannie's envelope to Etta? She sighed and walked out of the courtroom.

＊ ＊ ＊

"Stephen Fitzhugh said he knew nothing about his grandfather's first wife, Anna," Helen read. "When asked how his grandfather, Blayden Fitzhugh, could have had no knowledge of the skeleton in his cellar, Mr. Fitzhugh answered the skeleton might have been there when Blayden and Anna moved in. Yet, Blayden had the house built. So, the mystery remains." Helen handed the paper to Douglas. "I wonder if Jannie Pratt's descendants will get those three pieces of jewelry?"

Douglas opened the paper. "Hard to say," he said. "The law sides with those who know the law."

"I don't think that's always so." Helen sat forward in her chair and looked at Douglas. "The law should be for everyone, not just..." Helen shifted her gaze, pointing to the newspaper. "That's Terrell Jackson, the boy who helped you at the Shiloh cemetery."

Douglas turned the paper over and looked at the picture Helen was pointing to. The headline read: Spotsylvania man charged with assault, breaking, and entering. "What boy? When?" Douglas examined the mug shot.

"You remember. It was probably ten years ago by now. He helped you with that job you had at the cemetery. He had to do service for breaking those gravestones."

"That's the kid?" Douglas continued studying Terrell's picture, then scanned the article. "He cut some kid... Wait right there. That's the kids I told you about. Joseph Parker. He has a sister, Justine. They're the ones who were looking for the jewels. An altercation, it says. I wonder what that was about? I bet it had somethin' to do with the jewels."

"Terrible thing breaking those stones. Maybe that was the start of his downfall."

"He was a bit of a wise-ass," Douglas said, folding the paper. "Not much in this paper, you know. Small town, small doins."

"Better to read a whole week's worth at once," Helen said, getting up. "You want some lemonade?"

# TWENTY-SIX

It was a Monday morning. Rachel wasn't due at the restaurant until ten. She promised she would take Justine and Joseph to the library. Etta would drive them there, then drop her off at the restaurant on their way home. Justine wanted to look at books on snakes. Joseph wasn't sure what books he wanted to look at. He just wanted to look.

"We should thank Katy when we get there," Etta said to Rachel. "She has been really helpful in all this."

"I know. I like her. She's a good person."

They drove under the bridge where Joseph recalled Shahin grabbing the shovel from Justine's hands. It was a long time ago, he thought. At least a few weeks, maybe a month. He looked out the window, watching the future come up and go by. They were on Dixon Street. Etta took it to the end and turned left on Caroline.

"This is where Nonna Jannie lived," Joseph said.

"Where she worked," Etta said. "Show me the house. I never saw it."

Rachel turned to her mother. "I thought you knew where it was."

"No."

"There it is," Justine shouted, pointing to the house with a gambrel roof.

Etta slowed, pulling to the side beneath the tall oak tree. A sale sign stood just beyond the sidewalk to the left of the door.

"I wish we could go in," Etta said.

"We could call the realtor and say we were interested in buying it," Rachel said.

Etta looked at her daughter and frowned. "That would be a fat lie. We couldn't afford the front door."

"Look!" Justine pointed. "That's Mr. Douglas." Through the open gate to the backyard, she saw Douglas kneeling. He looked out at the car. "Mr. Douglas is our friend."

"He must be sprucing the place up for the owners," Etta said. "How did you meet him?"

"He was just here," Joseph said, raising himself to see past Justine.

"He must always be here," said Justine.

As the car drove through the middle of town, Justine kept her eyes open for the landmarks she remembered when she and Joseph walked along this street in search of the library. They drove down Caroline Street past antique stores selling items from the past. Two men carried a treadle sewing machine from an open door and placed it on the sidewalk. In 1933, this same machine was sold to a woman. It was in good shape. The woman was happy with it—and the price. She took it home and cleaned out the drawers, finding a diary. She flipped through the small pages, reading a few entries and poems, then returned it to the drawer for no other reason than it seemed to belong there, in the drawer. Now, sitting on the sidewalk outside the antique store, the sewing machine is merely a curiosity in search of a collector who has room to display it.

"We're getting closer," Justine said. "It's just up here."

"I see it," Joseph yelled.

"There!" Justine pointed over the back of the seat.

Rachel looked over as the car passed several people loitering in the shade of a tree. "They have music concerts here sometimes."

Etta said, "I've even been inside once or twice."

"You have?" Justine said with some surprise.

"Sure."

"But why haven't you taken us?"

"I guess because there's always something else that's more important."

Justine led the way downstairs, Joseph close behind. When she entered the room, Katy was sitting behind her desk, peering at her computer screen, pencil in hand. She looked up.

"Katy," Justine shouted.

"Justine. Joseph." Katy walked around her desk. They ran up and hugged her. "What brings you guys here?" She looked down at Justine's shoe, the toe area wrapped with duct tape. She asked Joseph what happened to his cheek and got a shrug for an explanation.

"I was researching Fred Aldridge's family," Katy told them. "I want to see if there is a connection between his ancestors and mine."

Etta nodded, wondering who Fred Aldridge was, and said, "Ivie called me the other night and we got to talking. We're planning to have a big family reunion, an ancestor party. Ivie's got old photos and memorabilia, and she's kind of the family historian. We don't have much from Nonna Jannie's time, but that's OK. This was Nonna Jannie's town. We have it."

"That's wonderful," Katy said. "You could visit the house on Caroline—"

"You could come too," Justine said, looking from Katy to Etta and Rachel.

Rachel smiled. "Yeah. Katy could talk about the history of this town back when Nonna Jannie lived here."

Katy nodded, unsure of her place in this reunion. But she was game.

Joseph was antsy, tiring of this talk. "I got a book," he said, holding up a book on frogs.

Justine held up a snake book. "Me too."

Etta said, "We wanted to thank you for all you've done trying to help with the jewelry and finding out about our Nonna Jannie."

Rachel held Justine by her shoulder. "Too bad we didn't get Nonna Jannie's jewels."

The image of Stephen Fitzhugh appeared in Katy's mind, growing larger. She stared past Etta to the far wall with its microfilm readers. Readers of the past. "Don't give up hope," she said. "But you know, you have jewels that are far more valuable than anything anyone could have found in an old house." Katy looked at Rachel. "They're right here." Katy reached out to Joseph and Justine.

Rachel smiled. "You're right."

"And we know that the story about Nonna Jannie and the jewels is real," Etta said.

"You know more about her history. That the history you were told, that was handed down, was true. Now you can take it forward. Tell the next generations."

Etta and Rachel nodded. "The story is true. It's no longer a family myth," Rachel said.

"And it's because of the determination of these two," Katy said, nodding to Justine and Joseph, "that the story ever came to light. Never underestimate the power of the next generation if they're given even a hint of the truth. But let me thank you guys for allowing me to rummage around in your past. It was a privilege I will never forget." She turned and walked behind her desk. "I have something for you. I was going to come by but got caught up in…," she shrugged, "stuff." From the drawer, she handed Etta a photograph. "It's Jannie and Anna Fitzhugh. See, they're standing by the oak tree in front of the house."

"Oh, my," Etta said, showing it to Rachel. Joseph and Justine looked in.

"Where did you get this?" Rachel said.

"It was in Anna's diary. I'm afraid I took it without permission. I didn't think Stephen Fitzhugh would have any use for it. You all should have it. It's yours."

"It's the only picture of Nonna Jannie we have. She's so beautiful," Rachel said.

"She and Justine could be sisters."

"Me?" Justine said.

Katy pointed. "Look at the nose and the shape of her cheeks."

Justine held the picture, staring at it for several seconds.

"What happened to Anna?" Rachel said.

"Anna," Katy straightened, taking a breath.

Justine looked up and said, "Sarah killed her."

"How do you know that, Justine?" Katy's mind peered back through images that seemed to lose heft with every passing day.

"Who's Sarah?" Rachel looked at Katy, at Justine.

Katy took a breath and changed her gaze. "Sarah was Blayden Fitzhugh's second wife. They married four months after Anna went missing. In Anna's diary, Anna writes of her suspicion about Sarah and Blayden, and she asks her friend, Kate, if she should get a divorce… No. I'm wrong, that's not in the diary. But she suspects something untoward is going on." Katy turned back to Justine. "You think Sarah killed Anna? How do you know?"

"I think it was a dream. Dreams that tell me things. That's why Joseph and I decided to look for Nonna Jannie's jewels."

"Yeah," Joseph said. "I have dreams too, but they just go away when I'm awake. If I had dreams like Justine, then I wouldn't have to ask her about stuff."

Katy smiled at the boy as Etta and Rachel laughed. "Justine's dream is as good as we have for that mystery." She went to her desk and handed Etta a set of photos of Anna's diary and the photos of her jewelry, including Jannie's bracelet and the matching wedding rings, saying she would like to start a file on Jannie and that copies of these same photos would be part of it, if that was alright. When you get Jannie's letters and poems from Ivie, could I have a copy? They'll be a part of the archive stored in the filing cabinets there."

"That's real nice," Etta said.

When they had gone, the librarian sat back at her desk and looked over at the microfilm readers. With a sigh, she admitted to herself that she would never know the full story of Anna and Blayden Fitzhugh and their maid, Jannie. But that was to be expected, the norm, working in the cellar beneath the library.

She was most disappointed in herself, allowing her to get too close to the sun, crossing the boundary between reality and fantasy. She stared at the readers. "It took hold of my emotions—my whole soul," she whispered to the machines as if they were human. "Now I must disentangle the fingers of fantasy from my mind and try to re-enter the real world." She continued to stare, remembering Justine's words, the words from her dream. And the words from her own dreams. Were they dreams of a different sort? Might there be some force that ignores time, that conveys meaning through dreams? That completes stories begun, shrouded in an earlier era and passes them along to a future era? A force that binds generations.

\* \* \*

Douglas pulled off his gloves and wiped his brow, then brushed the dirt from his knees. He surveyed the flower bed, Beverly Langston's flower bed. He didn't know where Langston was. Her house was for sale. But the plants in her backyard were his. He planted them. He would tend them until the next owner arrived.

Then the plants would be their property. But, in fact, he knew the plants would always be his. This was his kingdom.

Overhead, a crow flew, silent, unseen but for its shadow, moving quickly across his sightline, drawing his eyes to the brown soil. Something with an odd shape, out of place in this garden. He dropped to his knees and reached. It was surrounded by the soil. In his palm, he blew the particles away. Dark metal. A small bird. Douglas lifted it closer to his eye, turning it. He recognized it as a charm from a bracelet. "Kingfisher." He dropped it into his palm and spit on it, then rubbed it against his shirt. Silver, he said to himself, putting it in his pocket. He would string it and give it to Helen. She always wanted a bracelet. Now she would have one.

# ACKNOWLEDGMENTS

Thanks to Mr. Paul Simpson, former practicing attorney, for his invaluable knowledge of judicial proceedings.

**Ben Raterman** spent his early years through high school in Virginia and India. He joined the Peace Corps shortly after graduating from the University of Notre Dame. He worked for the US Navy for many years prior to writing full time. His short stories have appeared in several periodicals.